Trading Paper

A Mystery Novel About The Horse Business

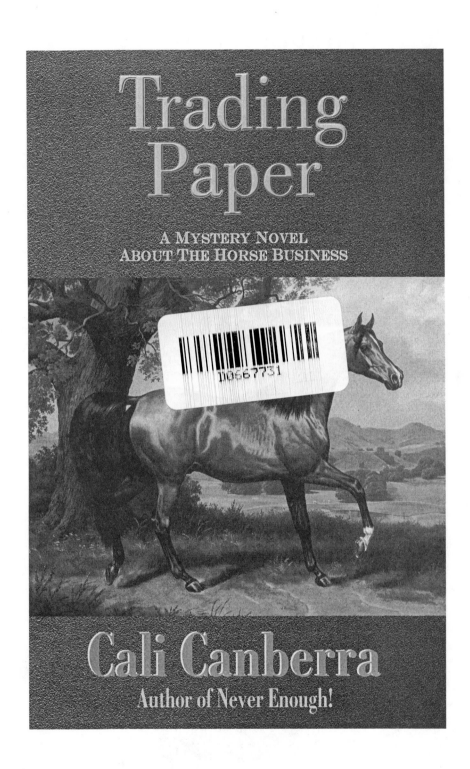

Cali Canberra

Author of Never Enough!

Praise for Trading Paper:

"...Author Canberra has a great feel for the people she writes about, as well as what went wrong with the horse business."
Hallie McEvoy - The Horseman's Yankee Pedlar

"I loved your story and applaud you for writing it! I can't wait to read your next book! Good luck & I'll support you any way that I can."
Bill Pennington - President, International Arabian Horse Association

"...I devoured the book - read it everywhere (even tripped a few times on the street reading while I walked). Pace was good, the drawing in of the characters to the mix really added flavor, and yeah, the ending was a kick in the teeth!" *L.A. Pomeroy - Equisearch.com*

"Just try & put it down before you're finished! Terrific fun, great dialogue, and characters you can really care about."
Stacey Mayer - Awhitehorse.com

Also by Cali Canberra...

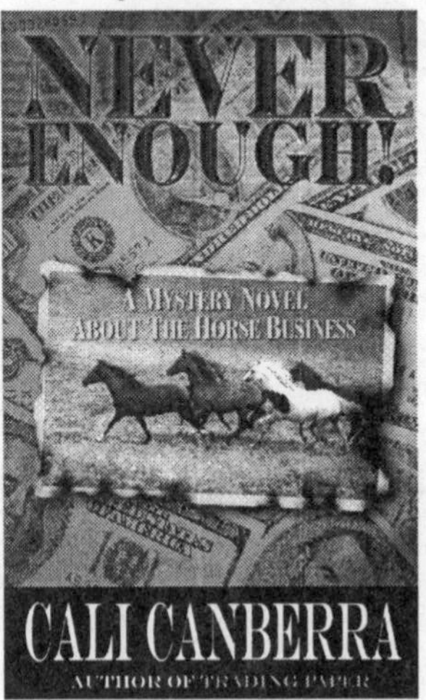

9th Annual Writer's Digest National Book Awards (2001)

Mainstream/Literary Fiction Honorable Mention - 8th place out of 350 entries

"This book is filled with charming and seedy characters who have no morals or scruples, and who will stop at nothing to get what they want. It's a fabulous read - I loved it!"
Hallie McEvoy - The Horseman's Yankee Pedlar

"A fascinating inside look at how the horse business really operates. I recommend this book to anyone who enjoys a good fictional crime mystery, but most especially to horse enthusiasts." *Stacey Mayer - Awhitehorse.com*

"An exciting story - just as interesting and entertaining as Trading Paper!"
Robbee Hueseth - Blue Ribbon Books

Published by

Newchi Publishing

11110 Surrey Park Trail
Duluth, GA 30097

ISBN: 0-97-05004-0-8

Third Edition

Printed in the United States of America

Trading Paper

A Novel

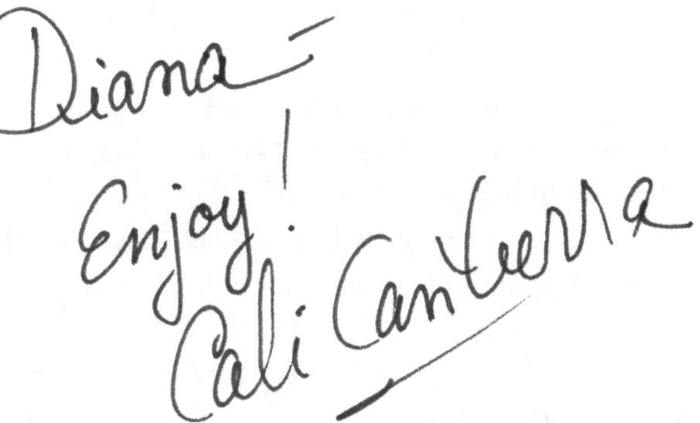
Diana –
Enjoy!
Cali Canberra

Cali Canberra

One

Johan Murphy used a monogrammed white cotton handkerchief to wipe the perspiration from his receding hair line, his face and his double chin, before he entered the law offices of Burger, Douglas, Steen & Cruise. Between the high humidity, the 97 degrees outside temperature and the fact that he was distressed about needing to work with a different attorney in the firm, it was amazing that he wasn't drenched in sweat from head to toe.

The receptionist, dressed in a conservative black pants suit, slid the chest high bulletproof glass door open so that she could greet Johan.

"Good afternoon Mr. Murphy. Alec is waiting for you in the conference room. Give me a moment... I'm just getting accustomed to the security measures," she said dismally as she pressed the button to unlock the new steel core wood paneled door, which now separated the reception area from the rest of the offices.

As she watched him pivot slightly sideways to barely squeeze what she guessed to be his 475 pounds through the door, she offered him a cold drink.

"I'll have a tall iced tea. Thanks," he said, too self-conscious about his weight to ask for sugar.

"Yes sir."

"I'll just go back to the conference room. I know the way," he said, wishing that he wasn't so familiar with the layout of the law office.

Johan was winded as he made his way down the long corridor, which had offices on the right hand wall and thick paned glass floor to ceiling windows overlooking the St. Louis arch on the left side. At the end of the corridor, the stately conference room was full of bookcases stuffed with law books and an oval table that could seat twenty people.

Three years before, during his first meeting with the firm's founder, Nathan Burger, he turned over a $200,000 cash retainer. No one at the firm made any mention of it, but by the time he arrived for his second meeting with Nathan someone thought to purchase a chair that was wide enough and plenty sturdy for Johan to comfortably sit. The chair was always available regardless of what room or office he was in at the firm.

Alec, a decidedly imposing man, stood up, dressed in a black custom tailored suit, with black shirt and a tie that was accented by a small garnet and gold tie clip. He offered his hand in greeting.

As they shook hands, Alec hid the fact that he was disgusted by the calluses that he could feel through the perspiration on Johan's puffy hand.

"Good afternoon. I'm not sure if you remember me. I'm Alec Douglas. I'll be taking over for Nathan," he said respectfully.

The firm bent over backward to retain Johan's business and the business of each of the five other people Johan had referred to them. The group accounted for almost 80% of the firm's business. Most importantly, they never questioned their bills and they always paid in a timely manner. Although the three minority partners in the firm were grateful for the group of clients, there was always informal controversy behind Nathan Burger's back about how they relied so heavily on the business from the small group of people.

"Yes. I remember you. Of course, I remember you," Johan answered, in spite of his difficulty in trying to catch his breath. He wondered if Alec was dressed in black for respectful mourning or if Alec wanted to look like he was a Mafia consigliere.

"Are you all right?"

"Please excuse me, I have asthma and the heat aggravates it," he explained.

"Have a seat."

"This room is huge for the two of us. Why aren't we in your office?"

Alec hesitated. He assumed that Johan would inquire, but he didn't know how to word his answer without sounding harsh.

"The FBI has it sealed. Crime scene. I can't even get to my own files and to things on my desk. Or my own computer."

"I suppose you're lucky that they didn't seal off the whole office, considering."

Alec straightened in his chair, his eyes squinting with anger and his lips pursed. He adjusted the knot in his tie as his posture noticeably tensed up. Leaning slightly forward in his chair, quietly, almost through his teeth he spoke with intensity.

"Believe me. They wanted to shut us down entirely while they investigated us. We had to get a court order. Finally, the judge said we could run business as usual, with the exception of my personal office, since that's where Nathan was gunned down," he confided.

His breathing was normal now.

"I can't imagine that you'd want to be in your office anyway, come to think of it," Johan said as he tried to picture the massacre.

Alec tried not to focus on Johan's double chin turning into a triple as his head looked down.

"No. No, I don't. But I do need my files and computer. I can't have access to anything. Those FBI agents are assholes."

"Yeah," he said as his face flushed. He was thinking about his own anger and frustration with the FBI.

"I saw you and your brother at the funeral services. Thanks for coming."

"I guess we had to see it to believe it."

Alec didn't have any idea what Johan meant by his comment, but he didn't want to open a potential complex issue, so he changed the subject. The receptionist brought in two large glasses of iced tea, a pitcher full for refills and a sugar bowl with two spoons and two cocktail napkins.

Johan drank down his entire glass of iced tea before he spoke.

"Nothing personal Alec, but I'm very uncomfortable working with you. Not that it's you... it's just that I've only dealt with Nathan. I confided in him. He knows me. I mean, knew me. Knew my business. My family. My colleagues."

Alec's posture relaxed and his eyes softened. "I understand completely," he paused for effect. "But even if you left our firm, you'd be dealing with someone you didn't know or trust yet. We would really appreciate keeping your business."

"I've thought of that. You're absolutely right. That's why I'm here. But keep in mind, I'm just not comfortable yet."

"Right."

"You understand that I have a variety of interests?"

"To be honest, I don't know much about what our firm has done for you. I couldn't locate your files anywhere. They aren't even in Nathan's office. Our billing records are sketchy."

"In that case, for right now, why don't we deal only with a financial problem I'm going through. Basically, everything else I've done with the firm is pretty irrelevant to this."

"Sounds sensible to me. Go on."

"Well, last February, I bought a pure bred Arabian show horse on four year terms. I don't have the funds to pay the next payment on the note. Is there any way I can do anything to avoid being sued?"

Alec didn't expect anything like this. He suspected that Johan dealt in some shady areas of business. This was just about a horse. He decided he shouldn't let his imagination run rampant anymore.

"Well, I don't know. Do you have a purchase contract with you?"

His short stubby fingers, irritated hang nails and all, fumbled to open his brief case. "Yeah. Right here," he said as he slid the contract, face down, across the table to his new counsel.

Seeing Johan's hands, it reminded him that he forgot to show up for his routine hair trim and manicure the previous morning. Before Alec picked up the document he couldn't help but see that Johan's open brief case had several files and brochures in it.

"Do you have anything else with you that relates to the purchase?"

"Well, you tell me. I'm not sure what you mean by *relates*... so I brought these," he said.

He carefully pulled out color advertisements, a small poster, the auction catalog, and a magazine with a photo of Love Letter on the cover. A manila folder contained clippings of newspaper and magazine articles about his acquisition of the mare.

Alec's piercing dark brown eyes opened wide as Johan started spreading everything out on the conference table.

"All of this is about you buying one lousy horse?"

"She's not a lousy horse," Johan said defensively, his voice raised a decibel. "She's the only female who's ever been a Triple Crown Winner in the Arabian breed!"

"I didn't mean *lousy horse* literally! It was a figure of speech for saying *one horse*. Sorry, I didn't mean to offend you."

"Yeah. I know. I'm just upset, 'cause I'd really like to keep this horse."

Alec unconsciously adjusted his tie knot. "Don't take this the wrong way, but I understood you have a lot of money. Why don't you just pay the note like you planned?"

"I don't have the money right now," Johan said, looking down at the floor as he contained his anger.

"Have you tried calling the party you owe the money to and explaining your situation? Requesting an extension of time?"

"Yeah. They'll give me an extension, but I'll have to pay penalties and interest, and I don't think I'll have the money in three months either. They said if I don't pay, they will be forced to sue. The mare is too important and it would set a bad precedent for the industry if they let me just give her back."

Alec didn't comprehend the importance of what they were talking about and the relaxed expression on his face showed it. "So they'll sue you. You'll pay in a few years when it gets to court.

Or settle in the mean time. Don't worry about it Johan," Alec said as if he were telling a little league player not to worry just because he struck out at bat.

He was relieved that he wasn't going to have to deal with anything complicated or with pressure or with anything that may disappoint Johan enough to leave the firm. The firm needed Johan to give them a fair chance to deal with Nathan being dead.

Johan shook his head; his jowls swung independently. He stood up angrily, reaching to gather all of his papers and magazines so that he could leave.

Alec tried to act relaxed, although he knew his blood pressure was rising. The partners would be furious if he lost this client.

"I'm sure we can work this out. Just have a seat and let me read the contract," he said as he turned over the document in front of him.

For dramatic effect, Johan continued to stack his paperwork, but not quite as aggressively.

A look of confusion washed over Alec's face. He squinted his eyes, cocked his head to the right and reread the part of the contract that spelled out the purchase price.

"First of all, the contract has an important typo error in it. That alone is in your favor."

"What do you mean?" Johan said as he lowered himself back into the chair.

"It says here that the purchase price is $2,500,000.00. Obviously, it's supposed to be $25,000.00."

If his problem wasn't so serious, Johan would have broke out laughing. Instead, his face looked pained, as if he were constipated.

"Turn the page." Beads of sweat were forming at his receding hairline.

Alec's soft skinned manicured hand turned the page. Nothing registered, as if time were in slow motion for a brief moment. In an instant, his eyes just about popped out of his head. Johan actually signed a contract to buy the mare for $2,500,000.00.

The terms of the agreement were 20% down payment upon the fall of the gavel, and equal quarterly principal payments for four years, plus 12% interest on the unpaid balance.

Alec swallowed hard, taking a minute to gain his composure that memorable Friday afternoon.

"So, what is a Triple Crown Winner, anyway?"

Two

Over the weekend, Alec studied every single page of information that Johan had left on the table. He glanced through the hundreds of pictures of the Arabians that were in the auction catalogs and magazines. He read all of the promotional materials about Polish Arabian horses. He learned about the investment aspects of breeding, showing and selling investment quality Arabians, and most interestingly, he learned about the tax haven that horse investments provide.

As much insight as he gained from the materials, what he still didn't understand was why his client had paid $2.5 million for a mare. Winning the Triple Crown meant that the horse had won the Championships in halter competition at the U.S. National Arabian Horse Show, the Scottsdale Annual All-Arabian Horse Show and the Canadian National Arabian Horse Show. What can the mare do now besides have babies? And, only one a year at that. No matter what Alec read, he couldn't reason out why Johan would pay $2.5 million dollars for a mare. He must be missing something.

He decided to call Dan Dunlop, another attorney in St. Louis with whom he was friendly. Alec knew Dan had clients with racehorses in Kentucky. Maybe he'd be able to give him the insight he needed.

"Hi Dan, it's Alec Douglas. Been a long time!"

"How the hell are you?"

"I'm doing fine, I guess," Alec said.

"I heard the Feds are camping out at your firm. Is it true?"

"More or less. Listen, do you have a few minutes to talk?" Alec said, wanting to change the subject.

"Sure. I'm just watching the kids play in the pool."

"You have some clients with racehorses, right?"

"Quite a few actually. It's an interesting business. Different at least."

Alec glanced down at his notes while he doodled in the margins of the legal pad.

"Do any of your clients have Arabians?"

"No. They're all in Thoroughbred racing."

"Is that the same as pure bred?"

"No," Dan answered with a chortle, remembering when he confused the two.

"My client has a pure bred Polish Arabian mare," Alec said slowly while reading from his notes.

"Totally different breed from what my clients have... although all Thoroughbreds do trace back to an Arabian stallion somewhere in their blood."

"Hmm. What breed the horse is, probably shouldn't matter. My client's trying to get out of paying off a note for a horse he bought."

"Really? I would think it would totally destroy his reputation in the Arabian horse business."

"Actually, I don't know if he's actually in the business. I didn't think to ask him."

"You mean you think this is the only horse he owns... the one he wants to get out of?"

Alec felt stupid. "I have no idea. Do I need to know, or are we just curious?"

"It depends."

"Okay. In the mean time, do you know anything about buying and selling horses on terms?"

"Not really. In Thoroughbreds, all sales are for cash, even stud services. But I would think that legally, a contract is a contract, regardless of what the goods are."

"I guess you're right," Alec said.

"I'll ask around my office Monday. Some of the other guys have clients with horses too."

"That'd be great. Call me... or give them my number. Good to talk to you."

"You too. Don't be such a stranger," Dan insisted.

"Sure. Let's grab a beer soon."

"Sounds good. I'd like to hear about Nathan from someone who actually worked with him... or about what really happened, I guess I should say."

"If I don't hear from you about the horse, I'll call you when the judge or the FBI says I can talk. Right now there's a gag order."

"Can I ask you one thing?"

"Depends," Alec said hesitantly, dreading the question everyone asked.

"Were you there when he was shot?"

"He was sitting at my desk. The blood splattered my face and suit."

"Really?"

"I'll tell you when the judge or FBI says I can," Alec repeated.

Alec rushed to hang up the telephone. Barely making it to his bathroom, he hurled vomit into the toilet. Again. He couldn't erase the traumatic scene of what he had witnessed. He was nauseated by the graphic memory of the raw flesh and blood; the stench of it, and the feel of it splattered on his own skin. His head whirled, remembering when he looked at his own starched white dress shirt, seeing chunks of flesh and dripping blood on his clothes, and later stripping down for the police to give them the clothes off his back. Then came the interrogation, which seemed to last for hours. He was still stunned that his partner and one of his closest friends had actually been murdered right in front of him.

Fairly confident that he purged his system, he raised himself off of the cold tile floor and meandered to the bathroom sink. Systematically, he brushed his teeth, gargled with a green mint mouthwash, and then changed into flannel shorts and a worn out cotton T-shirt that he wore since he was a senior in high school. Without giving it a second thought, he swallowed two Valium, chased by a tall glass of bottled water. Sprawled out on his king sized bed, he was desperate to fall asleep as fast as he could.

As the tranquilizer began its magic on his mind, he wondered...*when would people quit asking me about what really happened?* No one seemed to be thinking about his trauma. Not even his soon to be ex-wife. Fifteen good years of marriage. Four months of separation. She hadn't even called to see how he was doing. Not even after the police questioned her. He thought she'd come to his rescue. Come back home... even if only to leave again once he was doing better. But there was nothing. Not even a note or a phone message.

Three

Dan was gathered with everyone at his law firm's Monday morning meeting. At the conclusion of the meeting, he asked if anyone knew anything about the Arabian horse industry.

"I do. My parents are in the business and I used to show," said Garth Windsor, an entry level associate

"Great. Can we do lunch today? I'd like to pick your brain."

Garth eagerly accepted the invitation. This was his first opportunity to spend one on one time with a partner in the firm. He was twenty-six years old and this was his first job after graduating from law school.

"If one of my friends is available, do you mind if he joins us? It's actually information that he needs pertaining to one of his cases," Dan added.

"That's fine. Where do you want to go?"

"How about The Old Spaghetti Factory, say, at 1:00?" Dan suggested.

"I'll be there."

\`\`\`\`\`\`\`\`\`\`

Alec, Dan and Garth ordered food and had a beer before they got down to business.

"So Garth, Dan says your parents are into Arabians. Do they have Polish Arabians?" Alec asked.

"Pure Polish actually. They have eight broodmares right now... meaning eight foals due next February and March. They also have some three and four year olds in training and the show ring. I'm not sure exactly how many because they keep buying and selling. They love it," Garth said, excited about the topic.

"Great," Dan chimed in.

"Here's what I've got. My client bought some mare for $2.5 million..."

Garth cut him off.

"Johan Murphy's your client?"

Alec was impressed.

"Yes. Do you know him?"

"No. But everybody who's anybody knows OF him! My parents showed me the video of the auction highlights and I read the magazine articles that featured him and the mare."

"Why so much publicity about one horse?"

"Because he bought Love Letter for $2.5 million!"

Alec laughed and gulped down the last long swallow of his beer.

"So now Johan is as famous as the horse?"

"Pretty much so. That's how the business is," Garth said, sounding embarrassed by the admission, as if it were his fault.

"Is the mare any good?"

"Sure. She's a Triple Crown Winner."

The waiter wordlessly placed two assorted platters of appetizers in front of the three men, and stood at the table long enough to give them an opportunity to ask for another beverage or to add onto their order. They were obviously deep in conversation and he didn't want to interrupt them.

"Did Johan pay a fair price?" Alec asked in a way that insinuated that he expected an honest answer.

"Fair?"

"Yes. I want to know if he paid a fair price."

"Well, the value is what ever a buyer is willing to pay," Garth answered with conviction.

Alec didn't mean to, but he started questioning Garth as if they were in a deposition.

"Would the average person in the Arabian business have paid that?"

Garth cocked his head and tightened his face in deep contemplation before he answered.

"The problem is, there's really no average person in the Arabian business... especially the high end of the market."

"In your personal opinion, do you think that Johan got ripped off?"

"Ripped off? No! He bid the horse up at auction until he was the final bidder. How could someone get ripped off at an auction? Even privately, people only pay what they want to pay. No one gets ripped off."

Alec was hoping for a different answer.

"Okay. That makes sense." He adjusted his tie knot as he contemplated how much to disclose. "What my problem is, is that I'm trying to find a way for my client to stop paying on the contract without getting sued. He knows he'll have to give the horse back, but the person who holds the note is entitled to sue him for the balance due, regardless of possession of the horse."

Garth was intrigued. He'd heard about situations like this before, but never with an extremely valuable horse or with a famous horse.

"Let me give it some thought. Do you want me to call you directly or go through Dan?"

Alec removed his American Express platinum card from his Gucci wallet and placed it on the table to signal the waiter he was ready to pay the bill.

"Call me direct, if Dan doesn't mind," he said when he handed Garth his business card after writing his home phone number on it.

"I'll do it. By the way, does Johan Murphy own other horses?" Garth asked.

"I don't know. Why?"

"It may make a big difference if he's trying to stay in the business. He'll need to seriously consider protecting his reputation in the Arabian industry if he has other investment quality horses," Garth reasoned.

"That makes sense. I'll call him today and find out. If he does, I'll get some details and let you know right away."

\`\`\`\`\`\`\`\`\`\`

"Johan?"

"No. I'm Jordan, his brother. We're twins, so we sound alike. Do you want me to get him for you?"

Alec hoped they weren't identical twins. The food bill must be incredible.

"Yes. Please. This is Alec Douglas."

Out of breath, Johan answered the telephone.

"Hi. It's Alec. Can you answer a few questions for me?"

"Yes."

"Do you own other Arabian horses?"

"No."

"Have you ever?"

"No."

"Do you intend to buy any more Arabian horses in the future?"

"I doubt it."

"Okay. That should help."

"What does it matter?" Johan asked.

"I think our next move may make a big difference if we don't need to protect your reputation."

"Oh. Did you find a way to keep them from suing me?"

"Not yet."

"Did you find a way that I can keep the mare?"

"I haven't gotten that far. I have no idea, but I doubt it."

"Try," Johan said in a demanding tone as he studied the framed and matted newspaper article hanging on the wall above his desk.

The full-page article featured a story about his acquisition of Love Letter. It had a trio of color photographs. The smallest picture was of Love Letter being presented her garland of red and white roses and the Championship ribbon at the U.S. Nationals. The second photo was of the shiny mare on stage at the auction, with massive quantities of dry ice giving the special effect of smoke in the background; and then the largest picture was with Johan patting the spectacular dark bay mare on the neck immediately after the auction.

"I'll try my best. But why is this horse so important to you? Do you even really know her? I understand she's still in Scottsdale."

"The trainers who convinced me to buy her said that for whom ever got her, it would be a special treasure. A once in a lifetime opportunity," Johan confided.

Alec could sense the melancholy in Johan's voice. He didn't sound like such a tough guy right now. A light went off in his mind. He hadn't even thought to ask how he came about acquiring the horse... going to the auction... actually bidding and getting the winning bid.

"Someone convinced you to buy her?" he asked with just a hint of enthusiasm.

"More or less."

"Sounds like a long story. Can you get together for dinner and tell me everything you can remember?"

"Tonight?"

"The sooner the better. I may bring another attorney along."

"Tonight's fine, but I don't like the idea of anyone else knowing my business."

"I'd really like to bring him. His parents breed and show Polish Arabians, and he used to show them before he went to law school. I think it would be very beneficial to have him with us. He might be able to give us a little more insight since neither of us really knows the Arabian business."

"Okay. But you tell him to keep his mouth shut or he'll regret it."

This tone sounded more like what Alec had expected... and feared.

\\\\\\\\\\

Johan, Alec and Garth met at the Marriott. Johan picked the location, knowing the seating arrangements could accommodate his size.

"Earlier on the phone you mentioned something about someone *convincing* you to buy the horse. Why don't you explain that and tell us about how you heard about Arabian horse investments in the first place. That'll be a good start," Alec said.

Johan didn't have a clue why it would matter, but he told the men the story.

"Well, lets see. I was flying in the first class section of the plane when I met these two young men that looked a lot alike. We got to talking, and as it turns out, they're brothers in business together.

"My twin brother and I are in business together too, so we compared notes about what it was like. I asked them what they did for a living. They said that they trained and showed Arabian horses."

"Polish Arabians?" Alec asked.

"They didn't say. They just said they trained expensive and high quality Arabian horses and that they were traveling around the country looking for horses for their clients, and horses to buy for resale."

Alec tried to picture the scene.

"Go on."

"I asked them if it was a good business to be in, and they said it was, but mostly they loved horses and having their own business."

"Did they ask you what you do for a living?" Alec asked.

"Actually, that was one of the first things we talked about. Even before we talked about them being into the horses."

"What did you tell them?" Alec inquired, not wanting to let on to Johan that he really didn't know what he did for a living.

Johan stiffened. "I was pretty vague. I just said that we have a variety of financial interests."

Alec stared at him, not knowing what to think. "Did they inquire about your finances in any way?"

He was slow to form his answer. "Not directly. They commented on me traveling first class." He rubbed his temples as if it would draw out more memory. "One of them commented on my diamond studded Rolex watch. I didn't think much of it at the time. Why?"

"In retrospect, do you think that they were prospecting for clients on the airplane?" Garth asked.

"Now that you mention it, I heard similar kinds of questions and comments that one of the brothers made to a passenger waiting to board the plane. I only heard bits and pieces of their conversation. Nothing actually about the brothers being in the horse business though."

Garth waited for a moment to make sure he didn't interrupt Alec. "Do you know their names?"

"Sure. They gave me their cards and we talked on the phone several times before meeting in person."

"Who were they?" Garth asked, assuming he'd know them.

"Dean and Brian Pondergrass. Nice guys. Really know what they're doing. They win like crazy in the show ring too," he said as if he were now an expert.

"I know of them. They're big time," Garth assured them.

Alec started taking notes. "How is it that you came about calling them?"

"They mentioned that they were going to Scottsdale, Arizona the next week. I told them that I had some business interests in Tempe that I needed to check on. Dean suggested we all get together if we were in town at the same time. They offered to take me to some of the big farms. I thought it sounded interesting, so I took them up on it."

"So, you went the next week?" Alec asked.

Briefly, Johan looked away, hoping to catch the attention of their waiter. He wanted more bread and butter. "Yes. The horses were gorgeous. And they treated me very well. Took me around. Told me all about the tax benefits of having investment horses. And they pointed out that when you have the horses for an investment, most owners don't even ride them or take care of them."

"Then why get a horse?" Alec asked.

"Just to know you own it. Like fine art. Yeah…that's what they said. They said that owning high quality Arabians was like owning fine art that reproduced itself."

"Hmm. So, you liked the idea of that?" Garth asked while attempting to divert his attention from the creases and sagging of Johan's face and neck.

"Sure. And the tax deductions. They gave me printed information about how quickly horses were appreciating in value… something like 30% a year! And you write off all the expenses and depreciate their purchase price in three years or five years."

"I can see how it would sound enticing if you're in that income bracket," Alec interjected.

"Yep. And the farms and the horses were so stunning. They treated me really well. Usually people try to ignore me. I guess because I'm so overweight it makes them uncomfortable. None of the people I met that were associated with the horses made me feel out of place. They were all such nice people," Johan fondly reflected.

"Did you ever indicate to them how much money you would be willing to spend if you decided to buy a horse?" Garth asked.

"Dean and Brian pretty much pre-qualified me early on... but that's just good business. It didn't bother me."

"What did you tell them?"

"A million or two, if the deal was right and if it was on the kind of financing terms which they described as common in the industry."

Taken back by his answer, Alec swallowed so hard the other men saw the protrusion of his Adams apple. "You came right out and said that much, barely even knowing these guys?"

"Sure. It's not like I wrote them a check. I just stated an amount if it made sense," Johan said in his own defense. He wiped the perspiration from his face with the white linen napkin.

"Okay. How did they react when you told them you'd be willing to spend that much?" Garth asked as if the numbers didn't phase him.

"Dean asked if I really needed to make money, like an actual profit, from a purchase, or if I just wanted tax deductions."

"What was your answer to that?" Alec asked, afraid to hear the answer.

"I told them that everybody likes to make money, but that I didn't actually *need* to."

"What did Dean say to that?" Garth asked.

"He asked if I had any interest in just being famous... so long as I could still get the tax deductions."

"And..." Garth and Alec said at the same time, intrigued by the drama.

"I asked how I could become famous. I'm certainly no athlete or talented person. How could a guy like me get famous?" Johan was reliving the moment in his mind. "Dean said that in February, there was going to be a first class Arabian auction, and that the only mare to ever win the Triple Crown was going to be auctioned off. They said if I paid a lot of money for her, I could write it off and I'd be famous in the business. Said I could go down in history if I paid over $1.5 million, because that was the highest price ever paid for a mare before. Dean said *that* mare wasn't even a National Champion, let alone a Triple Crown Winner! They told me I'd be in every Arabian horse magazine and newspaper and that I'd be the talk of Scottsdale during the big show..." Johan's eyes lit up as he recalled the actual auction and him being the successful bidder.

Garth and Alec's eyes opened wide in astonishment. Neither of them could imagine paying so much money for a horse just for the thrill of it.

"So, they never told you that you would be making a wise investment by purchasing the mare?" Alec asked.

"No. They didn't even insinuate that I would come close to making a profit."

"Did you ask if you'd make any income at all if you bought the mare?" Garth asked.

"Of course, I asked."

"How did they respond?"

"They said it was doubtful. They said that she hadn't had a recent reproductive vet examination, but chances were pretty slim that she could get pregnant and have a foal."

"Why?" Alec asked.

"Apparently, the extreme stress of conditioning, training and showing damaged her reproductive system. The current owners couldn't maintain a successful pregnancy the few breeding seasons that they were even able to get her pregnant. That's why they just kept showing her once they knew she had problems. They said the mare enjoyed the show ring and the applause of the crowds. They said she loved all the attention she got at her stall before and after she was shown. Love Letter sort of has her own fan club."

"Okay. Basically, you weren't misled about anything by the trainers to try to get you to buy the mare. Is that right?" Alec asked.

"Not that I know of. They just got me to really want to own her and really want to become famous. You saw all the magazines and newspaper articles. I was written up everywhere, just like they said. I've got nothing against them."

Alec's eyes shut for a few seconds. He gave up hope of being able to blame someone else for his client's seemingly reckless purchase. In law school and in practice, they always teach you to look for someone else to blame. Or at least share the blame. It was rare that a client or their attorney couldn't at least twist things around to make someone else appear to be at fault.

Garth picked up the lost momentum. "Were Dean and/or Brian your agents at the auction?"

Johan shrugged, causing the fat on his upper arms to wiggle. "What do you mean?"

"Did they represent you in purchasing the mare?" Garth clarified.

"No. I was there. I did most of the bidding."

"Most? What do you mean?" Alec asked.

"Well, Dean and Brian were sitting with me, one on each side, encouraging me to keep bidding if I really wanted the horse, so I kept bidding. Each time the auctioneer stopped to talk about the qualities of the mare, the bids went higher and higher. There must have been a lot of people wanting her... that's what they said. When the bidding got up to $2 million, I was going to stop, but they asked me if I really wanted her or not. I told them I could go up to $2.5 million, and not a dime more. But then, I had to go to the bathroom and couldn't wait. They offered to bid for me up to $2.5 million."

Garth leaned in closer to the dinner table. "And that's what they did?"

"Yes. They got me the winning bid. I was so elated and grateful!"

At first, Garth and Alec couldn't move or speak. It was beyond their wildest imaginations that someone would think on the terms that Johan was.

Garth broke the uncomfortable silence. "Did they get a commission or any type of compensation for you being the successful buyer?"

"I don't know. I didn't think about it." Johan looked down at the flaking skin on his hands. Bumps were appearing and started to itch, but he resisted the urge to scratch them.

"You didn't think about it?" Garth asked.

"We were just all together, drinking and enjoying the evening. Photographers took all kinds of pictures of us while we bid, and even more when we went to the stalls and pet my new horse. I don't know how many people came up and congratulated me. I have to admit it, it was exciting… they even gave me a bottle of champagne!"

Alec fought to control shaking his head in amusement at his client.

Garth hoped he didn't make Johan seem reckless when he asked him a very direct question. "Did Dean or Brian, or the auction house, have you sign an agents agreement or disclose to you that they were making a profit from you purchasing the horse?"

"No."

"Okay." Alec said, finally seeing some potential daylight at the end of the tunnel. "That's the first thing we'll dig into. We'll file an affidavit saying we intend to file a suit, then subpoena all records that have to do with the mare; and all records that have to do with Dean and Brian, and the auction company, and all related parties."

"None of these people have anything to do with the fact that I can't make my payments!" Johan said, flustered by the entire situation the lawyers were creating. He put his hands under the table and feverishly started scratching at the bumps on his hands and fingers.

"Trust us. We know what we're doing. We're on your side," Alec said.

Four

"Who was at the door?" Marcie Bordeaux asked as she pulled on her riding boots.

Her husband, Greg, stood motionless with a blank stare, looking at the envelope in his callused hand.

"Did you hear me? What's wrong?"

He was speechless.

Marcie abruptly grabbed the envelope from him as if she was in a rush and he was being foolish.

"It's a subpoena. The guy that handed it to me said I was being served…" Greg said as his voice trailed off.

"Oh my God! What's this about?"

"I have no idea," he said, dropping his seat onto the rustic antique wooden bench in the foyer.

"You didn't open it?"

"Not yet."

"I'll open it," she offered since he was obviously too shaken to deal with it.

"Go ahead."

Marcie read the entire document to herself before she spoke. "All of the records from last year's auction are being demanded," she said slowly, as if she were confused. "I wonder why…"

"The auction records?" he said, bewildered to the point of being motionless.

"Yeah. Why don't you come in the den with me," she said, reaching to support Greg's arm in order to encourage him to follow her.

Trading Paper

Marcie sat at her desk while her husband of seven years collapsed into the overstuffed leather chair near the adobe fireplace. After rationally thinking about what they should do, she searched her Rolodex for her Uncle Dolan's number but couldn't find it. With one push of a speed dial button, she reached her father on the phone.

"Hi, Dad. How are you?" she said lovingly, trying to sound calm.

"Better. The doctor said I can start walking around more and going places. How are you and Greg?"

"That's why I'm calling. I need Uncle Dolan's phone number. We've just been served a subpoena deces tecum. I need to talk to him."

There was silence on the other end of the line. Drake Holloway had expected that eventually his daughter and son-in-law would be sued. The prices they were getting for the horses and the stallion syndicate shares were outlandish. He knew it would catch up with them eventually.

"Dad? Are you there?" Marcie asked, sounding panicked.

"Yes. I'm here! What... did you think I had another heart attack?" he said, not even knowing himself if he was teasing or not.

Marcie was paranoid now that her father, at only 60 years old, had just survived his second heart attack.

"Well..."

"I'm fine honey. Don't worry about me. What's all this about?"

She didn't want to worry him, but she owed him an explanation. "I'm not really sure, dad. That's why we need to talk to a lawyer. Ten minutes ago Greg was served a subpoena. It says that they are demanding that we produce copies of all records related to last year's auction."

There was silence from her father again.

Drake tried to remain calm. "Marcie, have you or Greg done something wrong? Are you in trouble?"

"No dad. We didn't do anything!"

"Then why do you want to talk to a criminal attorney? You're uncle's a criminal attorney," he said.

"I really didn't think about that. I just assumed that he'd be a good place to start since we don't even know what this is about. He's your brother, after all. Obviously we can trust his discretion," Marcie said reasonably.

When he answered, he told her what he never wanted to disclose. "Honey, your mother and I have suspicions that your uncle is a criminal attorney for some pretty unsavory characters. I don't want you mixed up with him, professionally."

"Well dad... of course most of his clients are going to be *unsavory*, as you put it... he's a criminal attorney!"

"I still don't understand why he didn't follow in the family tradition. I guess being a doctor wasn't good enough for him... couldn't make him rich enough...he always wanted to stand out from the rest of the men in our heritage..."

"Dad, don't start on that again! He's a great guy!"

"You don't understand. Your mother and I think his clients are Mafia-type people. You know, he used to practice civil law, then all of the sudden, he starts making really big money... the next thing we know, it somehow comes out in a conversation that he'd switched to criminal law. Dolan told us it was more profitable..." he said, obviously worried about his own brother.

"Why didn't you ever tell me your suspicions before?"

"He's your uncle. You're his favorite niece. You've always adored him and he's always been great to you. I didn't want his profession to hinder our family relationships," he said, wishing this never came up.

"Dad?" she said, sounding worried.

"Yes, honey?"

"He helped us do some business before." Her heart felt an imaginary stabbing pain. Her mind was spinning. "The farm in Kentucky. He hooked us up with an Italian finance guy out of Florida so that we could do the development."

Drake fell silent again.

"Dad? Are you there?"

"Yes. I'm here. I'm just thinking. You know, he loves you very much... I can't believe that he'd ever get you involved in something or with someone that you should be worried about," he said, wanting so badly to believe his own words to his only child.

"Yeah. You're right. He loves us too much. Besides, you're really only speculating that his clients are Mafia-types... right? I mean, you don't have any real proof do you?"

His voice was arid. "No, I'm just speculating," he lied with a lump in his throat.

"I need to start somewhere, Uncle Dolan can at least explain to us exactly what this means and what's going to happen. If we need an attorney, he can refer us to someone he trusts that deals in civil law."

"You're right. How about you and Greg join us for dinner tonight and I'll see if I can get Dolan to come too. We'll make it casual... like you said... you guys didn't do anything wrong. No sense in making a huge ordeal out of asking him a few basic procedural questions."

"Sounds good. I feel better already. We'll come over tonight even if Uncle Dolan can't. How about sevenish?"

"I'll tell your mother when she comes home from the club. She misses you so much now that she can't ride with you anymore."

"I miss riding with her also. See you guys tonight. Love you."

"Love you too."

\`\`\`\`\`\`\`\`\`\`

Drake and Deirdre Holloway's live-in chef, Rousseau, was content to be retired from the position of head chef of *Steven's Bistro,* in Scottsdale. A long time patient of Drake's, Rousseau was battling high blood pressure and other stress induced physical illnesses caused by his job at the exclusive restaurant. When Drake suggested his patient retire, Rousseau said that he didn't have enough savings to live on, therefore could not retire yet.

One fall evening two years ago, when Drake and Deirdre were dining at *Steven's*, Deirdre suggested to her husband that since Rousseau was such a spectacular chef, perhaps he could retire and take residence in their guesthouse. Deirdre wouldn't have to grocery shop and cook. In exchange for the housing, utilities and meals, Rousseau would only be working minimal hours compared to what he had been accustomed to. The guesthouse was rarely used, and when it was, it was used by people who could certainly afford to stay at any one of the luxury resorts in Scottsdale. The arrangement turned out to be ideal for everyone.

This evening, Rousseau prepared a lovely meal that he served on the stone terrace overlooking the natural rock pool and waterfall. Flowering cactus in large terra-cotta clay pots dotted the area, adding color and texture to the resort-like setting. A small koi pond was only steps away from the eating area. They started out with chilled seviche served in ice-cold frosted pewter bowls. In the center of the outdoor dining table, as the main course, served family style, a chafing dish was filled with mouthwatering paella. For dessert, he presented everyone with chilled melon cubes soaked in champagne and poured each person a tall glass of peach flavored iced sun tea.

After the sumptuous feast, Marcie directed herself toward the refined dark haired (although the color was out of a bottle) man to her right. When he was sun tanned, as he was tonight, he reminded her of George Hamilton.

"Uncle Dolan?"

He smiled faintly, as if not wanting his wrinkles to reappear. A warm glow swept his face, which looked at least ten years younger than his age. Face-lifts are good for that.

"Yes."

"We were served a subpoena this morning. Can you look at it?" she said as she removed it from her drawstring tan leather purse, which was hanging from the seat back of the padded chair.

A pulse began pounding in Dolan's ears. He hoped it didn't have anything to do with the project in Kentucky that he helped orchestrate the funding and the zoning approvals for.

"What's this all about?" he asked as he glanced over the boilerplate document.

"We don't know. We didn't do anything wrong," Greg answered defensively.

Dolan studied Greg's demeanor. "Why do you think someone would want the information?"

Marcie frowned. "We have no idea."

"Well, let's get you together with a partner in my firm that deals with civil matters. I'll at least come to your first meeting with her. Her name is Jessica Sellica. She's excellent."

"Do you think we can meet tomorrow?" Marcie asked.

"I can make myself available, but I'll need Jessica to let me know her availability."

"The Zellers are flying in tonight for an appointment tomorrow morning. They're looking at some horses to buy. I'll need to spend the morning with them. Maybe even lunch," Greg interjected.

"We'll shoot for two or three o'clock then. Sell them a horse... if this is serious, you'll need the money for legal fees!" Dolan said half kidding, half serious.

Drake impulsively raised his voice and his eyebrows. "You're going to charge them?"

"Dad!"

"Not if it's just a consultation and evaluation, but if Jessica takes them on as a case, yes. It's all billable hours that she would have collected from someone else."

Drake abruptly pushed his chair back and stood up as he threw his linen napkin down onto the table in front of him. If the napkin had been a ball, it would have bounced at least ten feet into the air.

"I can't believe you're going to charge your own niece! My daughter! I don't charge you when you come to see me as your doctor!"

"Calm down Dad! You're going to give yourself another heart attack!" Marcie pleaded.

"Yes dear, calm down," Deirdre said almost in a whisper.

"Some kind of doctor you are... you can't even keep yourself healthy!" Dolan yelled at his brother.

"Stop it! Everyone just stop!" Greg demanded as he stood up to take control and get everyone's attention. He put his hand on his father-in-law's shoulder and gave it a gentle squeeze. If Greg could calm excited or scared horses, he could certainly calm this man who he'd grown to care about as much as his own father.

"Okay," Drake agreed as he lowered himself back into his seat.

"Okay."

"Look you two... I'll represent you for free. I'm happy to, but I'm not going to be able to do as good of a job as Jessica. It's your call."

"We'll pay Jessica if it gets that far and we like her," Greg said without giving it a moments thought.

"Of course we'll pay her," Marcie added, in support of her husband.

Drake shook his head in disgust at the whole situation, but held his tongue. Looking away from everyone, he pursed his lips in anger.

"How about if I try to call Jessica right now and see if she knows her schedule tomorrow?" Dolan suggested, addressing Marcie and Greg while trying to ignore his brother.

"That would be great," Greg said.

Dolan went inside to use the telephone in the foyer so that he could have a little privacy. He was able to reach Jessica and tell her what was happening. While Dolan was on the phone, Drake made a suggestion.

"How about I tag along with you guys? I'm tired of being in the house, and I do have a vested interest in this situation."

"Vested interest?" Greg asked.

"Sure," he said as if it were a given. "I gave both of you my three pure Polish broodmares and $250,000 to help you expand the business back in 1980."

"Not to sound disrespectful sir, but those were gifts as I recall. Not a loan or investment," Greg said nervously, afraid to upset him.

"Yes. What's your point?" Marcie's father's lips drew tight as he responded.

"Again, sir, no disrespect intended, but you don't have a vested interest here. I think I'm speaking for Marcie also when I tell you that this is our business. Our private matter."

"You ungrateful son-of-a-bitch..." Marcie's father said as he stood up to leave the room.

"Dad! Wait! We're grateful for everything you've done for us. Greg didn't mean it the way you took it. And for the record, he doesn't speak for me. If you want to be there, come with us. It's fine with us."

"Don't speak for me either Marcie!" Greg said in a slightly raised voice.

Deirdre had tried to stay out of the conflict, but this was too much. She unclenched her jaw and finally spoke up. "Stop! Everyone just sit down and calm down before anything is said that can't be taken back. You're all under a tremendous amount of stress and pressure. Put this into perspective."

"You're right mom. Sorry everybody."

"Me too."

"Me too."

Dolan strolled back to join the family, no longer considering that their problem had anything to do with the Kentucky financing or zoning changes. He could feel the tension in the air, but he chose not to comment about it.

"Two o'clock tomorrow is fine. As it turns out, Jessica's husband bought a mare from your farm for her. She says he thinks he was ripped off. I hope she was kidding. You never know with her dry sense of humor!"

Greg tried to place Jessica Sellica's name as a client, but couldn't. "Who was the mare?"

"I didn't ask the horse's name. Sorry. But her husband's name is Turner Lloyd," Dolan said, as he reached for the white chocolate covered strawberries which Rousseau had just placed in the center of the table, next to the fragrant citronella candle that was now burning bright.

Greg clenched his teeth and shook his head in disgust. He felt compelled to discredit his critic. "Turner Lloyd is an asshole... and no, he didn't over pay for the mare he bought. He is just a cheap jerk. When it's not show season, he'll only pay for pasture board, just so he can save a few bucks. The mare hates to be outside all the time... especially in the summer heat, so we go behind his back and put her in a stall during the day anyway. She's happier, and he'll never know. All he really cares about is the money he's saving anyway."

"How much is board?"

"Board without training is $300 a month in the pasture and $500 for a stall with daily/nightly turnout time."

Dolan whistled through his full lips. "Sounds like a lot of money to me!"

"We keep the horse groomed, bathed and fly sprayed for that price. If they need training too, the horse has to be stall boarded and the training is an extra $250 a month," Greg said, justifying the price they charge.

"Still sounds like a lot of money to me!"

"Depends on how much money you have. This jerk, Turner, knew all the expenses involved, before he bought the horse. Hell, he looked around at every damn farm in Scottsdale for a mare to buy his wife... he came here four separate times in between comparing horses at the other farms. It took him three months before he came back to us and bought. Two weeks later, he's whining that he over paid and that the maintenance expenses are too high," Greg said without hiding any of his aggravation with the guy.

"Well, his wife's not like that," Dolan assured Greg and Marcie.

"I know. Jessica's always friendly at the farm. I didn't know she was an attorney. I assumed she used her husband's last name. All the paperwork is in his name, but she's the one who comes to ride the horse when we're not showing her. Turner rarely comes anymore now that I've made it clear I'm not refunding any of his money toward the purchase and now that he knows I won't lower the board."

"I don't know about any of you, but I'm exhausted," Marcie announced.

Greg nodded in agreement. "Sure honey," Greg said, addressing his wife, then added, "Oh, and dad, I'm sorry for how I spoke to you earlier. I'm not thinking clearly. Sorry."

"Apology accepted, son."

\`\`\`\`\`\`\`\`\`\`

Marcie was overwhelmed by the subpoena, Greg's heated argument with her father, and especially with learning that her uncle may be involved with the Mafia. Typically, she kept her thoughts to herself until she had things sorted out in her own mind. It wasn't like her to spontaneously blurt out something. Her self-control rewarded her with the benefit of never needing to regret her words. On the short drive home, Marcie and Greg rode in silence, each lost in their own thoughts, digesting what life was now demanding that they take on.

Once home, Marcie freshened up her face and hair, then brushed her teeth. In completion of her nightly routine, she undressed, dropping her clothes to the floor on her side of the bed. She slipped naked under the cotton sheets and light weight quilt, and promptly adjusted her pillows so that she could have a candid discussion with her husband.

Greg's unspoken job was to crank open the windows in the sitting room and turn on the ceiling fan over their bed. He performed his duty, turned out the lights, except the one on Marcie's nightstand, and then finally went to his walk-in closet to get undressed. He hung up his slacks, tossed his shirt in the basket that was for the dry cleaners, and then put his briefs and socks in the white laundry hamper. Usually he slept in the buff, but tonight he slipped on his silk boxer shorts with a bright tropical fish print. When he realized that he'd forgotten to get them each a glass of ice water, he went back downstairs to the kitchen and prepared them.

After he turned on the stereo in the master suite, he finally joined Marcie in bed. Laying on his right side and propped up on one arm, he turned to his wife and studied her face, grateful that he was there with her.

"Are you okay?" he asked with genuine concern.

Marcie sighed and then spoke gently, not wanting to start an argument, but needing to tell him what was on her mind. "I can't believe you're not grateful to my parents for how much money they gave us and for the mares. We sold those mares and their foals for at least $400,000 all together. They've been so generous and supportive."

"I am grateful, but look at everything *my* parents did. There's no way to even add it up. Plus my dad'll always be giving us his advice and opinions about breeding and training. He knows what he's doing... plus all the property, money and horses my parents gave us over the years."

Marcie expected to hear a brief apology. When she didn't, she sat up in bed a little more than she had been and talked in a more normal tone rather than the quiet non-confrontational tone she had used a moment before. "I know... but with your parents, a huge part of their generosity was for the tax deductions. Not to mention that the horses are their passion also... and on top of that, they live on the farm... and that we've given your brother a great paying job when no one else would hire him. It's not the same as my parents at all."

"Marcie... don't start up again. I'm too tired to debate any of this."

"I'm tired too, but we need to discuss this."

"Not now. Let's get some sleep."

Tears burned in her eyes when she turned her light out. This was the first time during their marriage that Greg didn't kiss her goodnight and hold her for at least a few minutes before he rolled over and went to sleep.

Five

Vintage Arabians is a desert oasis growing in the *Valley of the Sun*. Inhabiting over 150 acres in Scottsdale, Arizona, the facilities and the horses that grace it, are the envy of every horseman who has ever had an opportunity to tour the property. The farm has over one hundred acres of pastures for the breeding stock and the foals. Four rail PVC fencing is used throughout, protecting the horses from injuries that could be caused by traditional wooden fence or by wire fencing. Each stallion has their own individual turn out area that doesn't share a common fence line with any other horses. All of the pastures have built in irrigation systems, automatic drinking water tubs and large hay bins in addition to individual grain tubs for each horse. All paths from the barns have soft sand footing to insure horses don't injure their hooves or stress their legs, especially the new babies.

The open-air training barn is housed under a huge clear spanned structure, with five grooming and wash racks, two tack rooms, and fifty stalls. Laid out in two large rectangles, the smaller arena is nestled inside the larger. Outside of the barn sit four hot walkers, which mechanically exercise six horses each. Near the hot walkers are four round pens, a small riding arena and a large covered riding arena with ceiling fans. A covered viewing area with outdoor furniture sits between the two riding arenas. Today, a pool contractor is now in the process of installing an equine swimming pool.

The training facilities are sturdily built and attractive, but don't come close in aesthetic quality to the sales barn and marketing lounge, which are show places by anyone's standards.

The interior is built with tongue and groove hardwood, stained in rich brown, and is immaculately maintained. The exteriors of the stalls have solid brass trim work and stall signs, custom designed blanket racks, halter hooks, and park-like lighting in the wide barn aisles. The flooring in the aisles is constructed of cushioned rubber pavers laid out in a herringbone pattern. Championship ribbons and trophies are on display in glass cases at the end of each aisle of stalls and there are beautiful park benches scattered throughout the facility. The interior of the stalls is the same quality woodwork as the exterior. Each of the stalls contains an automatic water dispenser, a grain feeder and a hayrack. The stalls are bedded deep with fresh pine shavings on top of two-inch thick rubber stall mats that cushion the legs of the horse and add extra support. Each stall has a fan above it high enough for the horse to remain out of danger in the event that they reared up. The business office's marketing lounge complex is luxury beyond expectation.

Greg was in the training barn instructing his brother Patrick and his five assistant trainers on what he wanted them to accomplish today. In the meantime, the Zellers gawked over the world famous imported mare, Starterra, a twenty-nine year old mare from Poland who had finally given birth to a beautiful filly. The reproductive specialists spent four breeding seasons trying to get the mare pregnant with no success. Finally, last year she conceived. Everyone at the farm eagerly awaited the birth of this long anticipated foal. It didn't matter that she was born in the summer, they were just happy that she was born healthy and that the mare didn't have any complications. This would definitely be the last foal that the mare would carry. In Poland, she produced three National Champions and five colts that did exceptionally well on the racetrack in Warsaw.

Greg gave Will Zeller's hand a firm shake, then, embraced Heddy in the barn aisle in front of the foaling stall.

"It's great to see you. How was your flight?"

"The plane actually arrived early last night, and so did the limo driver. We were very fortunate. Maybe we'll have enough time to beat the extreme heat since we're starting out this early," said Will.

"If it was up to me, we'd just buy this stunning baby and leave!" said Heddy in baby talk.

"I told you before she was even born, Starterra's foal would never be sold, no matter the price," Greg said.

"Good. We don't need more babies," Will stated with finality.

"This filly is so special...being Starterra's!" Heddy melodramatically whined to her husband.

"You really want another foal? I thought we were here looking for either another broodmare or a performance prospect!"

"I know, but if Greg would sell this baby..." Heddy's voice trailed off.

"Not for sale folks. Sorry," Greg said, knowing exactly what was going through their minds.

People with a lot of money to burn always want whatever they think they can't have... and they'll pay dearly for it. He was reeling them in.

"Okay Greg, but if you change your mind, please call me first," Heddy demanded as she placed her hands on her narrow hips.

"You don't know how many people have told me that!" Greg lied. Well, actually, the way he worded it... come to think of it, it wasn't really a lie! They could take the comment however they wanted.

"Do you want to pet her before we go look at the horses that *are* for sale?" he said, really pulling at her heartstrings... and purse strings.

An hour and a half later Heddy made an offer to Greg without consulting her husband.

"Would you consider selling us Starterra's filly if we also bought your two Bardon daughters and the three year old chestnut colt?"

Greg chuckled, insinuating that Heddy was teasing around.

"Heddy, we're not spending that much money right now! You just had the yacht redecorated!" Will said before Greg could respond.

"You won't tell me how much we'll spend! Community property..."

"I can't sell you the filly. She's priceless to us," Greg said, reeling her in even more.

"Did you hear that Will? I want that baby. Please, work it out with Greg while I use the powder room and get us cold drinks," Heddy begged.

By the time she returned with cold cans of soda for each of them, the two men had struck a deal. When Will told her that the package of horses was hers, but not to expect to ever buy another horse again, she jumped up and down in excitement the way a girl a fraction of her age would have.

"Thank you sooooo very much for selling us that filly Greg. I know you never wanted to part with her, but she's just the kind of horse I've always dreamed of. I'm so honored. So grateful that you've sacrificed her to us."

\`\`\`\`\`\`\`\`\`

"Marcie! Where are you?" Greg called from the side entrance of the house while he was using the bootjack to remove his dusty boots.

"In the kitchen!" she yelled loud enough for him to hear.

Greg walked in with a grin on his face.

"So... tell me... how much did you get for Starterra's filly?"

"$275,000!"

"How did you decide on that amount?" Marcie asked.

"That's how much we'll need for the foundation and framing of the stallion barn in Kentucky," Greg said as if he had given it a lot of thought.

"Great... that's not bad for a two week old foal!"

"Plus, they bought..."

Marcie interrupted him before he could say anything else.

"The two Bardon daughters and one of the colts!"

"Yep. How did you know?" he said as he laughed.

"I know how you operate!"

Greg didn't respond.

"The Zellers are always buying young colts hoping they'll end up with a top notch breeding stallion. I can picture the whole scene. You take them down the barn aisle, one stall at a time... see eight or ten horses... tell them something about each, then the Bardon daughters are next to each other. You walk right past them and then start talking about the next horse. They interrupt you right away... Heddy says *'Greg, what about these mares?* Then you say *'Oh, don't even bother looking at them, I've got a very important client that's probably going to buy them for a lot more money than anyone else would pay. Don't even bother looking.'* Then Heddy insists that you tell her about them. You insist not to bother, but you tell her about them anyway. The next thing you know, Heddy gets Will to make you a ridiculous offer when you never even had anyone else in mind to buy them! Right!?"

Greg blushed with a big grin on his face.

"No comment. And the same thing with the colt."

"You're the best, honey!"

"Do you think it's wrong though?"

Marcie gathered her sleek hair into a ponytail and knotted the end to get it off of her neck. "No. They paid what they were willing and comfortable to pay. It doesn't really matter about the rest."

"You really think?"

"Yes. Don't worry. They buy what they want to buy."

"I know, but based on my tricks... maybe I shouldn't do it anymore."

"Greg, do you lie about the horse's pedigree or quality, or potential?"

"No! Of course not!"

"So, you're only creating a story that makes them want the horse," she said.

"And to pay more than they would have otherwise."

"It's so ridiculous! They're paying what they're willing to pay! It's not your problem the reason why. Take the money while we can Greg," she said, then planted a giant kiss on him and grabbed his butt with her right hand.

"Speaking of taking what you can get, how much did you get for the two mares and the colt?"

"$500,000! We lucked out. I thought they were only going to buy one horse and they ended up getting four!"

"So you sold $775,000 of horses today! Now we can start building the stallion barn at the Kentucky farm," Marcie said.

"Not yet. We'll deposit their down payment in the building fund account for now. We better wait until we have the rest of the money so we can finish the stallion barn, not just start it," Greg said light hearted.

"Why can't we use the money that'll be coming in from the buyers at the auction?"

"Because that really only covers our operating expenses here and in Kentucky, the mortgages and our living expenses."

"But it's so much money every quarter... we've got to have extra," Marcie said.

"Not really. We've got a huge nut to crack. And remember, out of the payments, we're paying commissions on a lot of it."

"But still..."

"Marcie, believe me. We're doing fine, but we keep building more, advertising more and buying more horses. Your ideas and tastes are very expensive... and hard to justify sometimes."

"But we make a huge profit," she said with a giant smile. She winked at him the way she did when she flirted.

He ignored the wink. This was serious.

"Not really. Sure, on each horse we sell we make a huge profit, but our overhead is incredible. You ought to look at the spread sheets for yourself," Greg said, starting to feel overwhelmed.

"I believe you. I just didn't realize it. You know I'm not detail oriented."

"You've got a great eye for horses, a fantastic instinct for marketing and you're an excellent rider. Those are enough qualities for me. I love you."

"And?"

"And what?"

"Am I a good wife?"

"The best I've ever had!" he said as he winked at her, grateful that she wanted to be with him.

"Do you think I'll be a good mother?"

"Of course, when the time is right," he said.

"I hope the time will be right soon. I love you..."

"Love you, too."

They had talked about having a baby on and off for the past two years. She felt ready and he didn't. Marcie couldn't bear the longing for child.

When she confided in her mother that she wanted a baby and that Greg wasn't ready to deal with all of the sleepless nights, crying, and diapers, her mother suggested that they seriously consider adopting an older child, perhaps three or four years of age. Marcie told her that she honestly didn't think she could love an adopted child as much as her own blood relation, and therefore wasn't willing to think about adoption.

The next evening, she and Greg went to her parent's house for dinner. Out of the blue, her mother confessed that they had adopted her when she was a newborn. It was their intention to make the point that love is love. They told her that you fall in love with any child you raise, regardless of blood and genetics.

Days later, when the shock of her being adopted finally faded, the yearning for her own baby intensified by the day. She desperately wanted to experience a life growing inside her womb and to give birth to her own flesh and blood that she would love with her entire being.

Six

"May I ask who's calling?" the raspy voiced man asked. This was his first day on Market Street in St. Louis.

"Just tell him it's a call he better take."

The man kept his cool. Working the phones for three years at the main headquarters in Washington D.C. prepared him for everything he'd ever encounter in a field office. "I'm sorry, but I can't direct your call without giving a name."

Johan's tone was firm and even. "Tell him it's Mr. Murphy and that if he doesn't take my call I'll contact his superior."

Out of nowhere, a high pitch hummed in his ear. He held the phone away from his head and waited until there was no detectable sound. The noise was a glitch in the FBI's new security scrambler that confirmed that the incoming phones lines weren't tapped.

His voice was hesitant. "It's my understanding that you've been directed not to call anymore."

Johan took a breath and then became forceful. "Tell him that if he doesn't take my call right now I'm coming down there and camping out until I see someone with the authority to deal with me. That's a promise... not a threat. Am I making myself clear?"

"Yes sir. Please hold."

At least two minutes passed before Caleb Anderson came on the line. The concern in his voice was more for himself than for Johan. "I've only got a moment. I'm not the person you should even be talking to."

"I've tried calling for the past two weeks. No one has answered. I need to talk to you," Johan said, obviously irritated.

FBI Special Agent Caleb Anderson was instructed by his superiors to cease any communications with the Murphy brothers. Caleb's job would be in jeopardy if anyone found out that he disobeyed orders. But something told him that things weren't going as planned if he wasn't to speak with them anymore. Of course, they didn't actually say they had dropped the case. They only told him to cease communicating. Did he do something wrong? Something that warranted them taking him out of the loop? He couldn't think of anything. His reports back to headquarters were always on time. His communications with the local authorities were consistently praised. And his immediate superior had recently discussed how they needed to get together to plan out the strategy they would use for the court case.

"I can't talk now. Meet me in the Hospitality House at Anheuser-Busch. Just find a seat and act like everyone else sampling beer," Caleb directed him, wanting to get off of the phone as quickly as he could.

"I've never been to the brewery. It's near the Arch, isn't it?" Johan said.

"It's about a mile from there. But don't get off on the Exit that says St. Louis Arch. Just exit the I-55 at Arsenal Street and go to Pestolozzi and Broadway. Turn on Pestolozzi where there are signs for the brewery. When you get to Pestolozzi and 11th Street, you'll see the free standing building... it's all brick and it'll say Hospitality House. There's a parking lot next to it. You won't need to walk far," Caleb said quietly into his phone because a secretary walked near his work area.

Johan was edgy now. "Why can't I come to you?"

"You can't. I need to take care of a few things before I meet you. I can be there in twenty minutes... I guess that would be about 4:30. Can you get there that soon?"

"We'll be there."

"Don't act like you know me. Sit down with a beer sample and I'll join you when I know it's safe," Caleb instructed.

"Are you serious? Why can't I come in?" He sounded angry.

"You can't. I'll see you in twenty minutes."

``````````

Johan and his twin brother Jordan left their house within minutes of hanging up the telephone. Jordan drove the black Cadillac at least twenty miles over the speed limit until they got off of the interstate. Even with their windows sealed closed and the air conditioner on, the nauseating odor of imported hops permeated their nostrils and made Johan queasy.

As they were keeping an eye out for 11th Street, Johan spotted three Clydesdales in their outdoor turn out area. If the Murphys weren't in such deep shit, they would have taken the time to visit the horses and the beautiful barn they were kept in at night. When the brothers were in high school, their parents took them to Grants Farm, just a half an hour from their house. As a teenager, Johan was enamored when he saw all of the beautiful Clydesdales and their shiny working tack. He speculated that the huge draft horses would be the only breed of horse that could hold his weight. Frequently, he found himself waking from a dream where he was on one of the giant equines, riding bareback in a full out canter. In his dream, he felt elated. When he woke up, he hated himself more than ever because in real life he was so fat and out of shape.

In utter contrast to Johan who was only 5'7", Jordan stood tall at 6'4". His 210 pounds of lean muscle showed through his clothes. The only physical traits the twins share are thick red wavy hair and green eyes. In his adolescence, Jordan loved sports and excelled at everything he tried. Swimming, track and field, tennis and skiing. For over a year he had a girlfriend who owned horses, but Jordan never rode even though he really wanted to try it. Sensitive to the fact that his brother would feel even more opposite if he did the only thing that Johan ever wished he could do. It
``````````

would have been a slap in the face. Johan was always reading Louis L'Amour westerns, watching John Wayne movies and anything else with horses in it.

Through their school years, Jordan was referred to as Jordan the Jock, while Johan was the outcast year after year because of his excessive weight, his acne and his asthma attacks. Jordan was the only person Johan was close to, so they went into business together. They never dreamed that they would be involved with the FBI after their documents were seized and the USDA filed an administrative action against them. Even the Teamsters were getting in on the action.

\`\`\`\`\`\`\`\`\`\`

Jordan waited at a table with two samples of ice-cold frosted glasses of Busch beer while Johan went to get a basket of Eagle Pretzels and a bowl of nuts.

Jordan spotted Caleb Anderson. Caleb was acting as if he was browsing over the historical company pictures and memorabilia on the walls and in the display cases. As Caleb moved closer to the Murphys, he legitimately admired the mint condition, restored bright red truck, which was the first motorized vehicle that delivered beer for Anheuser-Busch. The truck was so clean he could see his reflection in it. The instant he was confident that he hadn't been followed, he joined the Murphy brothers. He sat with his back facing the wall.

"Why isn't anyone taking our calls?" Jordan asked hurriedly.

Caleb hesitated and looked around the room one more time. "I don't know about anyone else on your case, but I was instructed not to communicate with either of you again."

Jordan squirmed in his chair. "Why?"

"I can't ask these guys why... I just follow orders," Caleb said, feeling like a wimp.

Jordan took the last swallow of his beer and said, "We're worried that we're caught in the middle of all of this. We need access to our bank accounts."

"I don't have anything to do with your money. I never did. It was my understanding that they would take the freeze off your accounts when you provided all of the evidence for trial."

Johan clenched his fists. "Forget the money for now… did your people take out Nathan?" Johan demanded to know.

Caleb contemplated his answer. For the past two weeks he ran every scenario that he could think of in his head. Nothing made sense.

"I don't think so, but I'm not sure," Caleb admitted.

In a fit of anger Johan reached an open hand toward Caleb, ready to grab the agent's neck. Jordan grabbed his brother by the wrist, pulling his arm back down to the wooden table before they attracted any attention.

"What is that supposed to mean?" Johan said too loudly.

Jordan stood up, put his hands on his brothers shoulders and said, "Calm down, we're supposed to be inconspicuous. We'll get this straightened out."

"I'm not worried about the money! I want to know if the Feds took him out… and if I'm next," Johan said as his face reddened.

"What do you mean *if you're next*?" Jordan asked his brother, stunned at the slant the conversation was taking.

"You've been worried about the money this whole time… I've been worried about being taken out of the picture like Nathan," Johan confessed. Sweat rings started appearing around his armpits.

"First of all, I had no idea that you were concerned about your own safety! I thought you were worried about the money too… you're the one who's gotten into debt you can't handle by buying that horse!" Jordan said.

Caleb listened to the brothers continue. Was it possible his own people killed Nathan? They needed him. They needed the information he was going to be providing. Why would they kill

Nathan or Johan? They were helping the FBI in exchange for their own immunity from prosecution.

"You're worried that whoever killed Nathan Burger will kill you also?" Caleb clarified.

"It's crossed my mind more than once," Johan said, breaking out in a full body sweat even though the room was chilly. His fingers were rapidly tapping the table while his right knee rose and fell at a nervous pace. The bumps started appearing on the palms of his hands.

Caleb considered the possibility, then shook his head and said, "It doesn't make sense. First of all, somebody from the law firm had to be feeding the shooter information to some extent. Otherwise, how would the shooter know that Nathan was in Alec's office?"

The brothers looked at each other with a hint of hope. Distracted by the stress of the situation, Johan wiped the sweat from his face with the sleeve of his monogrammed dress shirt, something he would have never dreamed of doing in any other situation.

"Besides, whoever was in the office feeding information to the shooter would have known about your 2:00 appointment. If they wanted you dead too, the shooter would have waited a half hour until you were in Nathan's office alone. He would have gotten you both at once," Caleb reasoned.

"You're right. It can't have anything to do with me or the FBI then," Johan said, his posture finally relaxing.

The three men sat silent, none of them wanting to ask the next obvious question.

Finally, Jordan spoke up. "What you're saying makes sense, but why aren't you allowed to talk to us?" He was getting worried again. "Why aren't they calling us to get their evidence and why are we suddenly not able to contact anybody from the bureau?"

"I don't know," Caleb said, with a complete loss for words of explanation. "And I don't know why I don't know!"

"Now that we have the hard evidence they want, they won't acknowledge us!" Jordan said.

Caleb squinted his eyes and pursed his lips as he shook his head in astonishment.

"Right. And now I've been told in no uncertain terms not to be in communication with you..."

"This is really crazy. And we need our money. Johan owes some big money to someone. We need at least $350,000 to cover us until we can get everything straightened out."

Caleb knew there was nothing he could do. He couldn't go to bat for the brothers. He was supposed to stay out of everything. Absolutely no contact. No exceptions. How could he now go and plead their case? He couldn't.

The agent looked apologetic when he said, "Look guys, you've got nothing in writing. You can't even prove it was the FBI that froze your bank accounts. If you check it out, the records say that the IRS did it. The only thing you can do is give them a little more time to contact you and hope they live up to their end of the bargain."

Jordan turned ghost white as he felt the blood drain from his face.

"I should have known," Jordan said, with more than a hint of his temper. "I don't know why we got involved in this operation in the first place! I knew it would be a fiasco! God damn it!" His raised voice and the pounding of his fist on the table drew enough attention for the bartender to peek out the swinging double doors that were behind the bar.

"I've got to get back to the office," Caleb said, as he stood up.

The three men noticed that the beer tasting room was deserted, with the exception of a janitor. Apparently, they had closed and no one made an announcement about it.

"So, whose side are you on?" Johan demanded to know.

Caleb was taken back by the idea. "Whose side?"

"Yeah. That's a good question! Are you just doing whatever they tell you to do... or are you going to help us?"

Jordan chimed in, as he stood up and leaned in toward Caleb in a manner that was intended to intimidate him.

"I work for the FBI."

The brothers looked at each other and rolled their eyes, a habit continued from their childhood when someone said something they thought was stupid. Jordan straightened his body, lengthening his spine as he pushed out his chest, with the intention of appearing dominating. Caleb thought he was adjusting his spine.

Jordan spoke a decimal or two lower than he normally did when he said, "We know you work for the FBI, asshole! But you're here… aren't you?"

Johan interrupted before Jordan's temper elevated even more. "Jordan, there's no need to talk to him that way. He's here… and risking his career at that! Doesn't that say something?"

"I guess so. But now what? We're no further now than we were an hour ago. That's what pisses me off!" Jordan explained in a voice that wasn't intended for secrecy, since no one else was around except the janitor.

Caleb had a guilty conscious even though he had no control over anything about this. He knew if the brothers were ever going to have the Federal criminal charges against them dismissed in exchange for their cooperation, he'd have to find a way to the bottom of this. They were so upset about not getting their money and about the possibility that Johan might be next on a hit list, they weren't even thinking about how and why all of this came about. Their own corruption caused the roller coaster ride in the first place.

"I'll do what I can from the inside. Don't call me. I promise, I'll call you as soon as I know anything. Anything at all," he emphasized. "Your telephone lines are probably still tapped though, so I'll say that I'm your tailor. You ask if your suit is ready. I'll say that you need to come in for another fitting."

"Another fitting?" the brothers said together.

"Yes. That will mean that we'll meet again here at whatever time we set up on the phone," Caleb said, accustomed to creative communication.

"Sure. But why *another fitting*?" Johan chuckled.

"Well, you are a big guy. You've got to be tough to fit for a suit... and this will give us the opportunity for more than one meeting, using the same thing about me being your tailor. It's called discretion, gentlemen," Caleb explained as they all headed toward the elevator.

"When the elevator opens into the parking lot, don't talk to us anymore. Johan and I will stand and talk for a few minutes so that it doesn't look like we were all together," suggested Jordan, really getting into character, dealing with the FBI.

"Good idea. Wait until you actually see me start to drive away in my car..." Caleb said, thinking that they may as well do it the way the FBI trained him.

When the men entered the elevator, the janitor threw away their trash, wiped down their table and chairs and then spoke into the ink pen that stuck from his uniform shirt pocket.

"Could you hear them?"

"Loud and clear."

"Good. I couldn't get that close to them. I'm glad this thing amplifies the sound. I couldn't even hear half of what they said."

"What was their general demeanor?"

"At first, they seemed pretty nervous, but then they relaxed some. When Caleb pointed out that they have no proof they are dealing with the Bureau and that they don't have a written immunity agreement, the Murphys started to get pretty pissed off... "

"Okay. See you back at the office," said the FBI's regional director.

Seven

Marcie and Greg Bordeaux weaved through traffic in their metallic red Porsche 911SC to downtown Phoenix, for their first business meeting with Jessica Sellica and Marcie's Uncle Dolan. One minute they seemed to be on pins and needles, the next minute they were just aggravated to be wasting so much time and energy. Then, they'd relax and reassure each other that they just needed to go through the motions. Everything would be fine soon, once the attorneys saw that they hadn't done anything wrong or illegal.

"There it is. The stucco building on the left with the fountain in front," Marcie pointed out to Greg.

"Oh yeah! I guess I have been here once before. You were right..." Greg admitted as he pulled the car into one of the reserved parking spaces.

Marcie laughed to herself, then asked Greg, "Do you remember how many hours and weeks Uncle Dolan and I searched for office space for him? I thought nothing would ever suit him... until we found this place. It was this colossal fountain that sold him."

Greg opened the trunk of the car and pulled out a cardboard file box that weighed at least twenty pounds. "I remember. And it was bad timing too, for you to be away from the farm that much. It was right when we were trying to organize the group."

"I know. You were busy with that and I should have been running the farm. Your brother couldn't handle it alone and keep up with conditioning and training at the same time. Everything was a mess!" said Marcie.

Greg hefted the box onto his left hip and locked the car. "We all understood though. As if it wasn't painful enough for him that his wife died in a car accident, he couldn't go back to practicing in the same offices anymore. Whenever they weren't in court they were working in adjoining offices. I can see why he wouldn't want to be reminded of her absence day in and day out."

"I think he just was lonely. He wanted to be with someone who cared. That's why he kept wanting me to go office hunting with him," she said in retrospect.

"I'm sure."

The receptionist escorted the couple to Jessica Sellica's office. Standing out from the upscale Southwestern motif, Marcie immediately recognized the original Remington bronze sculpture showcased on a handcrafted pedestal. The couple settled into the upholstered furniture, melting into the sandstone colored brushed suede. Jessica sat relaxed at her desk, which was crafted from rich and heavy dark wood. Marcie admired each piece of furniture, studying the hand carved antiques with silver drawer pulls and silver and turquoise inlay work.

After the greetings, Marcie changed the subject. "Your pottery collection belongs in a museum."

Four unique and stunning hand woven Indian rugs hung on the three walls. The fourth wall was more like an atrium, filled with flower blooming cactus in clay pots. The final touch of intimacy and sophistication was the natural rock running water garden. The water was trickling, offering a peaceful escape from a normally hectic life of an attorney. Marcie was most impressed that there wasn't a file folder, law book or law magazine in sight, nor any diplomas or other certificates. Jessica's office felt more like a comfortable home.

Dolan greeted Marcie with a gentle hug and Greg with a firm hand shake as he tried to evaluate their moods. This was the first time he represented a relative and wasn't quite sure of the appropriate way to conduct himself. Should he be strictly professional and down to business? Or should he be supportive the way a relative outside of the case would be?

"First, I'm going to have Jessica tell you a little about herself so that you'll feel like you know who you're confiding in. She's a wonderful woman and an outstanding attorney. The best litigation track record in the firm. She's got everything going for her... except that husband of hers. I want her to dump him and marry me, truth be told!"

No one, including Jessica, knew what to think about that last statement. They all wondered if he was joking around, just flattering her, or if he was actually serious.

Jessica wasn't prepared to talk about herself beyond her legal experience, so she kept it short and sweet.

"I grew up without a father. My mother raised me and we were poor. We always had food on the table and a place to sleep, even if it was on someone's sofa or in a sleeping bag on their living room floor. I always excelled at school. I had plenty of time for studying because we didn't have a television and I never had money to go out with my friends very often. In high school, I got a part time job at a Saddlebred farm a few miles from where I lived. I rode my second hand bike back and forth most days. My job was as a groom and once in a while I helped with feeding and stall cleaning if they were short handed. The owners were really nice. They paid me a little bit more than everyone else and they gave me free riding lessons when they had time. In the summer, I probably got 3-4 lessons a week; the rest of the year, maybe once or twice a week. Eventually, they let me start showing a few of their geldings in saddle seat and in equitation... all on their dime! We stayed in first class hotels and ate haute cuisine, at least to me. They said that they were modest compared to some of the other operations.

"I got a scholarship to Pepperdine, and didn't need to work because the scholarship paid all of my expenses. Now, as you know, I'm married to a tight wad. I'm a partner with Dolan. That's it. Let's get to work."

Marcie liked her style. "One question?"

Jessica smiled. "Sure."

"Who decorated your office? It looks like it's from a magazine. I love it!"

"Actually, one of my first clients owns an interior design firm and art gallery. She was sued for selling what was claimed to have been a forgery. I won the suit in court, including appellate. After I had worked so long on her case, I took a short vacation. She knew I admired the Southwestern style and that I was just getting started with my career. When I got back from my trip, I found my office just as you see it. Except, she had a lawyer's cabinet for basic law books. I took it out and put it in the conference room."

"Okay you two. I know you've never been involved in anything like this before, so I'm going to walk you through it. It's always easier on a client if they know pretty much what to expect," Dolan said.

"I thought we just needed to bring these documents and go through them with Jessica," Marcie said, getting a little bit worried.

"Legally, at this point, that is all that you are actually required to do. The subpoena states that you must produce all documents relating to the auction..." Jessica spoke up, wanting to take control since this was supposed to be her case.

"I don't understand," Greg interrupted. "You're saying there's more to it ?"

Jessica took a deep cleansing breath and slowly exhaled. "Well, let me be honest with you. I've never seen an issue raised and then dropped solely because someone produced documents!"

Dolan cut in. "That's why we're going to explain how the process works. So that there hopefully aren't anymore surprises."

"Right. Cut to the chase," Greg said, definitely getting nervous about the unknown.

"Here's what typically happens. Someone gets upset about something. They talk to their lawyer. The lawyer decides if the person has a legitimate cause for a complaint..." Dolan started to explain.

Greg interrupted him. "I don't understand. Why wouldn't the person at least confront whoever they have a problem with first... before they go running to a lawyer?"

"They should. They really should. But, unfortunately, not all people do what's most sensible. Anyway, the lawyer will either know he has a justified complaint that he thinks has a fair chance or better to stand up in court or not," Dolan continued. He raised his right hand in the air, with his palm toward Greg because he could see that he was going to be interrupted again. "Just listen to me for a minute Greg, then you can ask your questions. We'll get through this a lot faster that way."

"Jot notes if you need to, honey," Marcie suggested to Greg as she put her hand on his thigh.

"Anyway, sometimes a dispute isn't really cut and dry or completely understood. That's what I think has happened here. They are demanding the documents for evaluation of a potential claim. When I called opposing counsel, he was very forthcoming. He says that Mr. Murphy is concerned about the $2.5 million he paid for a mare named Love Letter. You're not the only ones involved. They also served the same subpoena on some trainers named Dean and Brian Pondergrass, who I assume you've done business with. They are also planning to contact all of the other people who were successful bidders at the auction."

Marcie put her hand over her mouth and widened her baby blue eyes. "Oh my god! They can do all that?! Why?"

Greg stood up with clenched fists as he leaned onto Jessica's desk. "Do you know how mad these clients are going to be?" he said in a raised voice.

"Hold on. Let me finish. I know this is hard."

Greg sat back down, but this time at the edge of the chair, ready to pop up out of his seat again if something triggered it. "Hard? It's a pain in the ass and we can't get involved in this!"

"You are involved. Like it or not. Just calm down and hear me out," Dolan said. When it was clear that Greg was ready to calm down, he continued. "Right now, your client, Johan Murphy, probably sees you as deep pockets. He wants to see what he can get. I don't think his lawyer, Alec Douglas, has determined what their actual case is, let alone if he could win it. He says that all he knows is, that his client thinks he's been cheated and that it looks that way to him also… "

"I never advised the guy how much to pay!" Greg offered, flabbergasted at the entire situation.

"Good. That's an excellent start. Anyway, this Alec Douglas is doing what we call a *fishing expedition.* They try to get everything they can and then try to create a case around whatever they happen to find. Basically, it's an overly broad use of the discovery process that the legal system permits."

"I still don't understand. What are they claiming that we did?" Marcie asked. Her heart was fluttering.

"At this point, they aren't actually naming any particular cause of action… which basically means, they aren't specifying yet. It's pretty much a thing where they say *hey… something doesn't seem right… let's check this out,*" he explained.

"And the court allows that? The person doesn't even have to know or think you did anything in particular to them and you have to give them all of your confidential documents?" Greg was incredulous.

"Yes," Jessica finally spoke, almost apologetically.

"And they're allowed to talk to all of our clients that bought at the auction?" Marcie asked, completely astonished at the prospect.

"Yes."

"And we have to take all of this time and pay for an attorney! They don't even need to lie and say we've done something in particular that's illegal or wrong?" Greg asked again.

"No, they don't even need to make up a lie," Jessica said.

Tears formed in Marcie's eyes and her face flushed. "What a stupid ass legal system!"

"In a way, yes. But, that's the discovery system. The U.S. has the best legal system in the world. Look at it that way," Jessica said.

Everything hit Greg like a ton of bricks. "So, what you're saying is that it's inevitable that this is just the beginning?"

"Yes. There will probably be documents that you didn't even think about producing that they'll demand. And interrogatories…" Jessica said.

Greg interrupted again. "What are interrogatories?"

"A written pretrial discovery device consisting of written questions about the case submitted. You answer all questions as a sworn statement under oath. They'll probably submit the interrogatories to each of you, to key employees, and buyers at the auction. Sometimes they can get an even broader scope. You never know," Dolan chimed in.

Greg was ready to beat his head against the wall, but the office was too perfect looking to seriously consider doing any damage. His hands trembled as he rocked his upper body in the chair.

"I wish that were all. Anyone even remotely involved can be required to participate in depositions and to provide documents. All of this is pretrial discovery. Hopefully, they won't find anything and it won't go that far. You never know," Jessica explained.

The tears streamed uncontrollably down Marcie's face. "But we didn't do anything wrong!" she insisted.

Greg was so wrapped up in his own rage at the situation that he didn't pay attention to how upset his wife was until she was barely able to speak. "You're right, Marcie… we didn't do anything wrong, so, it's not going to go very far… we'll just have to deal with it. Everything will be fine." He tried to convince himself as the words rolled off of his tongue.

Jessica and Dolan shot a glance at each other, hoping the other would continue with the unpleasant news. Finally, Dolan took the wheel.

"I hate to tell you this, but sometimes a very good case can be built against someone that didn't do anything wrong. If you don't settle out of court, you'll end up in court and risk losing. Sometimes you just can't consider who is right and who is wrong. It's an emotional journey and a financial burden if the other side won't fold their cards."

"But Uncle Dolan, how could it get that far? With us, I mean?" Marcie asked, now calmed down a notch or two.

"Sometimes people do things against the law without realizing it. Sometimes a plaintiff can make false claims that you can't prove to be invalid and with a preponderance of evidence, and the judge or jury rules against you." He paused for effect. "I'm sorry... but this is the way it is."

Greg found himself popping his knuckles one by one. "We get the picture. Now what?"

Jessica took control again. "First, I'm going to ask you questions that help me better understand your business. Then, you can explain any documents that aren't self explanatory."

"Can I get a little air and a few minutes alone to absorb all of this?" Marcie asked, feeling more overwhelmed than she ever had in her entire life.

"Sure. Ten minutes?" Jessica said.

"That'll help. I'm going to the lobby," she said as she stood up.

Greg started to follow her, but her body language told him that she wanted to be completely alone... not just away from Jessica, Dolan and the office.

He couldn't help but wonder if they could be in the category of people doing something illegal without realizing it. He contemplated how soon he should tell his own parents what was happening, but knew that he needed more time to accept and understand the situation himself before he told them anything.

Jessica hadn't had time to discuss with Dolan how much of a retainer his niece and her husband would be paying; about the hourly charge; or anything that may be a variable to the norm. She would address the financial issues after Greg and Marcie left.

Normally, after an initial consultation, the client pays the retainer before any additional time is expended. She didn't feel it was appropriate in this case to be the one to get involved in Greg and Marcie's payment, just as long as she got compensated the same amount that she would from any other client.

She really wished that she didn't need to tell Turner about her handling this case, but she had to. He always took a great interest in her cases, regardless of how commonplace they were. The particularly interesting ones were equally as fascinating to him as they were to her. He even watched her in trial when she thought that there would be something of consequence to see. She couldn't just not even mention this case. Turner was going to start to rant again about how Greg overcharged him for the horse he bought her. She could just hear it now.

Dolan used the time to check in for messages and faxes. When he didn't find anything of importance, he went to the refrigerator in the employee lounge to get the prepared platter of fresh fruit that was delivered from the deli. He removed the plastic wrap and arranged it on a large tray along with a pitcher of sun tea and four tall glasses filled to the brim with crushed ice. Distracted while visualizing himself spending far too many hours of his own on this case [hours that he wouldn't be billing his niece], he cut the tip of his finger as he sliced lemon wedges with his Swiss Army knife. Applying a bandage, he was aggravated that he couldn't find the only sharp knife that was normally in the lounge.

Dolan tried to set aside the fact of Marcie and Greg being family. Deep inside, his gut told him that they had to have done something illegal, or at the very least, unethical, in order to have built up their business so dramatically in such a short period of time. He really never took any interest in the business aspects of what they were doing until a couple of years before, when they inquired whether he knew anyone in Kentucky that had influence in rezoning decisions. Even then, he didn't ask many questions or get that involved. All he did was call a guy who owed him a favor. Within a week, they had a zoning variance for 2000 acres in the heart of Kentucky bluegrass. The land was originally for hunting in certain areas and for tobacco farming in others. For them to acquire the property, they needed the zoning changed. The plan was to develop fifty executive-style equestrian estates, a five hundred acre farm of their own, a marketing center, and an auction pavilion.

After the zoning issues were resolved, when Greg told Dolan that their next step was to get financing, and that they planned to go through their files to determine if any of their customers were in that business, Dolan offered to hook them up with a business contact he had. They agreed and didn't bother looking any further. A month later, all of the financing for the land acquisition was in place through a private investor out of Florida. The interest rate was fair. Dolan didn't tell them that the money came from Japanese investors. He led them to believe that the money was from Tony Valdachelli, when in the strictest sense of the term, Tony's business is simply a holding company that funnels money from Japan into the U.S.. There really was no need for Greg or Marcie to know the details.

Marcie wandered around the lobby wishing the entire meeting was a nightmare that she would wake up from any minute. It was horrible enough that they were going to be involved in an inevitable lawsuit, but when their clients and the trainers they worked with were going to be involved, it was just too much. She couldn't imagine that anyone would want to do business with them again if they were reeled into the situation.

With this happening, she wished she knew more about how the financial operations of their farm worked. Until now, as long as she had everything she wanted, she never cared to be informed, let alone involved in the business or details of the financial side of the business.

Jessica brought up the idea of a settlement. They didn't even own Love Letter, so they couldn't just let Johan out of the contract and refund all the money he paid in. All but five of the horses in the auction, including Love Letter, were consignments from their clients.

Marcie recalled that after the auction, during the buyer's party, she had a few too many celebration drinks. In the brief moment that she caught Greg without a buyer at his side, she told Greg that she couldn't believe that they had made a half a million dollars in consignment commissions just from Love Letter. She remembered Greg saying something about them really not making nearly that much money off of her because there were so many hands in the pie that had to be split. When she asked him why, he only had a moment to tell her that it was the only way Love Letter could have been sold for a record price.

Now, in retrospect, she realized that at the time, she was so stimulated from being in the temporary world of glamour and sensationalism that she didn't even ask him what he meant.

Marcie was forcefully driven to the rude awakening that she couldn't stay in the dark about how the farm operated and its finances.

Her dream world was over. The nightmare was beginning.

Eight

As the glass elevator that stood dead center in the atrium was easing down to ground level, Dolan spotted his niece in the lobby with the remnants of tears streaming down her face. It appeared that she was making an effort to compose herself, blotting off the smeared dark brown mascara that circled her eyes like war paint. Her eyes were glassy and her nose was red and irritated from crying and sniffling. There wasn't a trace of make-up left on her face to conceal her large pores and blackheads. She always prided herself for wearing her foundation and blush in such a way that anyone would think she was going au natural and had a beautiful complexion. Thank God for quality cosmetics and trained professionals to teach women how to apply them properly. If only she kept them in her purse to touch up with...

Marcie caught a glimpse of her uncle out of the corner of her eye as he hesitantly stepped away from the elevator doors that were closing behind him. She took a deep yoga-like breath in preparation for clearing her spinning head and returning to the business at hand. Even though Dolan was her uncle, she was embarrassed to be caught in such an emotional state and looking the way she knew she did. When their eyes met, she unconsciously looked down toward the tile floor as if in shame for a sin that the parish priest caught her at before confession.

"I didn't mean to get you so upset honey," he said apologetically. "You guys just need to understand what's really going on here. I'm sorry."

"I know. I appreciate it. Really, I do. I just needed a few minutes to myself," Marcie said through her sniffling.

"We really need to get started with the questions. It's been a half an hour," Dolan informed her as he led his distraught niece by the elbow toward the elevator. He was finding it increasingly difficult to act professional with the girl who taught him how to play with *Barbie* dolls and build forts in just about every room in his house.

Greg tried not to look shocked at his wife's skin when she returned to the office. He'd never seen it look that way before. In spite of all that they were going through, he wondered if she wore make-up *all* of the time. Could it be possible that she even wore foundation and blusher to bed and put it on fresh in the morning before he woke up? Most of the time she was out of bed before him, even if it was only to empty her bladder and then go back to sleep. Was she really touching up her complexion? If she was, seeing her as she looked right now, he could understand why she would do it. Starting the night of their first date, he always told her she was a natural beauty… the eighth wonder of the world; he now supposed she didn't want to disappoint him that it wasn't natural at all. At least no more natural than a halter horse being shown to a judge. It was amazing what a small amount of skillfully applied cosmetics and shaving could do for a woman and a horse.

Greg swallowed hard as he looked at his wife with new eyes. "Ready?"

Marcie's voice was so soft that everyone else in the room only knew what she said by reading her lips, *'Sure, I'm ready'*.

"There are several areas that we are going to need to cover so that we know what we are up against," Jessica informed them. "Know that everything you tell us is considered work product and is completely confidential. We legally can't tell anyone, not even a judge. So, everything you tell me must be 100% truthful, with no sidestepping or sugar coating, no matter what."

"Attorney and client privilege?" Greg asked.

"Absolutely," Jessica assured him.

Jessica weighed her words carefully before she said, "The first thing that I have to do is put myself in the shoes of Alec

Douglas, the Plaintiff's counsel. What would I be looking for that could be damaging? I would make a list of questions and build on that."

The Bordeauxs nodded their heads in understanding, but didn't repeat the words that were going through their minds... *but we didn't do anything wrong!*

Jessica was certain she knew what they were thinking, so she continued without waiting for a verbal reply. "My next step is to have a complete understanding of how your business works, how the industry works, and if you operated within the norm, using acceptable and legal business practices." She sat silent and studied their expressions to see if they understood what she was getting at.

Greg and Marcie nodded in unison but remained silent.

Dolan interjected. "I don't know about Jessica, but I think it's really important that we find out how the horses that you deal with went up in value so dramatically." He looked at Marcie. "I remember back when your dad was importing fabulous horses from Poland. He was selling their offspring for only $5,000... and grateful for that price."

Greg's adrenaline pierced through his veins. "What's the difference how the prices went up. It's just the market, like real estate. A worthless piece of land one year and the next year..."

Jessica interrupted, serving as an intermediary before he got off track. "Don't get defensive. It won't help anything," she said with the patience an adult would need to calm a child whose temper was about to flare.

"I'm not getting defensive. I just don't have time to waste," Greg said. He hoped that his voice didn't portray his conscience.

"What Dolan has asked about is precisely at the heart of the issue. From the looks of things, if I were representing a client who paid $2.5 million for a horse, I would sure want to know what made the horse worth that much money. And given that Mr. Murphy bought the horse at a public auction, I would want to know who was bidding against him… legitimate people or shills," Jessica said frankly.

Marcie's expression didn't change since she didn't know how the business operated. Like a spectator, she sat with her perfect posture absorbing the interaction between the three other people in the room.

The color drained from Greg's face and he tried to hide the quiver of his lips. A barely perceptible twitch of his eye started. He bit down lightly on his bottom lip as he thought about his response.

"Where do I start?"

"From the beginning, and don't leave anything out," Jessica said, now relaxing some since Greg had accepted that he needed to tell them everything.

"It'll take a while."

Jessica selected a pen to take notes with. "That's what we are here for."

Greg looked out the window for a moment to gather his thoughts and decide where to begin. His brother always teased him about being a winded storyteller, so today he weighed his words carefully to avoid wasting more time than necessary.

"Well… my parents always loved horses and went to farms that had Arabians, here in the United States. Long story short, they fell in love with Polish Arabians after an intense study of their genetics and physical characteristics. In the early 1940's they bought their first Arabians. Later, they bought a horse for each of us to train and ride. My brother and I lived and breathed horses, so it was a great family activity. We started showing and excelled in everything we entered.

"We all decided to try our hand at breeding, so we wanted our own stallion. The whole family went to Poland in 1963 and selected a stallion that we all agreed on. His name was Lodz. Naturally, the next step was to buy more land to have a big farm instead of a few acre set up. Lodz was a hit here in the U.S. We sold lots of breedings to him just through people seeing him in the show ring and from word of mouth… keep in mind that there weren't many Polish Arabians in the U.S. at the time," Greg explained.

"Then what?" Jessica asked.

"Well, we started buying more of our own mares and breeding to our stallion, producing more and more foals each year. Eventually, by the time that we had a lot of horses for sale, and so did our clients who bred to Lodz, we decided to hold an auction..."

Dolan was curious. "Was this the first auction ever held for Arabians?"

"No. There were others, and they did pretty good. That's where we got the idea."

"Do you remember what year that was?" Dolan interjected, pen in hand.

"Sure. 1971."

"How did it go?" Jessica asked as she was jotting notes.

"Pretty damn good. The top-selling mare went for about $50,000."

"Really?" Dolan paused for a moment, doing the math in his mind. "In 1971?" he clarified.

Greg raised his chin up a couple of inches and looked Dolan straight in the eye. "Yes," he said feeling insulted. Did Dolan think he was fabricating facts?

"What was the sale average though?" Dolan pressed for a more accurate picture of the times.

Greg answered curtly, even more insulted. "At *our* sale," he emphasized, as if his family were superior geniuses, "the Pure Polish mares averaged almost $30,000. The Polish-bred, meaning not 100% Polish blood, averaged about $10,000."

"Who was buying these horses?" Jessica asked.

Greg couldn't tell if she meant that only someone who was crazy would pay that much for a horse. He tried to remain calm on the exterior, but his gut started churning. She had no right to judge him or any of his clients. "Lots of people. Mostly people who already had horses. They just wanted better ones, once they saw the quality of what we were producing and importing from Poland."

"Then what?" Jessica said, now learning how arrogant that Greg was. She couldn't tell if Marcie shared his ego.

"Then, my family and I held at least one auction a year," he explained as if he were reviewing a history lesson. As an afterthought, he added, "The prices paid were higher each time. The value of our horses and our clients horses appreciated an average of 30% a year."

Marcie sat perfectly erect, looking at him admiringly.

Jessica nodded, waiting for a crown worthy of a King of his own country to appear on his head.

He decided to get off of the subject of money for a moment so that he wouldn't get more worked up about them judging him.

"Well, Marcie and I met at one of the shows. We were competing against each other... it was all friendly competition. The first day we met, we hit it off. Went on our first date about a week later. I knew I was in love then," Greg said, obviously recalling a very fond memory.

"I watched Greg showing in at least a dozen shows before we were ever introduced. I was in love with him before I even met him!" Marcie admitted in an adolescent-like manner as her eyes radiated. At least there was a little something she could add to the session now.

Jessica assumed that Marcie was attracted to Greg because of his talent with horses, and perhaps his resources. It certainly wasn't for his looks. Sure, he was in great shape, but his face and hair were unquestionably on the dorky side.

"After we dated for a while, Marcie and I decided to get married and start our own farm and marketing program. We didn't really have our own money though."

Jessica looked at him quizzically, but he explained himself before she needed to ask him to.

"Everything I did was really with farm money. I got compensated, but not really based on any kind of a salary or commission or formula. When I was old enough to need my independence, my parents built me a house on the farm, but at the opposite end of the farm as their house. I used credit cards and got cash whenever I needed or wanted something. Everything just came out of the farm bank accounts. Even though the horses and the farm evolved into a full-fledged business, it was run very casually as far as money and responsibilities went. Everyone made sure everything got done, and everyone had the money to live comfortably. We never really thought about money until Marcie and I decided to get married," Greg said.

"It was actually because of my father," Marcie clarified. "He asked us about whether I was going to need to get a job; where we were going to live, and all those kind of questions."

"That's when we decided that since we both loved the horses and you could make a decent living working with them, we'd start our own operation," Greg said.

"Was your family upset?" Jessica asked Greg.

"No. Not at all. I think they were almost relieved. When the family started everything when we were kids, it was just a hobby. The horses accidentally snowballed into a business."

Marcie expanded on the subject. "In fact, Greg's father suggested that he consult with his attorney and his tax advisor to see how he could help. It wound up that his parents gave us 150 of their 200 acres. They kept 50 acres for themselves... the land that surrounded their house, and the house Greg and his brother grew up in."

Not that it mattered for the case, but Jessica was curious about the family dynamics. She directed her question to Greg. "Wasn't your brother upset?"

Greg answered with complete honesty and it showed in his expression. "No. We discussed it at length. He didn't want his own business. All he cares about is being able to keep training and showing. It's his only passion and interest. Marcie and I decided to run our new farm as a real business, paying my brother a salary and bonuses, and giving him specific responsibilities... just as any business would," Greg said, not implying that he was doing his brother a favor.

Once again, with this line of questioning, Marcie could chime in. It made her more relaxed. "The land that his parents gave us was the land that had the barns, the pastures, and the riding arena," she explained as she pictured everything in her mind. "They were so generous, I don't know how we could have done any of this without them."

"Right!" Greg said, quite relieved to hear his wife volunteer the admission, especially without them being in a completely private situation.

"So, your parents are still in the business, right? Do they operate separately from you?"

"Actually, they're legally minority partners in the business and all of its assets, but they also personally own about fifteen to twenty horses at a time that they keep mostly on their fifty acres. My father does consulting on selection of horses to buy and breed. I handle all of the rest of the business aspects myself," Greg said.

Jessica didn't understand this attractive, talented woman's admiration of her husband. Marcie came from a family that would be considered wealthy by most people's standards. It seems that Greg has himself on a pedestal. Vintage Arabians is a horse farm, not IBM!

"I understand. Let's talk about how the prices got so high," she said diplomatically.

Greg knew better, but he hoped that Jessica wouldn't bring up the escalating prices again. He drank down the last of his bottled water as he composed his thoughts. Honesty and truth are two different things, he thought to himself.

"There were several other farms in Scottsdale at the time. All of us owned a lot of land because it was so undervalued when we bought it. From time to time, we'd end up talking at a show or some function, and it would get around to how expensive it was to add fencing and more barns to accommodate more horses, whether they were our own or our client's. None of us could even come close to breaking even financially… especially with the labor and feed costs to take good care of the animals," Greg said.

"Go ahead," Jessica said, trying to keep an open mind.

"So, one night, a group of us went out to dinner together after a local show and got talking about forming a consortium. The purpose was to turn this expensive hobby into something we could all turn a profit from. We discussed having about six or seven farm owners in the group. By the end of our long dinner and drinks, a couple of them didn't want anything to do with our plan, but five of us survived and formed the consortium," Greg said, intentionally omitting the details of the plans they schemed.

"What did the five of you do?" Jessica asked.

"A week later, we had a twelve hour long closed door meeting. No interruptions. We ordered in food and beverages and we stuck to business. We decided that it would be easy to take a leadership role and turn Polish Arabian horses into an actual industry. We just needed to devise a plan and follow it. We agreed to be friendly competitors, but we also all needed to work together to grow an industry from what was, at that time, a casual hobby. The horses were a hobby that we couldn't make a profit at.

"I still don't understand how you got people to pay such high prices for the horses," Dolan interjected, getting impatient. He could see that Greg was skirting around the details.

Greg took a deep breath before he continued. He needed to set the scene, or they would never understand how and why things happened as they did.

"I'll get to that in a second. First, we decided that it was fine to have just the everyday kind of person buying and showing the horses, but we needed to get more wealthy people involved…like the Thoroughbred business. We talked about how wealthy people wanted everything to be first class… their country clubs, cars, houses, boats, clothes, jewelry… everything. So it was obvious that they would want the farms they did business with to be first class also."

"Makes sense," Jessica admitted. Now that she had money, she didn't want to have her horse at a run of the mill looking barn.

"So, we needed to build fancy facilities and have fancy marketing materials. We would have to wine and dine our clients. That would cost us a lot of money," Greg reasoned.

"So, it was a catch 22?" Dolan asked.

"Not really. The other three gentlemen in the group were quite well off on their own. They just didn't want to pour even more money into their farms than they already were, if it wasn't going to make a profit,"

"I can see that," Jessica said, nodding in agreement while she sat back in her chair. There was nothing to really take notes on in this point of his explanation.

"So, anyway, we all agreed to build our farms as spectacular and prestigious as we could imagine and afford… and to have professional people do our marketing materials in a first class style and quality."

Jessica shot straight from the hip. "What about you? How did you and Marcie come up with the money?"

"A couple of ways. After I explained my business plan and our goals to Marcie's parents, they wanted to help us expand the business. When I told them that we needed to upgrade and add on to the farm to accommodate all of the potential business that was out there, they could see that it was necessary also. To help us out, they gave us a gift of $250,000 and three Pure Polish mares that were in foal.

"We spent some of the $250,000 on working with architects drawing up plans… and they made us a detailed model to display in my barn office. While the architects were working on our project, we bought and imported Lancelot, a Swedish National Champion Stallion. We paid an equine attorney to take care of the legal end of a stallion syndication… we offered the very first stallion syndication in the Arabian breed. We also spent, what at the time, was a lot of money, on marketing materials to market the stallion syndication."

For a change, Greg was just describing the facts without a hint of arrogance, Jessica thought. Maybe she jumped to an unwarranted conclusion earlier. She would reserve her judgment for later when she got to know him better.

Marcie's eyes showed that she shared her husband's pride of accomplishment as she listened to him continue. Jessica was surprised that she seemed to be listening to him as if Marcie were hearing the story for the first time herself. Was there a chance that she didn't know very much about how her own husband had built up their business? Jessica couldn't imagine herself being that uninvolved in the details of her and Turner's life. They shared almost everything.

Greg kept talking. "Each of the other people in the consortium bought one or two shares of the Lancelot syndication to help me get it rolling. Then, just by my reputation and Lancelot's show record and pedigree, along with people seeing my plans for the farm development, they were impressed with the syndication. All of the shares sold out within about six months. I guaranteed to buy any shares back at a ten percent discount if they later wanted out of the syndication and there wasn't an actual resale market developed yet," Greg boasted as he sat up tall and puffed his chest out just enough to display his self-confidence.

Here comes that arrogance again, Jessica thought.

"Sounds like good business," Dolan said, knowing that Jessica thought the same as he did about their client's attitude.

"How much money did you bring in from the syndication?" Jessica asked. She was taking notes once again. The details might be important later. There was no way to be certain at this point in the game.

"There were 75 shares at $75,000 each..." Greg started to explain as if he were totally numb to the incredible dollar amounts.

Jessica interrupted him. "I thought a syndication was when someone buys lifetime breeding rights to a stallion... when they get one breeding a year until the horse dies or becomes sterile."

"That is how it works," Greg said, confused by her statement.

"Why would people pay that much money?" Dolan asked.

"Because we did projections showing that each breeding would sell for $10,000 the first year, $20,000, the second, $30,000 the third. The projections didn't show any further appreciation past the third year."

"So what you're saying is, that according to your projections, in the first five years people would make back $120,000?" Jessica asked, adding the figures to her notes and double-checking that she wrote them correctly.

"Even better than that... we let people buy the shares on five year terms. That way, *every dollar* they invested was fully depreciated on their taxes for that year... including their mortality insurance and their pro-rata share of expenses, *and* even trips to Hawaii for syndicate share holder meetings," Greg said with a huge grin on his face. Somehow, he forgot about the circumstances that led him to his explanation.

Jessica wrote furiously. Dolan asked the next logical question. "So, did your projections pan out?"

Marcie had to chime in and answer. "Yes! In fact, in the fourth year, the breedings were selling for $35,000 each, *if* someone could even buy one. Lancelot was such an outstanding sire that most people used the breedings on their own mares. I think there were only about 20 breedings for sale the fourth year." Her eyes were sparkling now, with no trace of the tears that consumed her earlier, other than the fact that her make-up had disappeared.

Greg jumped in before Marcie could continue to recount the success of the syndication. "In the fifth year, several people sold their shares and got $300,000 a share. Keep in mind, they had already used four or five breedings... or sold some of them." He got excited, telling his success story. He couldn't sit still any longer. Standing up and trying to find somewhere to move around in the office, even he was impressed with his coup.

Jessica was sure that if her office was large enough, Greg would have been strutting around with his peacock feathers spread wide open in the '*look at me*' position.

"Why didn't you just syndicate Lodz, the stallion your parents bought?" Jessica asked without giving him the satisfaction of indicating that she was impressed with his accomplishment.

"A few reasons. One, his age. By this time, Lodz didn't have enough predictable fertile years ahead of him to justify a high dollar share price. Second, we picked Lancelot specifically to cross with the daughters of Lodz. Dad and I thought it would be an excellent cross…and it was…"

'Wow,' Jessica thought… *'he finally gave some credit to his father. It's about time.'*

Greg barely stopped to take a breath as he described how incredible everything was. "Keep in mind, there weren't all that many Polish Arabians in the U.S. at that time. We needed to infuse new blood so that people wouldn't inbreed too heavily. Another reason was because a new stallion spreads renewed excitement and hype. Half the business is about hype. Everyone already knew and respected Lodz and they were already able to breed their mares to him. Lodz wasn't exclusive or a novelty anymore. We needed high quality, hype and exclusivity to make the syndicate work."

"So that's where you got the money to do the overhaul on the farm?" Jessica asked.

"The first overhaul… not the later additions," Marcie said, feeling like she wanted to be part of the conversation again.

Dolan did a quick calculation in his head. "You brought in over five and a half million dollars from one stallion! And all your clients made a big profit. That's impressive."

Greg sat back down since there really was nowhere to pace. "That's one of the reasons why my clients became willing to pay a lot more money for quality horses every year. The more they profited, the more they would spend on buying more and breeding more."

"It sounds almost like people just followed along with what everyone else was doing… but who started paying the really high prices in the first place? What I still don't understand is, how you got enough people to do it in the first place, to establish what others considered the 'market value'?" Jessica said, tapping the point of her ink pen on the yellow pad.

"It was easy... the other people in the consortium bought the first four shares of the Lancelot syndication the day I had it ready..." Greg said.

Dolan interrupted. "So you made $300,000 the very first day? I should be in your business!"

Greg paused and rubbed his forehead. He had to phrase this answer properly. "No. Not really. They signed the contract to buy the shares, and I signed contracts to buy horses from them of equal value. We were just trading paper... none of us really spent any actual cash..."

Jessica wrote *'Trading Paper'* in extra large block letters, making the words bolder through doodling, as she spoke. "So, really, you traded syndicate shares for horses?"

"No. We didn't take the horses, except for one mare," Marcie answered for Greg before he got a chance to decide what he wanted to say.

Greg couldn't believe Marcie admitted it. If she hadn't volunteered the truth, things could have gone a lot smoother. He could imagine what Jessica and Dolan were thinking of them.

"I don't understand," Jessica said, confused.

"We just traded paper so that we could honestly say that these other successful business people and breeders were excited enough to buy shares. It implies that whoever you're trying to sell to should do what the experts are doing," Greg said, not meaning to let the guilt in his voice come through. He sounded like a little boy with his hand caught in the cookie jar.

Jessica and Dolan looked at each other with concern. From a legal point of view, these were really sham sales conducted to mislead potential investors. In legal terms, it was fraud and misrepresentation. The Bordeauxs were fortunate that everyone really ended up making a profit... no one would have reason to complain since everything worked out in the end. Still, it is against the law to conduct business this way.

"What about the actual sales of horses?" Jessica asked, afraid to hear the answer.

Confession time. "Well… sort of the same thing. Each of us in the consortium would allow the others to tell people that one of us bought one or more of their horses, for a specific price… a very high price. We'd call each other and make sure to get the stories straight in the event that a prospective buyer or current client asked. When the clients thought other people paid the high prices, they were willing to do it too. At least most people," Greg said.

Greg's own explanation hit him in the stomach like a medicine ball. Telling the process out loud made it sound bad. Really bad. He hadn't thought anything of it at the time… it was Marcie's idea, and he thought it was a good one. So did the others in the consortium. None of them felt guilty. They didn't think it hurt anyone… as long as enough real buyers followed along and it continued to snowball, that's what the real market would be. They just needed to start it somehow.

"We did it at our first really prestigious auction too… it created so much excitement," Marcie offered enthusiastically. She didn't grasp the full import of the deception from a legal and ethical perspective.

Greg cringed. This wasn't what they need to expose.

"What do you mean?" Dolan asked her, afraid to hear his niece's answer.

"Well, we had the others in the consortium bid up and buy several of the horses at the auction. In fact, they even had some relatives and close business associates bid up and buy also," she said proudly.

Greg couldn't believe Marcie was elaborating. In most ways, she was very smart. What was she thinking?

Jessica tried not to change her expression when she asked, "So, the people you were referring to didn't actually pay for the horses? They just appeared to be successful big spending bidders?"

"Yes. And it made everyone else bid high too! Our plan worked perfectly. After the first several auctions, we didn't need to do it very often anymore, because there were enough real buyers to actually sell the majority of the horses for really high prices," Marcie bragged.

Jessica couldn't make herself look at Dolan. It wasn't the time.

"So, what you're saying is that you never really got paid for the horses by the people in the consortium? Did you give them the horses for free in exchange for bidding?" Jessica asked.

Marcie was a motor mouth now and Greg couldn't think of how to stop her. "No! We just reciprocated, doing the same thing at their auctions. But we did move the horses to the farms of the successful bidders. If we didn't, that's when everything would have looked fishy. We're all within a few miles of each other and we knew the horses would be well cared for," Marcie said.

Greg's heart was beating hard, his blood pumping fast through his veins. Hearing the story told, he realized that they had done unethical things. Somehow, at the time, it didn't seem like any big deal. It was just a means to an end. But now, hearing it out of Marcie's mouth and in the presence of lawyers, it sounded like big trouble. He was astounded that Marcie didn't seem to grasp it.

"Marcie, don't you see that you were scamming people by doing all of that. It was all a set up. A con. An elaborate scheme to trick people into buying horses for more money than what the market would really bear..." Dolan finally said, hating to have to tell his own niece that she was in big trouble if anyone else found out.

Marcie defended them with a raised voice, as if that would make the lawyers comprehend everything. "You don't understand... no one got hurt! All the people who followed along made money. They love the horses. The social aspects of being in the business. They get the tax deductions. No one is harmed in any way!"

"You did it all by fraud and misrepresentation. That's wrong. Illegal. Actually, it's even criminal," Jessica said.

Marcie started crying because she couldn't get them to understand. She tried to think of another way to get them to comprehend.

"Why can't you see we did a good thing by creating an industry that made middle class people rich... and rich people richer! A strong industry creates lots of jobs too... trainers, assistants, grooms, farm help... it goes even further than that. The suppliers make more money... the tack stores, the feed stores, the farmers who produce the feed... it goes on and on. Because people were able to profit, we could produce more horses. Now, the entire industry has become a dynamic force in the entire U.S. economy!"

Jessica couldn't believe her ears.

"Marcie, if you guys did it all without coercion and deception, I would admire you. But you and your group are nothing more than a bunch of crooks!" Jessica said emotionally as she thought about her husband always saying that they overpaid for the horse they had purchased from Greg.

Marcie stormed out of the office, slamming the door behind her.

"I'm sorry for how she's being. I understand what you're saying. I'll get her to understand. She's upset because neither of us looked at it that way before... and neither did the others in our consortium," Greg said in an embarrassed quiet voice.

"Do you think that Johan Murphy found out how you conduct business?" Jessica asked.

"No. We all swore we'd never tell anyone, no matter how well the industry went. I trust that no one told," Greg said, confident in his answer.

"Do you need to get your wife?" Dolan asked, restraining himself from going to comfort his niece. Right now, he was her lawyer, not her uncle.

"No. She needs time alone to absorb all of this. I know her."

"Are you up to answering more questions?" Jessica asked, almost as if the emotional scene hadn't even occurred.

"Sure. Let's get this over with," Greg said, resigned to the fact that they had in fact done something wrong.

Jessica turned to a fresh page in her paper pad, prepared to take more notes. "What about the auction last year? Did you have all legitimate bidders?"

Greg got a sinking feeling in the pit of his stomach. "What do you mean?"

"Were there any shills?" Jessica said bluntly as she elevated her head and stuck out her chin slightly in an accusatory manner.

"No," Greg said, then hesitated about answering with complete honesty. "Not shills. But we did entice several clients to keep bidding up on horses that they really wanted."

"What do you mean?" Jessica asked.

Greg felt mortified to answer, but his demeanor didn't show it at all. "Well, I offered about fifteen of our best customers... ones that were very wealthy, and had already made a lot of money from doing business with us... I offered that for every time they bid an additional $50,000, I would give them services, such as training, showing, and breedings to our stallions, that equaled 20% of the final selling price of the horse, regardless of who bought the horse."

Her eyes widened and her eyebrows suddenly raised a half an inch. "And they agreed?"

"Yes. Because I told them only to do it on horses they'd really want to own... just in case their bid ended up being the final bid. They really did have to buy the horse if the bidding stopped with them. And it did, several times. They understood the conditions."

Dolan found the explanation hard to believe. "On horses that expensive, how could you compensate them fully... the 20% formula you talked about?"

Greg looked Dolan straight in the eye and never broke eye contact. He spoke as if he had been caught cheating at school and was now addressing the principal who had the authority to expel him. "Well, we worked it out, one way or another. Each of the clients knew I would. They trusted me. It just worked out so that I kept my word..."

Jessica interrupted him. "Specifically, *how* did you keep your word?"

He didn't have to think about his response. "Like with some, I gave them a free colt... one I couldn't sell easily and that they liked a lot. In fact, one of the colts went on to become a Reserve National Champion and is now worth at least $300,000. That's what they've been offered for him, at least. But they don't want to sell him."

Dolan and Jessica waited for more examples. When Greg didn't offer anything else, Dolan looked down at the rug, closed his eyes, and pinched the bridge of his nose at the inside of his inner eyes. The gesture told Greg that Dolan was getting tired and was about ready to lose his patience.

"With some of the bidders, I sold some of their horses for them and didn't charge my standard 20% commission... so, say on a $100,000 horse, I didn't deduct the $20,000 commission."

Dolan finally shot Greg a look that implied that he didn't think that Greg was helping his own case.

"Everyone's been totally and completely satisfied with how they've been treated. I swear!" Greg said, wanting very much to gain the approval of Jessica and Dolan.

"I don't believe you," Dolan said honestly. The skin over his face tightened. "Not that I wouldn't have worked with you anyway, but what was all the bullshit about you and Marcie insisting that you didn't do anything wrong?"

Greg's mouth was suddenly dry and parched. He took a sip of the water that Marcie had left from hours earlier. The pit of his stomach churned. "Until this conversation, it didn't seem like we had done anything wrong."

Dolan and Jessica each looked at him as if he were out of his mind. They didn't say anything. By this time, they were almost entertained to hear Greg continue to put his foot in his mouth.

"Everyone loves their horses. Thanks to me, they're happy and making money… or could make money if they wanted to. No one has complained or questioned us. Our customers are treated like royalty and they're satisfied."

Jessica shook her head in both disgust and amusement. "Well, not *everyone* is satisfied. Remember Johan Murphy?" Jessica said with a hint of sarcasm.

"I don't know what happened. I never even met him until after the auction," Greg said, not elaborating, yet not actually lying.

"Was anything special done that got people bidding on Love Letter… to such an outrageous price as $2.5 million?" Dolan asked.

He didn't answer right away. Jessica could read Greg's face. She could see that he was deciding whether to be one hundred percent honest.

A flash bulb lit in her mind. "That reminds me of a quote by Champ Clark: *'While the percentage of fools in this country is not so large, there are still enough to fatten the swindlers…'* she said.

Before she could continue, Dolan abruptly stood up, walked behind Jessica's desk, and put his hand firmly on her shoulder. "I've let everything else insulting that you've said go, but that was uncalled-for. I think you're being far too judgmental. You shouldn't be speaking to a client this way."

"Dolan, they're cons. They cheat people…"

"Stop it! You don't talk like this to a client! Behind closed doors is one thing, but not to their face or right in front of them! What's gotten into you?" Dolan was angry and embarrassed. "We're criminal attorneys. Most of our clients do things that are illegal and immoral. Do you need to end this session and compose yourself?"

Greg reminded them that he was in the room. "Both of you, stop this right now. I know what Jessica's problem is. She's hearing all of this and not thinking of *me* as her client. She's thinking of herself as *my client.* Now, she knows more of the ropes to the business. And, I'm sure in the back of her mind she can't wait to get home and tell her husband..."

Jessica was impressed with his insight. She hadn't thought about it that way consciously, but she was sure that he was right.

"I can't tell Turner anything. Attorney-client privilege. You know that," she said in a surprisingly calm manner. "But, you are absolutely right. I've got to forget I've done business with you. Forget that I'm your client in something that, in a way, is completely unrelated. To start, I think I need to move my horse to another operation."

"If you want to, go ahead. I don't need your business!"

With those few moments there was a sense of relief in the air and each of them knew they had to continue with the line inquiry that was started.

"Greg. You have to tell us the truth. The whole truth. That's what this case is going to revolve around. The guy is going to sue you and you know it. We have to know everything... and I mean absolutely everything," Jessica said with authority.

"Fine. But, Marcie doesn't know any of this. It's not that she wouldn't approve... it's more that she's sort of greedy... she would have been upset if I told her how much of the action I was giving away to get the publicity of the highest sale," Greg said.

The suspense was intriguing Jessica and Dolan. Then, Marcie walked back in.

"I'm sorry that I walked out like that. I get emotional and lose my temper sometimes. I'm ready to deal with things now...in the proper frame of mind..." Marcie said, now that her Valium had taken effect.

"Did you take your tranquilizer?" Greg asked.

"Yes," Marcie said, wishing that Jessica and her Uncle didn't know.

"She doesn't have a problem with drugs... she just keeps tranquilizers on hand to relax her before she competes in an important show..." Greg said, defending his wife's integrity.

"And before I ride horses that like to buck! I only take a half dose. Don't worry. It's just enough to take the edge off. Greg's dad prescribes it for me… and he knows why and he knows I don't take them very often," Marcie said, not wanting to worry her uncle.

"I understand. I do the same thing before I go in front of a judge or jury that I'm nervous about," Jessica assured her.

"Honey, I was just about to answer an important question when you walked in. It's an answer that you're not going to like," Greg said.

"What was the question?"

"Jessica asked if I did anything special that got people bidding on Love Letter… to get her to sell for two and a half million dollars."

"Did you?" Marcie asked him, obviously worried about what his answer would be.

"Yes," he said, feeling the rush from his head to his toes.

Nine

In unison, the Pondergrass brothers speedily retreated behind the closed doors of their shared office when the process server left the building.

"Dad said this would happen!" Brian said, raising his voice to his younger brother.

Unable to look his brother in the eye, Dean faced the acrylic glass wall, looking into the indoor Olympic sized riding arena; he watched an apprentice rider on a gray mare. "How would he know? He hasn't sold a horse since an expensive horse was five grand!" Dean retorted.

Brian didn't want to lose his temper with his only brother, but he was tired of Dean acting like he knew everything about big business just because he had a MBA from Northwestern.

"Just admit that he was right... we should have retained a good business attorney before we started brokering and when the prices of the horses started skyrocketing," Brian said.

Brian's words lingered in the air for the amount of time it took the rider to circle the riding arena. Dean's cockiness and self-assurance wasn't going to be dampened by a subpoena, even when in the presence of no one but his own flesh and blood business partner.

"I don't get it! Why do you treat dad like he's some big shot successful rich guy... and you act like I don't know shit?" Dean said, with disdain toward his father.

"Why? Because unlike you, I respect our father. If it wasn't for his success, we wouldn't own this farm or have this business."

"You just don't get it, do you?" Dean said as he poured a shot glass of vodka for each of them, without needing to ask Brian if he wanted one.

"Get what? That dad got rich from owning half the county?"

"Yeah. And the mineral rights. If he didn't inherit all the land that the last three generations owned, he would have been working in the factory, lucky to be a shift foreman!" Dean said after letting the first shot go down smooth.

Brian felt his shot of vodka burn his throat before he answered. "You underestimate him. He was smart enough to hold on to the land and sell off enough mineral rights to keep paying the taxes and supporting our family until the timing was right to sell the rest. He kept us five hundred acres and didn't charge us a dime. To me, that's a smart man, college graduate or not," Brian said in defense of his fifty-five year old father.

"This argument is never going to change..." Dean said as he refilled their shot glasses.

"I guess we really do need to call an attorney now," Brian suggested.

"We do."

\`\`\`\`\`\`\`\`\`\`

Alec made arrangements for Garth to take a temporary leave of absence from his regular job in order to work full time on Johan Murphy's case. His experience and knowledge of the Arabian horse business would be put to use. As Garth said, he didn't feel that he was doing anything useful at the firm he was with. He was burned out from the monotony of working on boring boilerplate motions and objections to motions.

\`\`\`\`\`\`\`\`\`\`

"Alec here."

"My name is Jed Packard. I've recently been retained to represent Brian and Dean Pondergrass. Do you have time to talk?"

Alec wasn't surprised to hear from their counsel. "As a matter of a fact, I do."

"First, let me tell you that my clients have very little to offer you, but they are gathering the information you've demanded and they intend to be completely forthcoming," Jed said.

"I appreciate that."

"The purpose of my call is to inquire about the nature of the request you've made. My clients have no idea why they would need to turn over their limited amount of information to anyone."

Alec decided to be candid, since the sooner he could get a credible party related to the case to cooperate, the easier the case would be to put together.

"My client, Mr. Murphy, was induced by your clients to buy a horse for $2.5 million dollars. I assume, that given the nature of your clients business, they were financially compensated for having brought Mr. Murphy to the auction as a successful bidder. My client tells me that no disclosures were made to him about any compensation that your clients would receive if he purchased the horse, which he did in fact purchase," Alec began.

Before Alec could continue, Jed interjected a question.

"Is this your first case in the Arabian horse business, Mr. Douglas?"

Alec was taken back, but admitted that it was his first case.

"May I suggest that my clients and I fly to St. Louis at your earliest convenience in order to enlighten you and to personally deliver the documents requested?"

"Is tomorrow too soon?"

"No, it's not too soon. As you can imagine, our position is that we'd like to expedite our involvement in this matter as quickly as possible. We've already discussed our schedules. Tomorrow will be just fine," Jed said, confident he had the upper hand and could dispose of the case easily.

\`\`\`\`\`\`\`\`\`\`

The three men sat in the same row of the first class section of the 727 plane heading for St. Louis, Missouri. Brian listened as Dean explained to Jed the relationship between them and Vintage Arabians; Greg Bordeaux, in particular. By the time they finished disclosing the details of the Love Letter transaction, they knew they were in for trouble.

"Why didn't you tell me these things in my office yesterday?" Jed asked the brothers.

"We're stupid," Brian said.

"I slept on it last night and admitted to myself that if you didn't know the real facts, you couldn't represent our best interests. On the way to meeting you at the airport, Brian and I talked about it and decided to tell you the whole truth about how the sale happened," Dean said.

Jed asked several more questions and then reanalyzed their position. "Alec Douglas is under the impression that we're willing to cooperate fully because you have nothing to be concerned about."

"Right," the brothers said, simultaneously.

"Now that I know everything, I'm going to need to feel out the case they're trying to build. I need to find a way you can work with them in a manner that would totally eliminate your liability," Jed said.

"What we did is that serious?" Dean asked.

"Yes. It was fraud. Criminal, in fact."

"Criminal?" Brian said, with a frog in his throat.

"Yes. We'll have to hope that they won't call the District Attorney. You better pray that they'll keep everything in the civil courts."

Concentration lines formed across Brian's forehead. He remained as calm as possible under the circumstances. "You said no one would ever find out!"

"No one did find out! Apparently, we're going to be telling them on our own..." Dean said with a guilty conscience.

"I can't believe this!" Brian said.

Dean defended himself. "Look, no one got hurt by anything. It might have been illegal, but it wasn't really wrong. Johan bought the horse because he wanted to. And he paid the price he was willing to pay. We didn't make him pay $2.5 million... he chose to!"

\`\`\`\`\`\`\`\`\`\`

"I appreciate you meeting with us so quickly," Alec Douglas said, as he shook the outstretched hand of Jed Packard.

"As I said, my clients would like to dispose of this as soon as possible. They've got a busy show season starting soon," Jed said to Alec.

"Johan asked me to apologize for him. He couldn't be here today on such short notice. He had other business commitments to attend to out of state,"

"That's all right," Brian said.

"I'd like to keep this as informal as possible, if that's acceptable to you," Jed told Alec.

"For now."

"First of all, I'd like to give you a briefing about my clients. Do you mind?" Jed asked.

"No. As long as I can still ask them questions, it's fine. Go ahead."

"My clients have been involved with horses their entire lives. Both men are talented horsemen, trainers and showmen. Dean handles the business and financial aspects of their operation while Brian handles the daily operations of the actual farm... he manages the people that work for them, such as the assistant trainers, breeding staff and grooms. They have a farm manager, but he primarily deals with the people who do the maintenance, the people who clean the stalls and feed the horses, and he orders the feed and other supplies for the barn and the shows. They have an office manager that Dean oversees. She does payroll, pays the bills, and deals with getting marketing materials and contracts sent out...typical duties."

"I see," Alec said, as he was taking notes.

"Dean and Brian are the only ones privy to any details of the financial aspects and sales techniques implemented by their operation," Jed said, deliberately being vague.

"That stands to reason," Alec said.

"I guess that covers some basic background."

"Sure. Thank you. May I ask questions now?" Alec said in what could have been interpreted as a patronizing tone.

"First, would you mind telling us what Mr. Murphy is complaining of?" Jed said innocently.

"Our case isn't developed yet, as we discussed. That's the purpose of our meeting," Alec said, intentionally avoiding a direct answer.

"I understand that. But why did Mr. Murphy come to you in the first place?" Jed asked.

"That's between he and I."

Dean couldn't stop himself from speaking up. "Johan seems to really like Love Letter. The last I spoke with him he was very appreciative of having had the opportunity to buy her."

"And he said he was so excited to have been written up in all the magazines," Brian added.

Alec knew they were right, but his client's feelings about the horse didn't have any bearing on the case. "Let me begin asking you questions, gentlemen," Alec said, without any hint of it being a question as to whether or not they were ready.

"Did you receive any compensation in any form, for having brought Mr. Murphy, a successful bidder, to the auction?"

"Yes, we did," Dean said.

"How much did you receive?"

"To date, or do you mean including what Vintage Arabians still owes us?" Dean asked.

"Explain anything you think I should know. I want to know everything about any compensation that you received," Alec said, trying to sound patient. He was ready to write answers next to the questions he already had prepared in writing.

"We received 20%, which was $500,000, as commission, after Mr. Murphy's down payment check cleared," Dean said.

"Go on," Alec said.

"We're owed all of the interest payments on the entire note, payable to us as payment is received by Vintage Arabians," Dean said.

Alec glanced at Johan's purchase contract. "That's, what, 12% interest on the unpaid balance?"

"Yes, sir," Dean said respectfully.

"Is that normal in your industry? To receive the interest payments?"

"No. Greg Bordeaux discreetly offered it to anyone who brought a buyer who would spend $2 million or more," Dean said.

"Was that in order to induce you into encouraging a buyer to pay an outlandish price?" Alec asked.

Jed quickly held his hand up, palm facing out, signaling Dean not to speak.

"Don't answer that. First of all, nothing has been established to justify your statement about an 'outlandish price'."

"I beg to differ," Alec said smugly.

"We're not here to debate the value of the horse, are we?" Jed asked.

"Not specifically, no," Alec admitted.

"Let's get on with your questions then," Jed said.

Alec took a deep breath, intending to get in a better frame of mind. He still couldn't help but think that his client was totally ripped off, regardless how his own client felt about the issue.

"Did Greg Bordeaux offer to pay out all of the interest in order to get over $2 million for the horse?"

"It was my understanding that that was the purpose, yes," Dean said.

"To your knowledge, has anyone else in the business offered the same, or similar enticement before?"

"Yes. Similar. The farms in Scottsdale that hold auctions frequently offer a select group of trainers some of the interest payments as additional compensation," Dean said.

"Explain."

"Well, usually, they'll pick five or six horses in their auction that they want bid up. Since trainers commonly bid for a client, or are with a client who's bidding, they want us to work with them on particular horses. So, on those horses, they may offer 5% interest for the entire note... or sometimes they'll offer a few free breedings to their stallions. We can sell the breedings to our own clients, or include them in a sale of a mare, or use the breedings ourselves for our own mares. Sometimes, they offer to let us use maybe 20 stalls in their barn during the Scottsdale show, so that we can do presentations of our horses and have parties... all meant to sell horses," Dean explained.

"Let me clarify this. You automatically get 20% commission?"

"Yes," Dean confirmed.

"And these other things are bonuses on top, given only if specific horses sell for over a predetermined price?" Alec was taking notes as quickly as possible.

"Yes."

"Is 20% the standard commission at an auction?"

"For us it is. The most influential and successful trainers get 20%. The other trainers, who the farm doesn't try hard to work with, and buyers agents, they get anywhere from 5% to 10%, depending on the farm that's holding the auction," Dean explained, boosting his own ego.

"Did Vintage Arabians compensate you for you bringing Mr. Murphy in any other ways... in addition to the interest payment?"

"Not Vintage Arabians," Dean said hesitantly. It stuck in his mind that Jed had told them that they needed to tell Alec everything possible to get on his good side.

Jed interrupted, and told Alec, "Mr. Douglas, my clients have a good deal of information to give you. We'd like to discuss an arrangement."

"What sort of arrangement?"

"One in which my clients will be 100% excluded from any liability in a civil action and that you won't pursue criminal action," Jed said firmly.

Alec wasn't even thinking along the lines of criminal actions. Jed showed his cards too soon.

"Let me assure you Jed, if your clients are the only ones who can help me win a case against Vintage Arabians, and they've got valuable enough information, I'll seriously consider leaving them out of this."

"That's not good enough. I need a guarantee that you won't go after them," Jed said, staring directly into Alec's eyes.

"First I need to know what they can help with."

"You'll have to trust me. Otherwise, we aren't going any further. We'll give you the only formal written agreement they have... an agreement that spells out the compensation they've already disclosed to you."

Alec thought for a minute. Johan didn't want to harm Brian and Dean. He had to go along with his wishes as long as there was someone else to go after.

"Okay. I'll agree, but they better help me make a strong case," Alec said.

Jed opened his brief case and pulled out a hand written agreement that he wrote on the airplane. It was already signed by himself, Dean and Brian.

"Read this, and sign here," Jed said to Alec.

Alec cracked a smile while he signed the document that would prevent him from going after the Pondergrass brothers. Johan would be pleased.

"This better be good. Spell it out for me, boys," Alec said.

"A couple of weeks before the auction, I met privately with Greg Bordeaux and told him I had a client who said he'd be willing to spend up to $2 million on Love Letter, just for the fame," Dean said.

"What did he say to that?" Jed said.

"He was straight. He asked if it was someone in the business. I said *'no, just some rich guy.'* Greg said he didn't want any part of it. I really wanted the big commission and the prestige, so I pursued it. Greg asked me if I understood that the mare had practically no chance of ever getting pregnant. I told him that I was fully aware, and so was Mr. Murphy. Then, Greg said something about the fact that no one could ever make money from that mare. I told him I knew it and that Mr. Murphy knows it and he doesn't care. He just wanted the tax benefits and the press about him buying the horse. Greg expressed that he didn't like the idea of someone who didn't already own high quality Arabians buying the mare. So, I asked him why he put such a big incentive... 20% and the interest payments. He said it was because he assumed that whoever bought her would want to show her more... maybe try to win the Triple Crown again... to make history that way. And he said he wanted to keep his reputation of selling the highest priced horses in the breed," Dean said.

"This Greg... did you believe him that he wanted to be that honorable?" Alec asked, having not expected to hear any of this.

"Yes. I consider him honorable. A little greedy sometimes, maybe. But not dishonest," Dean said.

"I've never known him to lie about a horse's ability or production record or anything important like that," Brian added to the conversation.

"Okay. Then what?"

"Well, he said he had to give it some thought... about letting Mr. Murphy buy the horse. Greg said he felt pretty confident that someone who was experienced and who would want to keep showing her would buy her for the same amount if there were enough people bidding the horse up," Dean said.

"What did you say to that?"

"I said that I'd sure like to make the money myself! I didn't know if Johan would buy a different horse. My impression was that Johan was only interested in the first and only idea I threw out… him buying the Triple Crown winner."

"How did Greg respond?"

"Starting at the point that the bidding was over a million dollars, he offered to pay us $10,000 in green cash, plus one breeding to any of their stallions, for each and every time that Johan bid on the horse… if he wasn't the successful bidder," Dean said.

"I don't get it," Jed said.

"Well, like I told you. Greg didn't want Johan to be the buyer… he just wanted the horse bid up high. His offer would have given us an opportunity to make at least some profit off of Johan being at the auction."

"I see."

"I told Greg I'd think about what he said. Before I left, he asked me to tell a couple of other trainers, that were in our circle, about the same compensation for them getting their clients to bid up the horse. I told him I would."

"Then what?" Alec asked.

"The next day, I called Ron and Claudia Fitzsimmons, the owners of Love Letter and asked if they had any other exceptional horses that they wanted to sell privately," Dean said.

"Did you already know them?"

"Yes. I actually showed Love Letter to her Championship at the U.S. Nationals," Brian boasted.

"Congratulations. Why did you call them after you talked to Greg Bordeaux?"

"So that I could talk to them in person, alone."

"Did they have other horses you could see?"

"Yes. One. So I flew out to their farm and looked around. Then I brought up Love Letter. I asked them how much they expected her to sell for at the auction. They said about $500,000. They also said that Greg told them he thought he could get at least a million, maybe two. They just thought he was full of himself. They couldn't imagine any horse that wasn't Pure Polish would sell for that much, let alone a mare who probably wouldn't ever have a baby."

"Yeah. Then what?" Alec said, sounding bored.

"Anyway, I proposed to them that since they would have been satisfied with a half a million, less Vintage Arabians' 20% commission of $100,000, would they be willing to work out a deal with me. Then, they said that Greg wouldn't take the horse for 20%. They said he would only take the consignment if the farm would retain half of the money and all of the interest. See, usually, the seller gets all of the interest, unless it's otherwise agreed upon.

"Anyway, at first, they turned him down. But then Greg kept saying that he thought he could get over a million... so the fifty-fifty split would actually make them a lot more money."

Alec was intrigued but didn't show it.

"Makes sense. What did they do?" Alec said.

"They said they didn't want to take a chance. Then Greg offered to buy the horse from them on the spot for $400,000. They asked if he would pay cash on the spot. He told them he'd give them a promissory note, with payment due after the auction, after he'd received good funds from another buyer," Dean said.

"Did they trust him?"

"I don't know."

"Okay. Then what?"

"Greg offered to give them two syndicate shares of each of the eight stallions that Vintage had syndicated. The value of the syndicate shares alone was well over a million dollars," Dean explained.

"Why would he do that?" Alec questioned.

"Because it's just paper... and sperm. They didn't pay money for the shares. They owned the stallions, syndicated them, and retained shares for themselves to use for future sale when the price went up, and to use for special deals like this. It's like printing your own money!"

"If you've got someone who'll take it..." Jed said.

"There's always somebody that will take it," Dean explained.

"So, what did they say to that offer?" Alec said.

"They said they just wanted to get whatever the market would bear, in normal circumstances."

"What did Greg say to that?"

"They said Greg reminded them that his auctions aren't normal circumstances. That's why they were consigning her in the first place. They agreed that he had a point. Eventually, he convinced them to take the note for $400,000 and take the syndicate shares. But then, when he sent a written agreement to them, they sent it back unsigned, with a note telling them that they didn't want to do it after all and that they were pulling the horse out of the auction!" Dean said.

"Why were they going to pull her out all together?" Alec asked.

"They thought Greg was getting too aggressive. They said they didn't like his tone! Greg's trying to make these everyday people rich, and they practically slap him in the face. Anyway, eventually they all agreed that Vintage Arabians could have half of the sale price and all of the interest if the mare sold for over a million. If she didn't sell for over a million, Ron and Claudia would pay the standard 20% consignment fee."

"Were they well off already?"

"No! These people were small time. Three horses in their back yard in a little hobunk town in California. The husband is a plumber. The wife sells multi-level marketing products or something. Don't get me wrong... they're very nice people, but a little short sighted, if you know what I mean."

"How did they get a horse like Love Letter?" Alec asked, completely baffled.

"They traded his plumbing services at a huge mansion and barn being built by Mitch Henderson, this other guy in the Arabian business. Mitch is a wheeler-dealer. Love Letter wasn't born yet and horses weren't selling for nearly as much. When he saw Ron admiring his horses in the pasture, he offered to give him Love

Letter's mother for free if Ron would do the plumbing job at 10% above his cost.

"Ron showed the three year old black/bay mare to his wife, who fell in love at first sight. They never dreamed of having an Arabian. They agreed to Mitch's offer. As it turned out, Mitch didn't know that the mare was accidentally bred to his stallion. Mitch planned on waiting to breed her until she was a four year old, but his new breeding manager assumed that he wanted to breed all the mares that were old enough… three years old… so he bred her. The result was Love Letter. When Mitch found out, at first, he wasn't going to sign the registration papers since he didn't know he was trading her while she was pregnant. When Ron got an attorney to call him, he signed the papers before it went any further."

"That's an interesting way to get a horse!" Jed chimed in.

"Ron and Claudia Fitzsimmons are pretty typical of people with some great horses. Not to the extent of a Triple Crown winner, but of just every day people ending up making a lot of money off of their horses. It happens all the time. It's kinda cool though… with the market going up so fast, a lot of middle class people have gotten pretty well off from their horses. You see people from all walks of life in the business. Keeps things in perspective if you take the time to get to know a lot of people," Dean said in retrospect.

"How did they pay for the training and showing her? It must have cost a fortune," Alec asked.

"They paid for the first year or so, until she won Regional Champion Mare. Then, they had trainers begging to train and show her for free. They just wanted to be on the end of the lead line with her. Anybody who knew anything could see she was a star and that she'd win at any level as long as they could keep her attitude fresh."

"Did you train and show her for free?"

"Yes," Dean said, thinking very little of the idea.

"Interesting story, but let's go back to why you went to meet with Ron and his wife," Alec said.

"Sure. I planned on proposing something similar, although not on as big a scale as Greg did. Obviously, I didn't bother. But then, a few days later Ron called me. He pleaded with me not to tell Claudia about the call.

"I was really taken back, because he said all of what they had told me in person was really completely based on his wife's views and morals. Ron asked me, if on the side, without Greg or Claudia knowing, if I could bid up the horse. He offered to pay me $20,000 for each time I bid or had a client bid up in $100,000 increments… starting when the mare reached $500,000."

"And you agreed, I assume?" Alec asked.

"Yes. But he wouldn't put anything in writing of course. And, I never got paid from him," Dean said.

"Anything else you can think of?"

"Well, I know of at least two other trainers that were for sure bidding on Love Letter… trainers that I personally don't think had clients really ready, willing and able to spend nearly that much money. Other than that, there's nothing I can think of," Dean said honestly.

"Did you disclose to Mr. Murphy that you would be compensated by Vintage Arabians, Greg Bordeaux, or anyone else, if he bid on the horse or bought the horse?"

"No," Dean said.

"Brian, did you?"

"No," Brian said.

"Why not?"

"He didn't ask," Dean said.

"Would you have told him if he had asked?"

"Usually, if a client asks about how we get paid, we just say something like, *'don't worry about it, we're taken care of. You won't owe us anything'*, and we've never had a conversation about it go any further."

"You don't think you have a duty to disclose your compensation?" Alec asked.

"No. I don't go anywhere and buy anything where someone discloses how much they make from me," Dean said.

"What about real estate? Or registered securities? They disclose the commissions and fees that they make."

"We're just selling horses and breedings! This isn't a regulated industry. Show me a law that says someone who sells horses or livestock professionally is required to disclose their commission!" Dean said, getting very upset.

"Yeah, show us!" Brian chimed in, getting just as angry.

"Calm down guys. Alec can't use any of this against you. We've got a written agreement," Jed reminded them.

"I know, but he's making it sound like..." Brian started to say.

Jed interrupted him before he got in too deep.

"We'll discuss this out of the presence of Mr. Douglas. Let's get on with the matter at hand," Jed said.

"Excellent idea. Can you put together a list of names, addresses and phone numbers of the other trainers you were talking about?" Alec asked Dean.

"What for? I already told you how everything went down."

"I know, but if you only want to supply information and want to stay out of the case, other than helping me make the case, then I have to use other parties," Alec explained.

"He's right," Jed acknowledged.

"Do you promise that no one will know the information came from us?" Dean said, getting worried about the ramifications.

"I assure you, they won't know."

"I have my phone book with me. I'll write it down when we're done," Dean said, hoping Alec was being honest.

"Can I ask you a more personal question?" Alec asked.

"You can ask. I don't know if I'll answer though!" Dean said, curious as to what it could be about.

"Were you trying to financially screw Johan when you got him into this?"

"No!" the brothers said simultaneously.

"We were making money, but we were doing him a favor too," Brian said.

"How were you doing him a favor?" Alec asked, completely incensed.

"He wanted people to envy him buying a horse that most of the people in the industry would have loved to have had. After the fall of the gavel, back at the stalls, you should have seen the way his eyes lit up when he stood and pet her. Not that we knew him well, but we never saw him look remotely happy… or even content, let alone smile. When he was with Love Letter and surrounded by people congratulating him, and photographers taking his picture with the mare… you should have seen him! It took ten years and fifty pounds off him. He was smiling from ear to ear," Brian said.

"I even saw a couple of happy tears roll down his face," Dean said.

"Those moments are priceless," Brian added.

"You really think that moment or experience should cost someone $2.5 million, plus interest, plus mortality insurance at 3%, plus the board and training?" Alec asked.

"It's not up to us to decide if it's worth that… it's up to the buyer. Whatever the buyer is willing to pay."

Ten

Alec's hand written notes from his morning meeting with the Pondergrass brothers, the auction catalog, all of the advertisements for the auction and Johan's contract, were laid out neatly, covering almost half of the expansive oval table in the conference room.

"I can't believe they disclosed all of that without even being threatened by a lawsuit," Garth said after Alec told him about his meeting.

The naïve statement reminded Alec of his inexperience. With the intention of a mentor, he said, "It was obvious that they were actually the ones with the most liability to Johan. They had a fiduciary duty to him and were a party to using illegal business practices to make sales. Jed Packard knew the best thing they could do was to cooperate, so that we could go after this Greg Bordeaux character. He probably has deeper pockets anyway."

"Couldn't we have gone after them both?" Garth asked. He took off his suit jacket, folded it lengthwise and carefully draped it over the back of the leather chair where his briefcase lay open next to where he sat.

"Sure. But it would have been next to impossible to build our case if we had to try to discover and prove everything on our own. People are generally closed mouth about conning people out of their money."

Garth didn't agree that people were being conned out of their money. He had mixed feelings about the end result of Johan buying Love Letter. When all was said and done, no one lied to him about the quality of the mare or her inability to produce income, let alone a profit. Ultimately, Johan decided how much to spend. It shouldn't have mattered that the bidders weren't necessarily legitimate. Johan even said that the only way he'd get famous from buying the mare was to pay a record-breaking price.

Regardless of how he felt about the merits, Garth didn't intend to express his opinion. At this point in his career he was positioning himself with Alec. His short-term goal was to be offered a permanent job at Burger, Douglas, Steen & Cruise. Perhaps he could specialize in the equine industry since the firm, like most law firms, didn't have anyone who knew about equine law, let alone had an intimate knowledge of the business. Of course, the more he was finding out, the more he realized that he really didn't know about how people in the exclusive end of the market conducted business.

Garth spoke as if he and Alec had worked as a team for years. "The first thing we need to do is subpoena the records that show who all of the registered bidders and successful bidders at the auction were."

"We'll need all information that Bordeaux has on each bidder," Alec added.

"Not just names, addresses and phone numbers?"

"We need to know everything we can. What other business dealings that they've had with Vintage Arabians and/or Greg and Marcie Bordeaux... by the way... you'll need to word every request to include *Vintage Arabians and/or Greg and/or Marcie Bordeaux and each of their agents, representatives and affiliates*."

Garth remained expressionless, hoping that his ignorance about this didn't show.

Alec removed his tie and unbuttoned the top button of his starched white dress shirt. "We need copies of any contracts or agreements between their operation and all of the bidders. And I guess we should get all of the financial information that they have. Get specific where you can, but make the request as broad in scope as possible."

"Right. And I'll contact the list of trainers who were bidding too. What about the auction company? I think we should at least talk to the auctioneers and the pit men," Garth suggested.

"Good idea."

"I'll subpoena all of the parties that consigned their horses to the auction. Who knows what could have gone on!" Garth added, hoping he wasn't going overboard.

They were thinking on the same wavelength. Alec nodded his head and grinned. "You're going to be good at this."

Bridgette, Alec's secretary, interrupted the two men when she opened the heavy door and told Alec that Johan Murphy was returning his call.

"Thanks. Put him through," Alec said. His voice and eyes revealed a familiarity that extended beyond employer/employee.

\\\\\\\\\\

"Thanks for calling me back so soon. Where are you?"

"Jordan and I are in Jersey. We'll be back in a couple of days."

"Business or pleasure?"

"Business. So, what's going on about Love Letter?"

"We're progressing. The reason I needed to talk to you is that I want to convert this from an hourly case to a contingency case," Alec said.

"Why?"

"It would be better for everyone that way."

"For everyone? Who's everyone?" Johan asked skeptically.

"Everyone involved. My firm. Garth Windsor. You. The contingency would benefit everyone. This case is going to take a lot of man-hours. I'd advise you not to pay an hourly rate. It could break you if you're short on cash," Alec said as if he was looking out for Johan's best interest rather than his own.

"I just don't have the money to pay for the horse and don't want to end up being sued over it. How could working that out take so much time? And how could you collect anything from Vintage Arabians?" he asked, genuinely confused.

"Well Johan, as it turns out, we're going after them. We'll make you plenty of money," Alec said, wanting to elaborate, to explain to him that the whole Arabian horse industry is just a big con. This phone conversation wasn't the time to burst his bubble.

"I don't want to go after anyone! I told you. I just don't have the money to pay for the horse!"

"You said you didn't want to damage the Pondergrass brothers... and we're not. Fortunately, they've been very forthcoming and they're cooperating... in fact, they're assisting us in building a case against Bordeaux. There's plenty of..." Alec said.

Johan interrupted him. "I'm not signing any contingency agreement. I'll pay for what you've done so far. Give me the information you've got and I'll find another attorney. Send me a bill today."

Alec was stunned to hear a dial tone before he could respond to Johan's unreasonableness.

"Right. Sure. I'll have Bridgette draw up the contingency agreement and we'll courier it to your office as soon as you get back in town," Alec said to the dial tone, not wanting Garth to know his client's response and that he had just been hung up on.

Pause.

"Yes. I'll look forward to talking with you then," Alec said, then immediately used a finger to disconnect the phone before replacing the handset on the receiver.

Garth put everything in perspective and it finally registered what the case was evolving into. Alec intended to financially destroy Vintage Arabians. "I didn't know that Johan didn't want the Pondergrasses damaged."

"He was adamant about it. He really likes them. I guess a lot of it is because Brian and Dean are brothers who own the business together. Johan and his brother, Jordan, own their business together... I guess he feels it's something important that they have in common... who knows what the guy is thinking!" Alec said with a tone that revealed he didn't have a lot of respect for Johan's way of thinking in this matter.

"Johan wanted the tax deductions, right?" Garth reasoned.

"Sure he did. Who wouldn't?"

"Maybe it was the business that needed the deductions. Did Johan buy Lover Letter personally, or did his business technically buy the horse?" Garth asked as he reached for the purchase contract.

"Good question. I don't think I even paid attention to what the contract said."

"Here it is. Murphy Enterprises is the buyer," Garth said, pointing to the middle of the first page, hoping that Alec would appreciate the importance of his thinking of this angle.

"I'll be damned! You are on the ball! The contract is actually between Murphy Enterprises and Vintage Arabians Sales Company. Add Vintage Arabians Sales Company to all of the wording on the subpoenas and other documents," Alec said, mortified that he hadn't thought about the detail.

The more Alec was discovering, the more settlement money he envisioned going into his own pocket. He loved the judicial system. Who cares what anyone else thinks. Alec was confident in his persuasive powers. Perhaps he would contact Jordan. Surely, he would easily convince Jordan that they should pursue the case against Bordeaux. That might be easier than trying to change Johan's mind. In the mean time, he planned on proceeding as if he had a signed contingency agreement. No need to slow things down or discuss it with Garth. It was none of his business.

"I'm considering doing some phone interviews. What do you think?" Garth suggested, raising his eyebrows to emphasize the question.

"Let me think about it. It sure would expedite the process if they'll talk to you." Alec tapped his pen on his notepad, dissecting the case in his mind. "We need to find out who these people specifically are. Then, if they won't talk on their own, you can threaten the subpoenas."

"All I have to do to find out who the sellers and buyers are is to look in the trade magazines. I can get the right issues from my parents tonight."

"Great. Direct one of the legal aids to prepare all of the other paperwork and have the aid arrange for the process servers. Then, go ahead and start calling the successful buyers as soon as you get what you need."

\\\\\\\\\\\\

Garth placed the call from his temporary office at Burger, Douglas, Steen and Cruise. Dialing the high tech piece of equipment, he pictured an engraved brass plate on the door with his name on it.

"Hi Dad! How are you?"

"Fine. Is something wrong?" Davis Windsor asked as he thumbed through his most recent woodworking magazine.

"No. Why?"

"Usually it's your mother who has to call you! I can't remember the last time you called us just to see how we were."

Garth swallowed hard and felt a lump of guilt in his throat. He was uneasy that he had an ulterior motive to the call. Undecided as to whether or not he should make some small talk or if he should just get to the point, he hesitated before responding to his father. After his father's reaction, he didn't want to admit that the reason for his call was that he needed to come over to get their magazines.

"I'm sorry. You know how busy I get," Garth told him for the thousandth time.

"Your mother misses you. Why don't you come over for dinner tonight, if you're not too busy?"

"I'd love to. How about six o'clock?"

\\\\\\\\\\\\

Garth backed his steel gray Honda Accord out of his reserved parking space in the five story-parking garage. Distracted by his first real case in the legal profession, he didn't look out his rear view mirror; he came inches from knocking down a frail elderly man walking hunched over with a cane. Garth apologized profusely as his heart skipped a few beats over the near catastrophe.

Leaving the office at 4:00, before rush hour traffic started, allowed him plenty of time for getting home to feed Tuxedo, his black and white cat, and to change from his navy blue pin striped suit into jeans and a polo shirt.

Driving through downtown was always astonishing to him; street beggars pan-handling at the same intersections that executives crossed to enter their exclusive office buildings; and homeless people strolling next to business leaders. Garth was saddened at the sickening harmony to the workings of the city.

On days like this, when he experienced an acute awareness of his surroundings, he missed living with his parents in the peaceful country where you could see green grass for miles on end. Growing up, his parents reminded him that everyday was to be treasured in appreciation of living in the wide-open spaces. The memory of living where there was fresh air, beautiful horses and playful dogs and cats made him question the life path he had chosen for himself.

He especially missed his horse, Ameretto, who he grew up with and confided in as if he were the brother he never had. From the time he was four years old, until he left for college, he rode his chestnut gelding every day, rain or shine, whether it was hot and humid or bitter cold. His pets, including Ameretto, were his best friends; he was an only child and didn't live in a neighborhood.

Garth was unusually close to his parents because they all shared in the rituals of taking care of horses and the farm. His father taught him how to use his hands and enjoy building things from scratch. Together, they made wooden tack trunks, saddle racks and intricate gates to the pastures. During spring break when he was in middle school, they built new stall doors for the barn. They built their most spectacular project during the summer of his sophomore year in high school; they laid a beautiful flagstone entry to the property. His mother hand carved the entry sign with the farm logo and the silhouette of an Arabian horse. It was a work of art that took her two months to complete.

During foaling season they took turns staying up all night long, camped out in the barn aisle, waiting for the next miracle to be born. The moment that the mare due to foal looked as if it were inevitable that she would have the baby, the three family members huddled together in anticipation of delivery. Over the years, they spent many sleepless nights together during false alarms. They would always tease whoever was on foal watch if it was a false alarm. They drew straws to decide who got to be the one to imprint the newborn foal because whoever got to do it would have the closest bond with the horse.

Competing together in horse shows all over the United States, they cheered each other on and supported each other through glorious wins and heartbreaking losses.

Garth treasured his fond memories of how he grew up. He hoped that someday, when he married, he would be able to offer his wife and children the same kind of joyous lifestyle. That's one of the reasons he became an attorney. He assumed that the legal profession would provide him the financial resources to have his own farm and horses, along with the freedom of time to enjoy it with his wife and children. So far, he didn't make very much money and he hadn't met the right woman yet, but he knew he would discover her if he looked long enough and hard enough.

\\\\\\\\\\

"Do you want to go out to the back pasture and see the weanlings while mom's getting dinner ready?"

"I was hoping we'd all go together," Garth said.

Garth's mother had a tear in her eye when she said, "That's sweet honey, but it's going to get dark pretty quick and I can't leave bouillabaise to cook too long. You go ahead and go. They might be yearlings before you come back home again."

"Are you all right, mom?"

"I'm fine. Go with your father. See if you can tell which one is Charisma! She's changed so much from that scrawny looking suckling."

Davis Windsor drove the golf cart past the broodmare pastures to the thirty-acre weanling pasture. When they pulled up to the crystal clear pond near the gate, Garth melted at the sight. The view was pristine and belonged on a calendar of scenic America.

Black board fencing as far as he could see up the gently rising hillside of emerald green grass framed the picture. Patches of hardwood trees dotted the landscape with their bright cordovan, crimson, tangerine and ocher colored leaves. At least a dozen ducklings and their mothers glided in the pond, which was reflecting the canary yellow and amethyst sunset.

He didn't know why he didn't come back more often. The farm was the only place that he really felt he belonged. As he filled his lungs with fresh air that was tinted with the aroma of fresh cut grass, he envied his parent's life.

The gentle breeze caressed Garth and blew the scent of his father's Old Spice after-shave to his nostrils. It's funny how a familiar scent can send you back in time. Garth flashed back to the day his father made the announcement that effective the next month, he was taking early retirement. He told them that he wanted to stay at home with his family and pursue his dream of breeding and raising high quality Arabian horses on a full time basis. Lily, his mother broke down in tears. She was thrilled that he made his final decision and announced it on Garth's tenth birthday. Lily was lonely being married to a commercial airline pilot, and it was often too trying for her to take care of the farm in the winter during snowstorms when her husband was gone for days at a time. Garth was too young to be of much help, although she never let her son think that she wasn't dependent on him.

"Dad, how did you decide when the time was right for you to retire from flying?"

"Well, it's interesting that you're asking me right now," Davis said.

Garth looked at him, scrutinizing his father's response.

Not wanting to burden his son, Davis intentionally remained vague when he said, "Your mother was going through a very emotional time then too. I thought it would be better if I were home all of the time..."

"What do you mean, a very emotional time *then too*?" Garth said.

"Surely you can tell that your mom's not herself."

"She does seem preoccupied. Like she's covering up something that's bothering her," Garth admitted in retrospect.

Davis made a split-second decision to confide in his son. "We've never told you this before, because the time never seemed right, but your grandmother committed suicide when mom was nineteen. We didn't want you to know, so we told you she died as a result of a car accident."

"Why didn't you want me to know the truth?"

"Because you already knew that your Aunt Jennifer committed suicide when you were six years old. When the police came and notified mom, you were there, standing at her side."

"What's that got to do with grandma?"

"We didn't want you to worry that your mother would do the same thing."

His father's revelation socked him in the stomach. "Mom wouldn't ever want to kill herself! She's got us... and the farm. A life she loves. And the country club. She loves her tennis team and playing golf. She has a wonderful life," Garth said in defense of his mother.

"I know. And I'm glad that you know it. Mom knows it too... but, she's been haunted for years by something that happened before I met her. She gets really depressed about it once in a while."

Maybe being sheltered wasn't so bad after all. So this is what it's like to be a grown up... your parents confide in you. "What happened?" *Do I really want to know? Why did I ask? Now I'm afraid to hear the answer.*

"I don't know. She's never told me. In thirty- two years of marriage she's never told me," he conceded.

"Haven't you asked her? She is your wife!"

"In the first few years of our marriage, I used to ask her, because she practically shut down then. It was always in the fall. I didn't realize it at first, but later, I put it together that she got worse late in the summer and in the early fall."

"How did you figure that out?"

"Well, I realized that when I felt the greatest, she felt the worst! I was always at my best when the weather turned beautiful and the trees glimmered of color. I always wanted to be outdoors enjoying every minute I could. I'd garden. Golf. Go trail riding. She could barely get me to come inside for dinner.

"Then, about four years after we were married, I realized that she would practically shut down at the same time of the year. I'd usually find her sitting outside on the porch, gazing into the pastures or quilting yet another blanket. She barely cooked... we ate sandwiches or T.V. dinners almost every night.

"At first, tried to get her to come do things with me, but then, when I saw that my pushing her made her even more withdrawn, I stopped. By Thanksgiving, she would be pretty much back to herself. Active. Cooking. Outgoing. The mom you know."

Wondering how he could have been so insensitive, Garth confessed, "I don't remember her ever being like that."

"She wasn't too bad about it after you were born. She was so overjoyed to have you, I think she tried to erase what was making her so sad. I imagine that mom buried it even deeper so that you wouldn't be affected. She loves you so much."

"So, when did she start acting sad?"

"All of the time I've been with her. It's just that when you were born and lived at home, she didn't show it around you at all. Even when she was alone, it wasn't nearly as crippling as before you were born... but whatever the secret is, it's still there... muffled behind a strong exterior."

"Why didn't you make her tell you about it?"

"You can't make someone tell you. They have to do it in their own time. I kept thinking that eventually, she'll trust me enough to confide about what is so painful. Now, it's been thirty-two years, and I still don't know."

"Now that you're talking about it, mom looks depressed right now. Is this what you're talking about?"

"This is the time of year. She's obviously not herself, but believe it or not, she's putting on a front for you. I've come inside unexpectedly and found her crying or looking hopeless. It kills me to see her this way."

Garth took a deep breath and contemplated his words before he asked, "Do you think she would commit suicide... like her mother and sister?"

"No."

"You're sure? Has she ever talked about killing herself? Even hinted about it?"

"No. If it had gone that far, I would have absolutely insisted that she see a therapist."

"Have you ever tried to get her to see a professional?" Garth asked, not meaning to sound critical of his father's actions, or lack thereof.

"Yes. Every couple of years I suggest it. Obviously, to no avail."

The weanlings suddenly discovered that they had company and came barreling down the hillside to the golf cart. All five of them did a slide stop, just in time to not hurt themselves on the tires or the roof. They surrounded the cart, in a race for the search for bags of carrots or apples. When they didn't find anything, two of the most offended fillies walked a few feet away and started munching on the grass while the other three started to slobber on the cart. Davis immediately picked up the riding whip he kept on the golf cart. As soon as the three pranksters spotted the evil whip, they stopped munching on the cart. In an attempt to apologize for their wrongdoing, they nuzzled father and son in their hair and on their shoulders.

The faint sound of the ringing cowbell echoed all the way to the pond. Lily was letting them know dinner was ready. Davis shooshed the weanlings away with the whip so that they could exit the pasture.

"Do you think I should try to talk to mom?"

Davis didn't need to think about his answer. He knew his wife too well. "No. Not directly. But maybe if you come around more often, maybe go riding with her or something, maybe she'd offer something. That might help. I doubt it though. She's kept it inside for this many years… and she probably wouldn't want to trouble you… you're her son. "

"Well, she might tell me now. I'm an adult… I'm twenty-six."

"I know, but you're still her son," Davis said, resigned to the idea that he may never find out the cause of his wife's secret.

"Yeah. But I really should come around more. I love it here. And to be with you guys. I just get so caught up in my work, I don't take the time. Every time I come I feel replenished."

"I'm sure you're busy with the ladies too…"

"Well, sort of. No one special though."

"You still can't find anyone you want to be serious with?"

"Not yet. Not serious enough for marriage, if that's what you mean."

"How about even serious enough for a real relationship? You never know what it will lead to once you get to know each other better…"

"I do see one woman fairly regularly. But, I still date other people."

"Does she date other people too?"

"I've never asked her, and she's never volunteered it."

"You've told her clearly that you're dating other people?"

"Sure. I don't want to mislead her. If she wants to do something with me and I have another date, I just nicely tell her that I've got a date and suggest that she and I get together a different night."

"You couldn't do that in my day! At least not with a *nice girl!*"

"Yeah," he said with a grin. "I guess my generation is lucky that way. How everyone wants to be so honest and open about relationships and sex."

"Speaking of that, are you getting any?"

"Sex?"

"Sure. With a couple of gals. I don't sleep with everyone I date, if that's what you're wondering about."

Before the conversation could go any further, they were pulling the golf cart into the three-car garage.

Uncharacteristically, Garth walked to his mother in the kitchen and gave her a bear hug as he said, "I've missed you, mom. Can I come out and go riding with you this weekend?"

His mother was startled, but her eyes lit up when she answered him. "It's supposed to rain all weekend."

"I didn't hear the forecast," he said, genuinely disappointed.

She had another idea. "Why don't I come to the city and we'll go to the movies and dinner or something!"

"That would be great! Why don't you spend the whole weekend at my flat? You can visit some of your city friends too."

"I could use a change of scenery for a day or two," she said, with the hint of a smile forming on her face.

This was definitely not a visit where he should tell his parents why he really finally took the time to come out. Nonchalant was the key word.

After dinner, while his parents put away the leftovers, did the dishes, and fed the cats and dogs, Garth casually browsed through the Arabian horse magazines that they subscribed to. The March and April issues would have the auction results from the February auction sales in Scottsdale. When he located the issues that he was looking for, he took them back into the kitchen and thumbed through the pages, appearing to be only half interested in the advertisements.

"May I borrow these?" Garth said, expecting to simply hear an affirmative answer.

"Why? You haven't read an Arabian magazine for at least a year unless the article was about us or if it was the auction catalog or results," Davis stated as if he kept tract of such things.

Garth debated whether or not he should tell them the truth. If he did, it would be obvious that he had an ulterior motive for his visit, and he didn't want to hurt their feelings. On the other hand, it seemed like a ridiculous thing to lie about.

"It's for work."

"Work?" Lily questioned suspiciously.

"Yes, mom."

His father gave him a curious look while he decided how much to press the issue.

"How is work lately? The last time you talked about it you were bored out of your mind preparing motions for the attorneys who were doing the interesting work."

"Actually, a funny thing happened. It's a long story, but my firm loaned me out to another firm that's working on a case, which involves someone who bought an Arabian. I'm getting paid double what I've been getting at work... and of course, it's challenging to work on something like this!"

"What's the case?" Davis and Lily said simultaneously with a bright spark of interest. They weren't just making conversation now.

"I don't think I can discuss it. I'm not sure. Believe it or not, I never thought to ask Alec if this is supposed to be confidential... the general concept of the case, I mean," Garth said, surprised he hadn't considered it before now.

"Is it against anyone we know?" his mother inquired. She wasn't prone to listening to gossip, but this seemed different.

"Well, I'm not absolutely sure who all we'll go after. One big farm for sure, but there may be other people brought into it also," he said, hoping he wasn't saying too much.

Garth's parents tried to convince him that they wouldn't talk about it to anyone. They attempted to get more information out of him, but he stuck to his guns and insisted he first had to ask Alec if he could talk about it at all, and if so, to what extent.

"Who's Alec?" his father asked.

"Alec Douglas. He's a partner in Burger, Douglas, Steen & Cruise..." he started to explain before his mother interrupted him.

"Alec Douglas! Nathan Burger was gunned down in his office... it's in all the newspapers and on the local news," Lily said, excitedly.

"Isn't the FBI investigating all that?" Davis wanted to know.

The casual conversation suddenly turned intense.

"I only know what's been in the news also. Alec hasn't made a single mention of what happened that day, nor what the FBI was doing," Garth told them honestly.

Davis dropped the ceramic dish he was drying as a thought popped into his mind. "Son, it could be dangerous for you to be at their offices. I don't like the idea of you working with them right now."

"Dad..."

"He's right Garth. That wasn't a random shooting. What if the killer comes back and you get caught in the crossfire. Or held hostage? Or..."

"Mom! Stop it! You watch too many movies. I'll be fine."

He started doubting the confidence of his own words as soon as they came out of his mouth. At the time he was brought into the case, he was so appreciative to have something interesting to work on that he hadn't even considered any of the possibilities that his parents thought of. For now, he couldn't show any concern about it, or they would worry even more. He couldn't imagine anything happening, but then again, he couldn't imagine Nathan Burger being murdered.

Eleven

Elsie, the Danish live-in maid was just finishing polishing Greg's paddock boots when he strolled into the kitchen. He was irritated that she didn't clean and buff their boots the night before, as she was directed to do. Marcie would have to have a talk with her, *again.*

The phone rang and interrupted his thoughts about dismissing yet another maid this year.

"Hello."

"It's Dolan. We need to meet with you and Marcie, later today or tomorrow morning. Something's come up."

Greg's bad mood was reflected in his tone.

"What for?" Greg said, as if he didn't recall the extent of the trouble they were in.

Dolan let out a sigh before he informed Greg of the latest development. "We were just served an amended request for production of documents. Jessica and I need to go over it in detail with you and Marcie."

"Well, we haven't been served anything else," he said, as if it negated what Dolan was telling him.

"Nothing else will come directly to you. When you retained us, we notified Mr. Murphy's counsel that we are representing you in this matter. Now, everything will come directly to us," Dolan explained, trying not to talk down to Greg.

Greg walked around the corner, stretching the phone cord as far as it would go, hoping the maid or Marcie wouldn't hear him talking.

Out of a nervous habit that surfaced when he was stressed, he bit the inside of his mouth before he asked, "What do we need to provide that I haven't given you yet?"

"It's a long list, and they may not actually be entitled to everything on it. That's why we need to meet," Dolan persisted.

The maid took the copper water can outside to the terrace and doused the potted orchids and flowering cactus.

Greg glanced out the arched French doors of the kitchen and saw Marcie hand grazing one of the horses in their yard. Satisfied that she wouldn't overhear the conversation, he spoke freely.

"We can meet Tuesday."

"It can't wait a week. We've got to get on this now. If you're too busy to come back to our offices, Jessica and I can come to your house in the evening, when you're done working. How about tomorrow night?"

Greg slicked back his thick brown hair with his left hand while he gave the question a fleeting moment of consideration. "No. Not until Tuesday. Marcie's birthday is in two days. I've already bought first class plane tickets and paid for a long weekend at a resort in Hilton Head. It's a surprise getaway birthday present for her. We haven't golfed anywhere but Arizona in at least a year. I made these arrangements a couple of months ago."

Elsie was now shaking off the overnight dust and pollen that accumulated on the cushions of the terrace furniture. Before she replaced each cushion she fluffed it back up and then sprayed a light coat of lemon-scented disinfectant on the sun facing side. She never dared to skip the final step of *daily terrace maintenance*, as Marcie called it, since she knew that her employer often sniffed a random cushion to see if it was done.

"Reschedule it. Take her out to Mancuso's for her birthday and promise to take her on the trip when things slow down with this legal crap," Dolan said, as if it were an order, not an idea.

"She needs this trip more than ever with this going on. I can't cancel it. And, going to Mancuso's wouldn't be good enough for her birthday dinner anyway," he said adamantly.

"Mancuso's isn't good enough? It's the best restaurant in Arizona! Hell, if you're a connoisseur of Northern Italian cuisine, it's the best in the country."

Greg didn't care if he sounded snobby or not. "We go there at least two or three times a month, if not more when we're entertaining clients or prospective buyers. I need to take her somewhere spectacular that she's never been. And like I said, everything's already arranged. We'll be in on Tuesday. Don't say a word to her about this in the mean time."

Dolan was taken back by Greg's response. He had never come across a client that took a serious matter so lightly. Most people put their lives on hold until their attorney told them otherwise.

"Let me at least get a copy of the list to you later today so you can be thinking about what you'll need to put together. We'll meet Tuesday, first thing in the morning. But, keep in mind, you won't have long to gather everything and review it with us," Dolan said as a concession to Greg's outright refusal.

"Have Jessica bring it when she comes to ride her horse. I'll get it then. I'm not telling Marcie anything until Monday night when we get back," Greg said, not even considering whether or not Jessica had actually planned on riding that day or the next.

This didn't seem like the same man Dolan had known for almost eight years, which was disconcerting to him, while at the same time, understandable under the circumstances. Most people get edgy during legal problems and some people exhibit sides of their personality they never even knew existed.

"I'll ask her," Dolan answered, not wanting to start an argument this early in the game.

Greg finally calmed down. "Listen Dolan, I've been thinking. How about if I give Johan Murphy a call and try to resolve whatever this is all about? I think everything's gotten blown way out of proportion..."

"You can't. Once someone retains an attorney to represent them, you can't communicate with them directly anymore. Everything, every single word and piece of written correspondence, has to go through each parties' counsel," he explained regretfully. At least Greg wanted to take the initiative on his own... perhaps even admit responsibility.

Greg absorbed what Dolan had just told him before he answered, "Isn't this different though? Love Letter is still here at our farm. He's never moved her."

"We didn't even discuss that. I just assumed that he took her to St. Louis so that he could see her easily when he wanted to."

"Nope, she's still here, content as could be."

"My gut instinct is that you still can't talk directly to him, but let me see what Jessica thinks. Maybe if you call him under the pretense that it's about her training regimen or something. Perhaps if you only talk about her training, then see if he brings up the legal aspects of what he's pursuing."

"Okay. Well, call me and let me know as soon as you can. Maybe I can make this disappear before we have to go any further," Greg said, accustomed to being the leader and in control.

Dolan didn't want to tell him how unlikely it was that they could make anything disappear without a financial settlement.

"Have you ever spoken to him on the phone before?"

"Yes. A few times."

"Who called who?"

Greg neatly tucked in his button down denim shirt while the phone was cradled in his neck. "The first time, he called to see if he could continue boarding Love Letter here until he decided what he wanted to do with her. Then he called another time just to see how she was doing. I guess, maybe a couple of weeks later I called him to suggest we put her back into a conditioning program before she got out of shape. He said he didn't really want to. He didn't plan on showing her ever again, and thought she should just be allowed to be a horse again..."

Dolan interrupted, just out of curiosity. "What did you say?"

"I told him I thought she'd probably enjoy retirement and that the mare certainly deserved at least a vacation! And I assured him I'd see if she liked being turned out in the pasture all of the time or not. Some horses thrive on the freedom and some are insecure about not having a stall to go to at night. You never know. Anyway, he said he'd appreciate us finding out what made Love Letter happiest and was confident that we'd treat her right. He was quite nice, actually."

"Anything else?"

"Well, he called a couple of weeks ago and said he had a financial set back and wondered if he could have a year before he made his next payment. He seemed genuinely sincere, and embarrassed," Greg said.

"And what was your response?"

"I told him to call my CPA and gave him his name and number. I didn't hear from him after that until this legal hassle out of nowhere."

"I'll have Jessica talk to your CPA and find out about that conversation. Do you know his number off hand?"

Greg was reading the name and number from his personal phone directory as Marcie walked into their breakfast room with grass stains on her beige schooling breeches and white crew neck sleeveless blouse. She didn't seem to realize she had some abrasions on her right arm.

He raised his brows as he rolled his eyes, obviously planning on teasing her when he got off the phone.

"My wife just walked in, so I better get going," Greg said, clearly not identifying who he was speaking to.

Marcie asked who he was telling their CPA's name and number to and Greg told her it was someone that was new in town that had Andulusian horses. He said the guy assumed that they'd be using the best accountant in town, so he called.

"You're just trying to change the subject so that I don't laugh at you!" Greg said with a sparkle in his eye.

Trading Paper

"No, I'm not trying to distract you. I know you're going to laugh no matter what..." she said with a bright smile across her dirty face.

"Why do you even bring that horse to the backyard?" he said while laughing.

"He needs to learn not to be herd bound. He's just a big baby! I'm teaching him it's more pleasant to be eating grass in our yard than to be getting worked in the round pen or walking in endless circles on the hot walker," she said, just as she had defended herself at least a couple of dozen times about the same horse.

"You're not teaching him that! *He's teaching you* that he weighs a thousand pounds; you weigh, maybe a hundred and ten. *He's teaching you* that if you refuse to let go of the lead rope when he bolts to get back to his pasture, he can drag you through the grass until you can't hold on anymore! That's what *he's teaching you...* Ms. big time trainer!" he said lovingly.

"He's not teaching me that!" she said with a sparkle in her eyes.

"He sure in the hell is trying to though! You're just not smart enough to learn it!"

She punched him in the arm as hard as her petite frame could. He pretended it hurt, even though she knew he barely felt it.

"Pour me some coffee while I go change..." she said as she walked out of the kitchen.

"Yes dear. It would be my privilege," he said, as if he were kidding. In reality, he was desperately hoping that nobody would ever take her away from him.

Twelve

Although Garth wanted his mother to spend the weekend with him, part of him was relieved when she called to cancel, saying she felt a cold or flu coming on and that she thought she should stay at home and rest. Now, he'd have the time to work on the case.

He took the Arabian magazines to a copy center. First, he photo copied the page out of the April issue that showed the auction horse's name, age, sex, sire and dam, sales prices, consignor and buyer. He enlarged it to a size that would allow him to write notes to the side if needed.

When he returned to his flat, he hand wrote individual index cards with the same information for each horse so that he could take detailed notes about his conversations with each the consignor and the buyer and any other information that he thought would be of use. By the time he finished, he had thirty-seven index cards reflecting twenty-eight consignors and twenty buyers. He was able to get everyone's telephone numbers from advertisements in the magazines.

The sale total was an amazing record setting $15,250,000 and a lot average of just under $436,000. If Bordeaux received a 20% commission from each consignor, they grossed over $3,000,000 in commissions. Of course, he had no idea how much they netted.

Until Garth studied everything in print, he hadn't really fully grasped the enormity of the industry. When he was actively involved in the showing of the horses, before college, people talked about a $50,000 to $100,000 horse as if that were an outrageous price. Not caring about money, Garth enjoyed the horses in his own way, by grooming and feeding and cleaning stalls. He thrived on everything about being around the magnificent creatures.

Money never entered his mind when he thought about his family's Arabian horses. As an adult, his parents had occasionally mentioned something about how the horses were going up in value dramatically every year, but they never offered any examples and he never thought to ask. In his mind, the horses were just an expensive hobby for people with discretionary money.

Sitting on his brick patio, with the magazines opened in front of him, he reflected that in the past few years his parents had replaced their smooth wire fencing; now the entire farm is fenced and cross-fenced in four rail black boards. Two years ago they built a new twenty stall barn and a 100' x 250' covered arena. As the work was being done, he was so absorbed in his own life, he hadn't even considered the source of the money, let alone how expensive it must have been.

In his family, they rarely discussed finances, and when they did, it was really about Garth. Them buying him his first car and paying for his insurance; the cost of college and law school; how little money he was making at the law firm and how much his living expenses were.

Sometimes they boasted about selling a horse for 'really good money', but he never thought about how much they were actually talking about. Now, he couldn't help but wonder exactly how much money they make in the Arabian business and what their horses were worth. He hated himself for it, but for a fleeting moment, he couldn't help but feel exhilarated, thinking about the fact that he would inherit everything from his parents since he was an only child.

In the past, he'd glance through the Arabian magazines and occasionally read an ad or study a picture. Each April he read about the glamorous February Scottsdale auctions and resulting prices and took notice, but never related his own family's horses to what was happening in the business.

Today, Garth found himself reading every advertisement in each of the monthly magazines that he brought home.

Amazed at what he estimated to be eighty percent of the magazine being advertisement, he looked to see if the ad rates were printed in the publications. Sure enough, they were. Premium four-color ads are $1,100 per page, and include only one photograph. Most of the farms in the magazine have multiple page spreads with numerous pictures on several of the pages. He couldn't imagine what Vintage Arabians must be spending on advertising just in the two main breed magazines.

Garth went inside his flat to get a beer and some bug spray. As he passed his telephone, a thought hit him, so he dialed.

"Hi mom."

"What's wrong?"

"Nothing! I'm just calling to see how you're feeling and to talk to dad about something."

"Oh," she hesitated. "You scared me when I heard your voice. I can't help but thinking about you working for that Alec Douglas. I'm so worried something terrible is going to happen," she said, with no indication in the sound of her voice that she was congested or had a cold.

"I'm fine, mom. Don't worry about me. How are you feeling?"

"Tired. Run down. My throat is starting to hurt. I'm drinking plenty of tea and dad's here making me some of his special chicken noodle soup. Grandma's recipe," she said, referring to her mother-in-law.

"I'm glad he's there to take care of you," Garth said. In his mind, he meant about her emotional state, more importantly than a cold or flu.

"Did you call the police, like you promised?"

"Not yet. I'll call when we hang up. I forgot."

"How could you forget? A man was murdered in the office where you're working!" she said as if she were scolding him when he was ten years old for climbing a tree that was too tall for him to manage.

"I forgot because I'm not the one who is worried. You are. I'm sorry. I swear, I'll call as soon as we hang up," he said, sounding like an adult, versus the child she thought she was talking to.

"Call me back and let me know what they say," she insisted, as if he wouldn't get his allowance if he disobeyed her order.

"I will. Is dad handy?" he asked, now remembering why he didn't call home that often. He loves his parents, but his mother is always overprotective of him.

"He's right here. I'm watching him season the soup. I always have to remind him not to over salt, you know."

"Can I talk to him?"

"Sure."

He heard the clanking of the kitchen workings and faint voices in the background, but couldn't make out a word until his mother told his father that something was wrong but she didn't know what it was.

"Hi dad. Can I ask you some questions about the horse business?"

"Of course. I never knew you to be interested in the business aspects before," he said, surprised at the request. He mouthed the words *everything's fine* to his wife.

"It's for this case I'm working on," Garth said, not meaning to imply he wasn't personally interested.

"Did you ask your boss if you could tell us anything?"

"No, I didn't. I completely forgot. I'll ask him Monday. Anyway, can you talk right now?"

"Let me turn the heat down on the soup," he said as he adjusted the knob to simmer on their new Viking stove. "Okay, shoot."

Garth took another swallow of his beer and then tried to remember what he wrote in his notes. His mind drew a blank. Feeling embarrassed and unprofessional, he decided to fake it and hope the important questions came to him. If not, he'd dodge the mosquitoes and risk his life going back out to his patio and get his notes.

"Do you advertise regularly in the Arabian magazines?"

"Each year we've been advertising more and more."

"Because you get more money for the horses? You have to advertise more to sell them?" Garth asked, thinking logically.

"That's part of it. Sometimes we run ads when we don't even have horses for sale..."

Garth interrupted and said, "Why would you do that? It sounds like a waste of money."

"Good PR. We'll run a full-page ad congratulating a client for buying a horse from us, or for getting a major show win with a horse they bought from us in the past. Sometimes we'll just run a two page ad with a scenic picture of the mares or babies in the pasture."

"You spend a couple thousand dollars to run ads like that?" Garth said, stupefied.

"That's what people in the business do now days. The public always needs reminded we're here and they need to be able to find us easily. When they want to buy horses, they're not going to think of us if they don't see our ad that month. And if they're interested in our program, they're probably not going to go back months and months looking through old magazines to see if they can find our phone number."

"Yeah dad, but..."

"We need to fit in. You wouldn't believe how it strokes the ego of a client when you do an ad thanking them for buying a horse. If we can, we use a picture of them with the horse. When we don't have one, we'll use the picture of just the horse and print the buyer's name pretty large. They love it. They think they deserve it after they've spent $75,000 on a baby, or $150,000 on a broodmare. We feel like it's the least we can do if it makes them happy!"

"You've sold horses for that much?" Garth said, in shock.

"Quite a few. You know, most of our mares only cost us five to ten thousand when we bought them years ago. Or we bought their dams and we bred them ourselves," he explained.

Now, Garth could see why they could easily afford the advertisement that they were doing and to upgrade the farm so dramatically.

"Man, oh, man! I had no idea!"

"Mom and I don't like to brag, but you asked," he said modestly as he stirred the soup.

"Let me ask you this, dad. When you showed Astrella all the way to her Top Ten win at the Nationals, how much do you think it cost you? You paid professionals to do it, right?"

Davis thought for a moment before he answered, "Well, we bought her as a yearling for $50,000…"

Garth stopped him. "I thought you bred her!"

"We did. But we sold her when she was a week old. We got $20,000 for her then. Then, the people who bought her ended up getting divorced. They liquidated all of their horses and called us first to see if we wanted to buy her back. Obviously, we did."

"You paid them a $30,000 profit?" Garth said, not believing what he was hearing.

"We paid what the filly was worth at the time. She was really developing beautifully," he said, defending himself so that it didn't sound as if it was a stupid business move. "Our trainer convinced us that it was the right thing to do. To pay the price the filly was worth, and not worry about how much we sold her for eight months earlier."

"Okay. Then what?"

"I conditioned her here at the farm for about three months, then I sent her to Vintage Arabians for halter training…"

His heart dropped out. His father kept talking, but Garth's mind was suddenly spinning. He didn't hear a thing. He never thought to ask his parents if they had ever done business with Greg Bordeaux, and if so, what kind, and did they still do business with him.

He felt like the wind was knocked out of him. "Dad. Stop. I lost track of what you were saying..."

"Lost track? Are you okay, son? What's wrong?"

"Have you done much business with Vintage?"

"Yes. Quite a bit, in fact."

"Do you still do business with them?"

"Yes. We could never operate profitably without utilizing their program."

"I need for you to come to my place." Garth demanded in a panic.

"When?"

"Now."

"Now?"

"Yes."

"But your mother..."

"Now. Please."

Thirteen

Garth dropped his face into his upraised hands and rubbed his head, trying to relieve the pressure that was building up. His mind was reeling with disbelief of his own stupidity. How could he have never thought to ask his parents if they did business with Vintage Arabians before he took this case? How could he be so oblivious to how small the industry really was? He knew that quality Polish Arabians were rare. Why didn't he think about the possibility of all the directions this case could take?

An hour later his father was rapping on the tarnished brass doorknocker. Garth set his fourth beer of the day on the butcher-block kitchen counter as he passed it on his way to the entry hall. Even in this time of stress, he couldn't help but think about how he needed to strip down and refinish the hardwood floors. Before he bought the flat, he told himself that the red oak floors were a priority for refurbishing the place. Of course, at that time he didn't know that remodeling the kitchen and two full bathrooms, in addition to the entry hall powder room, were going to take so much money, work and time.

"Thanks for coming," Garth said as he shook his father's hand.

The handshake was a formality they never partook in before and it didn't go unnoticed by Davis.

"What on earth is going on? For the life of me, I don't understand you! One minute we're talking about advertising and the next minute you're in a panic… between you and your mother I don't know how much more I can take!"

"There's a big problem…" Garth started to tell him.

"Are you in danger? It's something to do with Nathan Burger being murdered, isn't it?" he stammered as he began trembling and scanning the living room to see if anyone else was present.

"No. I'm safe. It's not that. We're all safe. Calm yourself and have a seat. We need to talk. Do you want a beer or anything?"

Davis took a deep breath, preparing himself for whatever was to come. "Do you think I'll need one?"

Garth didn't give it a second thought. From his wet bar refrigerator, he grabbed another beer for himself and one for his father. He twisted off the caps of both bottles and dropped one of them into the trashcan under the sink and the second bottle top into a gigantic jar, one-third full with bottle tops. When he spotted the jar in an old country store, he knew it would look perfect on top of his wet bar. He bargained the young blond woman down to seventy dollars and hoped to get her phone number with the deal. Surprisingly, he wasn't successful at getting her number. After he strategically placed the jar at the bar, he promised himself that as soon as the jar was completely filled with beer bottle tops and wine bottle corks, he'd go on the wagon for three months.

He handed his father the ice-cold suds. "Listen, I can't tell you all of the details, but if you promise not to tell anyone what I'm going to explain, I'll tell you enough for you to understand…"

"What in the hell are you talking about, son. You're rambling like an idiot!"

"I know. I'm sorry. I just don't know what to do!" The pit of his stomach churned as he tried to find the words to describe the situation.

"Is your health in danger?"

"No! I told you…"

"If you're healthy, nothing could be so bad. Now calm down and tell me what is going on," he said in a kind, fatherly manner.

"You don't understand. This is monumental…" Garth said, still as distressed as a moment ago.

"Is it about money? Do you need money? That's what all of this is about. You're in debt and need to clear it up…"

"It's about money, but…"

"Don't worry. Every young man makes mistakes. You'll learn from it. Mom and I will take care of it, son. How much do you need?"

"Dad… you don't get it. Let me explain," Garth pleaded, but still not knowing the right words to use.

"Don't be embarrassed son, I'm your father. Do you think I've always handled my money perfectly? It's a learned skill, and even then, things can happen."

Garth leaned back, sinking into the seat of the worn out leather chair that he'd bought at a garage sale. He closed his eyes and took a deep breath.

"Just shut up for a minute and listen to me!"

"Don't talk to me that way! I'm willing to bail you out of whatever money trouble you got yourself into and you tell me to shut up!" he said as he stood up, half ready to smack his son across his face.

Garth crossed his arms in front of his face in defense. "Calm down. We both need to calm down."

Davis sat back down, glad that he hadn't struck his son. He reached his hands to the back of his neck and attempted to massage the tension from himself. He sat quiet and took a deep breath. "I'm calm. Talk to me."

"This case I'm working on. It's against Greg and Marcie Bordeaux, Vintage Arabians."

Davis' mouth dropped open as he leaned forward and slumped toward the coffee table. He set his jaw, unable to speak.

"First, let me say, that I personally don't agree with Alec about the case… about how he thinks that our client, the Plaintiff, was taken seriously advantage of and therefore has a right to go after Vintage," he explained, hoping his father believed him.

"If you don't agree that Vintage should be sued, why are you taking the case?"

"Well, it's difficult to explain. It all started out that Dan Dunlop, a partner in the firm I work for, asked everyone in a meeting if they knew anything about the Arabian horse business. Of course, I said I do.

"Then, he asked me to meet with his friend, Alec Douglas. Naturally, I said I would, without knowing anything about why we were really meeting.

"To make a long story short, it all started out that I just wanted to escape the boredom and monotony of sitting in my ten foot square cubicle writing motions.

"I was thrilled at the opportunity to do something else when Alec invited me to come on board and Dan approved it. I didn't even consider anything else except for the fact that I was really doing what I think an attorney should do... use his brain for something useful and interesting."

"I warned you what it would be like for the first few years..." Davis interjected.

Garth ignored his father.

"At first, we didn't know what the case really was going to even be about. Our client, and I can't say anything about him or his horse or you'll know who I'm talking about... anyway, it just started out that our client bought a horse at a Vintage Arabians auction last February, and now he doesn't have the money to continue paying on the note.

"It seemed so simple, but obviously better than writing meaningless motions. The next thing Alec and I know, there's information leading us to believe that there was fraud, misrepresentation and criminal activity going on at the auction, through Vintage's private sales and with the sale of our client's horse in particular."

"Are you serious? Like what?"

"I'm not at liberty to tell you. At least I don't think I am. I need to ask. The thing is, what started out as being a simple case, trying to find out how we could legally get our client out of his contractual obligation to continue paying for the horse, has turned into a can of worms. A serious one.

"Now, Alec and our client are inevitably going to go after Vintage Arabians and Greg and Marcie Bordeaux with everything they've got. Alec never said it in so many words, but he's proceeding like a pit bull, acting like he's going to destroy their business!"

"And you're part of this. Assisting Alec makes you part of this."

Garth didn't answer.

"You're helping to destroy Vintage Arabians?"

"I didn't know it was going to happen. We just fell on the information..."

"How do you just fall on information like that? May I ask you that?" he said, obviously aggravated.

"The trainers that were the agents for our clients spilled their guts in order to be left out of the loop of the litigation. Like getting full immunity."

"You've filed the suit?"

"No. We're conducting discovery right now so that we know all of the actual grounds we can sue on."

"So... then, you can drop it."

"No, I can't."

"You even said you didn't agree with Alec about whatever Vintage did. So, just drop it."

"Dad, even if I walk away, the litigation isn't going to stop. Alec will just find someone else to replace me. He's probably got the most critical information now anyway. Everything else will just be gathering the hard evidence to prove the case."

"Convince Alec to drop it," Davis demanded as he stood up and started pacing the room.

"I can't. He wouldn't even consider it. It wouldn't matter one bit what I said. What Bordeaux did was clearly illegal and criminal. I can't elaborate on it, but trust me. Alec has a strong case. He's not going to drop it for me or for you. He sees deep pockets and lots of money for himself and his firm."

"There's got to be something we can do to stop it!"

"There's nothing. I'm either part of it or not... but nothing's going to stop it. That's the problem. I had no idea that you do business with them," Garth said in frustration.

Davis grabbed his beer and drank the rest of it all in one long swallow. He trembled from head to toe from nerves. Despite the air conditioning, he broke out in a sweat, perspiration forming on his forehead and above his upper lip.

"Everything we're worth revolves around Vintage Arabians being the leader in the business," he confessed.

Garth swallowed hard, afraid of what he might hear next. "Why? Do you own horses in partnership with them or something?"

"No. But they're undeniably the market leaders. The innovators. They set the pace of the industry. Vintage Arabians provides the marketing tools their clients need to be successful. About six months ago we paid a million dollars, in cash, to buy a Pure Polish stallion and nominate him to their Medallion Stallion program. It's all worthless if they go out of business."

"You had a million dollars?" Garth said, shocked at the idea.

"No. We mortgaged the house and the entire farm. And, I put up *all* of our stocks and investments as collateral on a bank loan," he said, feeling a rock sinking into the pit of his stomach as the words left his mouth.

"Oh my God! Why on earth did you do that?"

"Greg says that we'll gross about $300,000 a year from breeding rights and that he'll sell all of the breedings for us. The stud's only three years old. He's going to breed for at least twenty years! It was a great investment... until this!"

"You believed him?" Garth asked, convinced his parents were duped.

"Why wouldn't we?"

Garth shook his head, then asked, "Why would Greg sell you a horse for a million bucks that he could have made so much profit from?"

"The stud wasn't a million. He was $600,000. The other $400,000 was for lifetime program rights to have him be a Medallion Stallion. Our choices were to pay a one time $400,000 fee or to pay $100,000 per year for every year he was in it. It doesn't take much intelligence to see that the opportunity to pay only $400,000 was a bargain."

Garth's mind was reeling now. "What on earth is a Medallion Stallion?"

"It's a legally separate entity of its own. An independent marketing program created by Greg, but operated totally independently of his farm. If Greg approves your horse for Medallion ratings, the stud gets a certain amount of Medallion symbols by his name when he's advertised and promoted. Spark, our stallion, received the highest number of possible Medallions, which are five.

"Anyway, it's basically saying to the public that Spark rates among the very elite in the Polish segment of the breed. The Medallion Stallion program will conduct it's own horse shows that will have only the resulting offspring of the Medallion Stallions... and their own auctions of the offspring of Medallion Stallions. The money also pays for first-class brochures, extensive advertising in the magazines, and elaborate trade show booths at the big shows. It puts us in the elite of big time! The program also gives us the contacts to sell our own horses to the big buyers."

"Sounds like horse shit, bull shit to me," Garth said.

"It's not. It's a great idea, and Greg put it all together."

"Why didn't he just do this all for his own farm?"

"Because, like he said, everybody has to make money in the business or no one's going to spend money on his horses or his breedings. *'Spread the wealth or there won't be any'*. That's what Greg says, and it makes sense to your mother and I."

Hearing it explained that way, Garth could see his father's reasoning. And Greg's. It shot like a searing bullet through him. Until this very moment, Garth had no idea the extent of the impact this would have on his parents.

"If Vintage Arabians goes out of business, can't someone else just take over the Medallion Stallion program? You said it was independent of Vintage Arabians."

"No. No one could take over. No one *would* take over. Greg complains that everyone else wants to make a fortune, but they don't want to be innovative or take a leadership role, let alone risk anything. It's all up to him and he's taken the responsibility. If he falls, we all fall."

"Dad, you've got to be exaggerating. Drastically. He's manipulating everyone into believing that they need him so bad that they couldn't survive without him! Don't you see it? Bordeaux needs to psyche everyone out in order for him to succeed the way he wants to."

"It makes sense what you're saying, but you don't really know the people in the business, Garth. You're wrong. We're totally dependent on Greg."

"Maybe you've let yourself be dependent on him, but you don't have to be! An entire industry can't fall with one guy!"

"No. Not the entire industry. Just the people with Polish Arabians. With rare, valuable, expensive, Polish Arabians. That's the market that will fall apart."

Garth thought about what his father was saying. He got them each another beer, opened a bag of tortilla chips, poured them onto a ceramic platter, and brought them to the coffee table. Next, he went to the refrigerator and got out a bottle of salsa and poured it into a matching bowl before taking it back to the coffee table.

He sat down and sorted out his thoughts. "Dad, I don't mean to insult your intelligence, but this whole thing is starting to sound like Jim Bakker or one of those overboard religious leaders who tell people they can't live without their guidance. The guys who preach and preach in ways that people are addicted to hearing their words… and put all of their faith in one man."

Davis rose to his feet as quickly as his body would permit, guzzled a long swallow of beer and headed toward the front door.

"You've got it all wrong son. You are going to destroy more people than you know. Including your mother and I. We'll lose everything. I have absolutely no way to pay back that bank note without the income from the horses. I'm too old to start another career that will make enough money for us to live on and retire with. You're not just bringing down a man you have no respect for. You're bringing down hundreds of people like your mother and I."

Davis stormed out of the flat without another word, the heavy entry door slamming behind him. As he frantically searched the pockets of his khaki shorts for his keys, he was overcome with the heavy burden of guilt, feeling he was abandoning his son, even though it would be himself that would be damaged, not Garth.

Garth never dreamed that his father would really leave without them coming up with a reasonable plan of action. The instant he realized his father wasn't coming back into the flat, he ran outside barefoot, in faded jeans, ignoring the minuscule pointy rocks that were imbedding in the soles of his tender feet. Even though he knew his father couldn't hear him, he yelled, "Dad. Stop. Wait a minute!" as loud as he could.

The abrupt contrast of the air conditioning inside of his son's home and the inferno outdoors made Davis lightheaded. He was soaking wet from the humidity before he even got settled into his driver's seat. The steering wheel burned his hand and made him curse out loud to himself. As soon as he turned on his ignition, he switched the air conditioner fan to high and he rolled down all four of the electric windows, allowing the heat to escape his car.

When Garth reached the car, he was out of breath. "I'm sorry. I had no idea it would lead to this or that you and mom were so involved. I'm sorry."

The desperation in Davis' face aged him another decade. As if pleading for his life he spoke in a dubious tone. "Then stop this whole thing!"

"You don't understand! I can't. I'm not in control. The ball is already rolling and picking up more speed every day."

Davis drove off without saying another word. He stared straight ahead down the two-lane street; his head pounding like a jackhammer was in it. Blinding tears streamed down his face by the time he approached the first intersection going seventy miles an hour.

Fourteen

Marcie glowed with satisfaction after their early morning lovemaking, which was automatic on birthdays and major holidays. Not that she and Greg didn't have an active and passionate sex life. They did, but it was almost always at night.

Having horses in Scottsdale meant that the majority of the year, horseback riding had to be done between dawn and noon. After that, it was too hot. Consequently, their habit was to jump out of bed by 5am, have coffee, juice and breakfast and then do some stretching. By the time there was enough light to see outside, they were each mounted on a horse.

Several years ago, they built an indoor arena, but it was still too hot to ride in the middle of the day. They justified the expenditure because the sun didn't beat directly down on them as it did out in the open, and when the wind kicked up, there weren't dust storms. Unfortunately, heat was heat, no matter how many fans were operating. Most years, from April through October, the heat in the massive arena was unbearable until at least nine o'clock at night.

This morning, Greg brought a large heavy rectangular shaped box to her when she was propped up in bed drinking coffee. Gently, he kissed her on the forehead as he set it on her lap. She untied the red satin ribbon. The florist delivered thirty-four long stemmed ruby red roses for Marcie's thirty-fourth birthday. The card read, '*Love, Craig*".

"I can't believe *you* didn't get me flowers for my birthday! At least my lover, Craig did though!" she teased when she opened up the small envelope and read the card.

Greg whisked the card from her manicured hand. The florist obviously misunderstood his name. "Craig's not whisking you away like I am!" he teased back.

"Why can't we just relax. It's my birthday. We should do what I want!"

"Get dressed in something comfortable after your shower. We're leaving in half an hour," he said playfully.

"To where?"

"It's a surprise that I know you'll love!"

"I always love your surprises... I'll get up in a little while. I just need to relax and have another cup of coffee," she said as she stretched out her entire body, not feeling at all self-conscious about her nudity.

Greg never tired of looking at her sensual body, clothed or not. Since the day he met her, she's remained in phenomenal shape. Marcie always claimed she did it for him, but he knew better. She did it for her own vanity, but he didn't care. All he cared about is how she looked and being able to feel her firm physique.

Thankfully, she never made him feel uncomfortable when he would put on an extra ten pounds, which was inevitable in January and February of each year. That was when they'd be entertaining clients and prospective buyers at every meal and happy hour. Every day for at least six weeks they had breakfast, lunch and dinner with different people. Then, of course, there was the nightlife scene, when they had to act like they enjoyed partying if a big spender type client wanted to go out drinking and dancing.

Whatever it took to get to know people better so that they'd want to do business with them, they were willing to do. By April, Greg always had his weight back down to where he looked and felt best when he was riding.

"Really. We need to leave in half an hour to make it to the airport..."

"Airport! Where are you taking me?"

"I told you...it's a surprise for your birthday. Our bags are packed and in the car. Get moving!"

In thirty minutes she was ready as ordered, wearing loose fitting alabaster colored gauze slacks with a contrasting fuchsia V-necked cap sleeve blouse. She slipped on a new pair of bronze toned Brazilian braided leather sandals and admired her pedicure as she strolled out of the bedroom. At the last minute, she rushed into the kitchen to pour a cup of coffee in an insulated travel cup. The clay tile floor was still wet as a result of the maid mopping and sanitizing it just minutes before. Marcie slipped and caught herself on a barstool at the tiled breakfast bar. When her balance was regained, she realized her ankle was twisted so severely that she needed to elevate it and ice it.

"I know it's not your fault, but we're obviously not going to make our flight. I'll call and cancel the trip," he said, deflated.

"Can't we just take a later flight?"

"No. If your ankle's going to keep hurting, we shouldn't even bother going."

Marcie's curiosity was peaked.

"Where were you taking me?" she asked, desperately wanting to know.

"Hilton Head, for a golf vacation. You haven't golfed anywhere outside of Arizona in ages. I thought you'd like getting away."

"Greg…" she said, drawing out his name. "That's so sweet. I really would have loved to. Maybe I'll be fine after I ice myself a few times. Should we just go and see? You can golf without me if I'm not up to it," she offered.

"No. We'll do it another time."

Marcie didn't want to bring up the legal problems, so she just said, "I really would like to get away from everything. How about cruising up to Sedona? Your parents aren't staying at the retreat this weekend, they're in Maui still."

"Sure! That's a great idea. Then, if it turns out you're up to playing golf, we'll go to that new course they opened. My mom really liked it."

Shortly after they escaped Scottsdale, a near miracle happened. It was the first day Arizona had seen rain in at least two months. The downpour cleansed the sandy soil and freshened the air to the point where a person couldn't help but take the deepest breath that their lungs could consume. It was almost a rebirth.

Fortunately, they only drove the Mercedes sedan in the rain for the first half of the drive. When they were closer to approaching the breathtaking red rocks of Sedona, the fresh air was dry and crisp. Putting on light jackets was a joyous occasion in the middle of the day.

Fifteen

Shawna Sanders sauntered out of Loren Blackstone's office, attempting to conceal her elated mood. Her agent successfully renegotiated her contract with the network. Now she could do her own story development and if she wanted to, she could co-produce her own segments.

From the first day that she came on board the primetime news show, the network suits ignored her tactful request to take part in the investigations of the stories she anchored. In fact, they wouldn't even listen to her story ideas, let alone permit her to develop a segment on her own. As much as Shawna enjoyed covering the assignments they gave her, she missed coming up with topics and doing some of the investigation herself, as she did when she broke into the field of news journalism.

Her growing frustration that the suits didn't consider how she got to where she was today, led her to seriously contemplate leaving the show when this second season ended. At the time that they made the lucrative offer to hire her, they raved about the in-depth coverage she did on unusual stories and how she had the rare ability to get people to open up to her.

Once her employment contract was executed, unexpectedly, from the first day of work, it seemed to her that all they wanted was a pretty face that could deliver a story in a manner that exuded trust and confidence to the millions of viewers that the show garnered.

Her first week on the job was an eye opener. Loren Blackstone, the producer of the show, had her interviewing and hiring hair stylists, make-up artists and wardrobe designers instead of getting her set up with her own office, a telephone system, fax machine and computer. She was flabbergasted at the fuss Loren was making over her appearance. Before the first show aired, Loren insisted that the stylists give her an entirely different look. He instructed the stylist to cut her shoulder length brown hair into a short conservative style, and that it was to be lightened to a medium blond color.

When she called her husband, Ryan Sanders, and described her frustration, he told her that she was overreacting. That day, Ryan didn't have much time to hear her out because he was in final contract negotiations on buying a movie script that he had been after for several months.

It didn't take long for her to see the direction that Loren mapped out for her position on the show. Increasingly dissatisfied that he never showed any intention of using her real talent... sniffing out a story, doing a comprehensive investigation, and *then* presenting a concise reporting of it, she went in search of a replacement producer behind the network's back. When she found the right woman for the job, she went directly to the suits and voiced her feelings and proposed an immediate solution. The suits told her that Loren Blackstone had an iron clad contract to produce the show and that they couldn't replace him.

After months of discouragement at her job, Ryan suggested that his in-house attorney at Soaring Productions review Shawna's contract. Even though his company was primarily involved in movie and Broadway show productions, his attorney is well versed in all types of entertainment law. She needed to know if she could literally demand to do investigations, or to see if there was a way to break the contract after the second season was over.

As of today, everything was resolved. She was free to pursue her own story segments, and she was given a budget and a staff of three full time people that she selected. A cameraman, an assistant and an investigator. They were given a suite of private offices that had over two thousand square feet of space with a conference room and small media room in which to work out of in complete privacy. Shawna was determined to make an impact on the show's success.

Trading Paper

The group gathered at Chantelle's on Harrison Street. Considered a special occasion restaurant, today warranted them celebrating at the contemporary French four-star restaurant. Paying at least fifty dollars a person for lunch and drinks was a treat from Loren.

Chantelle's owners, David and Karen Waltuch oversee the operation, making every guest feel welcome and relaxed, treating everyone as if they were the only customers being served. They pride themselves on offering an intimate atmosphere for privacy, as the tables are widely spaced and the chairs are unusually comfortable. Each table has an arrangement of gorgeous fresh flowers; the handwritten menu is a work of art in itself.

The Master Sommelier, Roger Dagorn, offered recommendations from the superlative wine list that he had assembled. Trish was the only one who ordered wine, and she only did so because she was so impressed by his descriptions.

"I'd like to toast our team and our inevitable success!" Shawna announced, holding up a tall spicy Bloody Mary.

"To us and our new venture together!" Wade added, holding his club soda, ready to clink the four glasses together.

"I can't believe you had to get legal representation and have your agent get involved, just to be able to utilize your real talents for the show!" Wade said.

"It's so ridiculous..."

Shawna's face lit up when she spotted her husband walking purposefully toward their table. She gracefully rose from her chair, fluffed up her wispy bangs, and smoothed her paisley skirt. He approached her, grinning ear to ear. They embraced and lightly kissed each other on the cheek

"Ryan... I can't believe you're here! Thank you!"

"I thought I'd surprise you."

Wade leaned forward and tapped his index finger on his glass to subtly capture Shawna's attention.

"I'm so glad you came. Now you can meet the crew. This is Wade Carlsbad, my video and photo man," she said as she directed her gleaming hazel eyes to her left.

"Nice to meet you. I know Shawna's relieved to have you. She didn't know if she could pull you from the network evening news crew," Ryan told him as they shook hands.

"And this is Trish Hart. She's my..."

"Your investigator," Ryan finished her sentence. He wanted the crew to know that Shawna valued them enough to discuss them by name.

"Yes. I'm her investigator. I'll warn you. You're my first assignment. Shawna thinks you're cheating on her!" Trish said, breaking the ice of the seriousness of their introductions.

Ryan laughed, knowing that she was kidding around. He'd never cheated on his wife. If he had, he was certain that Shawna would use an investigator who specialized in the field of proving husbands, or wives for that matter, were having an affair.

"And you are Alyson Hembree, right?"

"Yes. It's nice to meet you," Alyson said coyly as she lowered her pale blue eyes, looking at her lap. "I'm your wife's new secretary."

"Secretary?"

"Yes, sir," she said in her soft voice.

"Shawna tells me that you're going to be her right hand! I'd hardly call that a secretary!" Ryan said.

He was practiced at boosting people's egos and bringing out the best someone had inside them. He could find and develop potential people never knew they had.

Alyson lit up and sat taller with pride in response to his assertion. When she smiled, she looked like a different woman than the one who only a moment earlier appeared insecure.

"Listen Alyson, let me give you one important piece of advice. Speak up to my wife. Every once in a while she needs reminded that she's not always right or that she's not the only show in town. I trust you'll do that for me? For you?"

Alyson was so shocked at what Ryan told her that she was afraid to look toward Shawna for her reaction. Shawna could sense Alyson's unease, so she chimed in.

"He's right Alyson. My husband knows me! And everyone, remember, we're a team. Unfortunately for you, I'll be the one getting most of the credit and publicity for everything we do, but we all need to remember that we're a team that needs to work together through rewarding times and tough times," Shawna said sincerely.

Trish raised her glass of Merlot for another toast. "A-Team!" she said. She intentionally pronounced it with a hard *A*, as in the silly Stephen Cannell television show.

Everyone followed in the toast, pretending to be entertained by her failed attempt at humor.

"If we're the 'A-Team', then you must be *Ms. T*!" Wade said dryly to Trish as he tugged at his gray ponytail.

Shawna rested her manicured fingers on Ryan's forearm and gave him a gentle squeeze as she looked into his intense deep dark brown eyes.

"Oh! I'm so caught up about our good fortune, I didn't introduce you to my husband… this is Ryan Sanders… my soul mate for life," she said, obviously proud to be happily married.

Ryan removed a small Tiffany and Co. jewelry gift box from the inside breast pocket of his sienna brown Italian suit jacket.

Shawna opened the box and beamed with the glow of happiness. She admired the simplicity of the piece. It was a sterling silver and gold charm to hang from a necklace chain. The charm had the word *'Integrity'* raised in gold lettering and the *'i'* was dotted with a small ruby, her birthstone. Shawna appreciated that her husband was so thoughtful and generous, yet didn't go overboard with extravagant and flashy gifts that she wouldn't have felt comfortable accepting or owning.

Her face turned slightly blush and happy tears just barely appeared in the corners of her eyes. She gracefully reached over and hugged her husband and whispered 'thank you' into his ear, then pecked him on the cheek. They acted like a young couple newly in love for the first time in their lives.

Wade was entertained by their public display of affection. He drank his club soda, watching everything from the perspective of an outsider, as if he weren't even at their table. He viewed most of life that way, whether he had a camera lens to his eye or not. Perhaps that's why he's one of the top photojournalists in the field. He was protected and comfortable with the anonymity of recording an event instead of being part of the event.

Trish, an unmarried, unattached career woman, was leery about how Shawna and Ryan were acting. She couldn't help but speculate, wondering if it was all a show. Not just for the benefit of their group, but also just in case anyone else was taking notice. In spite of their fame, Shawna and Ryan Sanders miraculously somehow always managed to escape being part of any negative publicity or gossip.

Trish considered that if they were always on stage, creating a perfect picture for onlookers, maybe they could hide any skeletons that might be in their closets. In an instant, she was angered at herself for always thinking like an investigator. Why couldn't she just be happy that Shawna and Ryan had the American dream? True love. Career success. Financial success. Was she so jealous that she couldn't admit that some people really are what they appear to be? Maybe she should explore another profession. One that wouldn't require her to distrust people. Twelve years of being an investigator was long enough. Trish caught herself in negative self-talk and quickly brought herself back to reality.

"I hope someday I'll meet Mr. Right, like you have," Trish told Shawna.

"Me too," Alyson added.

"You too?" Trish said, exaggerating the sly grin on her own face.

"I know what you mean," Alyson said sheepishly, but still with a smile.

Ryan looked directly into Alyson's eyes and said, "We don't judge people. Being a lesbian is your business. Shawna, Trish and Wade feel the exact same way."

"Excuse me Ryan, but you're out of line," Shawna said, meaning it as an apology to Alyson.

"You're embarrassing me."

"I'm sorry. My husband only meant to make you feel comfortable to be open. When I was making a list... a very short list... of people I wanted to work with, you were first on the list. The other two-team members had to be people who were totally accepting of alternative lifestyles. Of course, I didn't want anyone who would be sexually or racially biased or prejudice. Besides all of the normal qualifications, those were my main requirements. You can understand that Ryan and I talked about it," she explained with all the sincerity she could muster.

\`\`\`\`\`\`\`\`\`\`

When the team finished lunch, Shawna was eager to start working. She suggested that they go back to their new offices to begin setting up and creating their personal spaces. Anxious to work on her own self-directed investigative report, she followed up on some interesting correspondence.

Martha Gentry wrote the letter. She had tried reaching Shawna by telephone, but the station refused to put her calls through because she wouldn't tell them specifically what the nature of her call was. In the letter, she wrote that she wasn't comfortable telling just anyone who answered the telephone about what she knew, but it had to do with the government. She suspected her husband was involved against his will.

After calling directory assistance, Shawna used her access code and dialed the phone number she was given.

On the second ring, a masculine voice answered with an abrupt, "Yo."

"Hello, is a Martha Gentry at this number?"

"Who's this?" he slurred hesitantly.

She assumed that Neil Gentry was the person that she was speaking with. For a split second, she considered hanging up and trying back later in the day.

"I'm returning her call. Is she in?"

"I asked who in the hell this is!" he snarled.

"Is this Neil Gentry?" she asked, hoping that she wouldn't inflame whatever had made him so angry that he'd be rude to a complete stranger on the telephone.

"It's none of your damn business. You called this number! Who are you?"

Shawna heard a loud belch in the earpiece that was cradled in her neck. She flinched and made a face as if she could smell it through the airwaves. The man made no attempt to cover the phone before he made a disgusting bodily noise.

"It sounds like I've called at a bad time. I'm sorry to have bothered you," Shawna said lightly, almost at random. The tone was one in which she learned in her early investigative days. Better not to alert the wrong people at the wrong time for the wrong reason.

Without waiting for a reply, she hung up and sat tapping the useless end of her pen on the letter. The more taps, the more the brain circulated. No tapping, no thinking.

Alyson heard the familiar tapping; she took the liberty to approach Shawna's desk since her office door was wide open. "What's the problem?"

"I'm trying to reach a woman who wrote me a letter requesting that I tell whoever answers the phones at the station to put her call through. She didn't want me calling her at home. I guess she tried to reach me, but couldn't. You know how I need my calls screened."

"Right. So you tried calling her even though she didn't want you to?"

"I have a gut feeling that I have to pursue this. I called directory assistance in St. Louis and got her phone number," she said defensively.

"What's her story?"

Shawna picked up the letter as if to confirm what it said. "The letter says she lives in St. Louis, that her husband works for the USDA and that she was worried he may be involved in criminal activities against his will... whatever that means."

"Hmm," involuntarily resonated from Alyson's lips. She wished she could respond with something intelligent, but nothing came to mind.

Shawna held the letter as far away as her arms would stretch in order to read it clearly through her slightly squinted eyes. "This says that he back handed her when she questioned him about him having gambling money and buying a brand new fully loaded black Lincoln Town Car, using cash that didn't come from their savings or investment accounts. He screamed at her to never question him again. She's scared to go to the police, but she wanted to talk to me."

"Wow. How long ago did you get the letter?" Alyson asked, making a mental note to make an optometry appointment for Shawna.

She buried her head in her hands feeling regretful. "About a month ago. I should have at least made arrangements to take her call. I don't know what I was thinking."

"You were all wrapped up in the work you were doing and in dealing with your lawyer and agent. Anyone would have procrastinated in the same situation. From now on, I'll be able to handle things for you. Nothing else will slip through the cracks."

"Thanks. Anyway, I guess I'll try the number again later. The guy who answered sounded like a total jerk. If it's the right number, it's probably her husband," Shawna said. Careful not to smear her make up, she delicately rubbed the inside corners of her strained eyes, wishing she looked better in glasses.

It went without saying that Shawna's phone call may have triggered another abusive situation. That was probably why Martha Gentry specifically didn't put her telephone number or address.

An hour later, Shawna dialed the number again.

The phone was picked up before the first ring was completed.

"Hello," a female voice whispered.

"Martha Gentry?"

More whispering. "Yes."

"This is Shawna Sanders."

More whispering. "I've been praying that you would call. Give me your number. I'll call when I can."

"Let me give you my office number and my home number," Shawna found herself whispering back. She spoke the numbers slowly and then asked, "Is your husband there right now?"

More whispering. "Yes. He's passed out, drunk. I don't know if he'll wake up."

"Has he hurt you again?"

More whispering. "I'll call."

A dial tone echoed in her ear before she could ask anything else. Shawna planted her elbows on her desk and pressed firmly on her temples to stimulate clear thinking. Tapping the pen didn't work today. With her eyes closed and taking deep breaths, she fought every instinct in her body that told her to catch the next flight to St. Louis.

Sixteen

"Martha?" Shawna ventured as she approached the distressed middle-aged woman who was alone at a large booth at the hotel restaurant.

"Yes. I'm Martha. I can't believe you're really here," she said, partly relieved and partly star struck. She nervously caressed her fingers on the gold cross that hung from her necklace.

"I told you we would meet you," she said with a reassuring smile across her face.

Wade, Trish and Alyson joined them at the booth as soon as it was obvious that the woman was indeed Martha Gentry. The group introduced themselves and made small talk while waiting for their waitress to get their coffee and juice and take their breakfast orders.

From their brief telephone conversation, Shawna pictured Martha as a middle aged, overweight mid-western housewife, that by day stayed at home watching talk shows and soap operas while she ate junk food until her husband got home from a drinking binge at a two-for-one happy hour after work. She assumed that Martha spent each night cooking up fried foods or heating T.V. dinners and catering to her husband in order to avoid being slapped around.

As it turns out, Martha is a lean, fit vegetarian who teaches Yoga at a Meditation Center two hours each morning and volunteers her time teaching intermediate tennis lessons at the Parks and Recreation Department near her house several days a week. She also volunteers at her church with anything they ever need help with. As a passionate gardener, she spends as much time as she can utilizing her degree in horticulture in her own yard. For the past eight consecutive years, their house won awards from their huge neighborhood development for having the most exquisitely landscaped property. Until recently, Neil spent his spare time working with her in the gardens and building a reflecting pond in the half-acre back yard.

Once they got to know a little about Martha, they got down to business.

"Do you think you should check into our hotel? Maybe get away from your husband. Your safety is the most important thing," Trish said.

Martha shook her head as if it would provide an explanation for her husband's behavior. "My husband is a God fearing man. He's never laid a hand on me before. Never even threatened me. I don't know what's gotten into him."

"Well, I'm glad you haven't lived in an abusive situation, but if he's done it once, you never know if it's going to happen again," Trish said.

"I'll be fine. It's him that I'm worried about," she said as she adjusted her headband to get her long loose strands of hair off her suntanned face.

Her hair was highlighted in several colors of blond and light browns giving it the look of someone who spent a lot of time at the beach. In reality, the closest Martha ever got to a beach was when she went on a church retreat to the Lake of the Ozarks. Martha had never seen the ocean and was unlikely to ever have the opportunity.

Shawna glanced in Alyson's direction to make sure she had her note pad ready, then gently touched her hand to Martha's forearm. "I understand. First, you need to elaborate on what you started telling me on the phone so that we know what to do from here. We have no idea if you're in danger or not. You contacted me because you're worried."

"I don't know where to begin," she said. There was so much to tell and so little to tell at the same time. Right now, everything was just a suspicion.

This is how most people are when talking with an investigative reporter. They have information, but don't know how to explain how all of the pieces fit together. Shawna prided herself on making people clarify their thoughts and identify the real issues that relate to their story.

"Since you think his problems revolve around his job, how about starting from the beginning of his career?" Shawna suggested.

Martha softly bit down on the right side of her lip as she decided where to start. "Okay… well, when Neil first graduated from college, he got a job with the U.S. Department of Agriculture and set his sights on working his way up in the organization. As he advanced, one of his superiors, a mentor in fact, suggested that he get an MBA, insinuating that he wouldn't get any further without it," she explained, now relaxed in her seat as she thought more about his history. "Neil's always been motivated and goal oriented. He's quite an achiever. In fact, every year he raises the most money for our church when they hold fundraisers."

"That's good," Shawna acknowledged since Martha seemed to expect a reply.

She shook her head and thought back to the days when her husband was never home. "Neil worked full time and attended extension courses at the local college for two years. Finally, on the brink of total exhaustion, he earned his MBA.

"After that, he was so frustrated. After all of his hard work, as it turned out, in St. Louis there weren't any upper level positions available. We had some tension in our marriage for a while because I refused to move away from here. We talked to our priest and he got us through it."

"You were born and raised here?" Trish asked.

"Yes. And we have a good life. Close friends. Our church. My parents and my sister and her kids. I refuse to move. It wasn't as if Neil was unemployed and we absolutely had to move for him to get work. He just needed to wait for an opening in the department," she explained without sounding defensive.

"Obviously, you didn't move or get a divorce over it," Shawna said.

"No. We worked things out," Martha said with a tender smile. "Neil's generally a patient man. He continued working in a supervisory capacity over the USDA's local inspectors. Shortly after his forty-third birthday, he was promoted to the position of Chief Inspector of the region. The promotion was bitter sweet because he didn't get an increase in pay or benefits. What he did get were more responsibilities; the opportunity to develop and institute improved guidelines and procedures that served as a test model for the rest of the country.

"Of course, along with that came longer hours, but at least he was independent. He was finally able to work when and where he wanted and rarely reported to his superiors any longer. He relished in the autonomy of his role with the USDA and could envision further advancement in his career," she explained with pride.

"That's good," Trish said.

"Neil set his sights on establishing himself in the top echelons of the organization. Not understanding the politics in top level management, he assumed that if he worked long enough hours and with enough diligence, he could eventually be named the next administrator of the USDA's Agricultural Compliance Division or head up the USDA's Agricultural Marketing Services Department."

"Is that when his personality started changing? When he realized he didn't understand the politics?" Shawna asked.

Martha had given the subject of her husbands personality change a lot of thought before today. In fact, that's what prompted all of her suspicions in the first place.

"Neil started practicing yoga three years ago when he needed to work on stress relief. The yoga seemed to have helped him until about a year ago. In a matter of months, he went from missing an occasional yoga class to completely dropping out. Eventually, he even stopped going to church. His frustration and stress from work were increasingly obvious."

"What signaled to you that it was beyond normal stress and frustration?" Shawna asked.

Martha didn't have to think about her answer. It was waiting on the tip of her tongue. "Rather than throwing himself into his work more, as was his normal habit, he began working less hours, but more random hours. What was worse was that we drifted apart."

Shawna asked the canned question that was required in just about every interview she had ever conducted. "Can you give me an example?"

Martha's eyelids puffed up and turned a pale shade of pink as she held back her tears. "Sure. For one thing, Neil was always concerned about money and never having enough to do what we wanted. Suddenly, last year he started buying higher quality and more stylish clothes, he'd golf, go on expensive hunting trips, go on trips to Las Vegas, and go out drinking with people I never met."

"Where did he say the money was coming from?" Shawna asked.

"I never asked. At first, I thought he was finally splurging for the first time in our lives. I thought it was great that he'd finally spend money on himself instead of putting away retirement money; and, before this, if there was anything left over from normal expenses, he would give an offering to the church."

"You mean you tithe to your church?" Shawna asked.

"An offering is over and above a tithe. It's our way of proving our sacred vow with God, according to Malachi 3:8. Of course, God loves us no matter what, but when we can, we like to make an offering."

None of them knew what to say as a response to her starting to talk more about her church and finances. Each had hoped someone else would say something appropriate.

Martha continued explaining the financial changes. "One day he came home in a great mood and announced that we were finally finishing our basement and using part of it as a game room. He told me to go shopping for whatever furniture and decorations

I wanted, as long as it wasn't feminine or new age looking. He said he already hired someone to build a custom bar with seating for six, bought a beautiful pool table, an overhead light and a hot tub for the new deck that was going to exit out our walk-out basement."

"That sounds extreme. Especially with everything else he was spending money on," Shawna said.

"I know! And then, when I saw that he was paying cash for everything and I questioned him about it, he told me that he'd won the money in Las Vegas."

"Was that plausible?" asked Trish.

"I guess. But I didn't feel good about his answer. On the other hand, I remembered him saying that he'd won big when he came back from that last trip. At the time, I asked him how much he won and he got defensive, asking me if I didn't already have everything I wanted and needed."

Shawna put herself in Martha's shoes. "So, in an attempt to keep the harmony, you didn't ask anything else?"

"I didn't want to start an argument. I dropped the subject and never brought it up again."

Trish didn't want to insult Martha, but she had to ask. "Anything since then?"

"Yes! That's when I finally realized how naïve I've been. Six weeks ago, when he showed up at home driving a brand new Lincoln Town Car, he had no explanation as to how he had the money to pay cash for it. When I demanded to know, he backhanded me... and scared me the way he screamed at me to mind my own business." Tears came gushing from her eyes just remembering what had happened. She looked up, eyes closed and did the sign of the cross over her chest. "It was so unlike him. I actually found him crying in the guest bedroom when I woke up alone in the middle of the night."

"Were you afraid of him after that?" Trish asked.

"Not afraid. Like I said, it was not like him at all. He's a gentle, kind man. But, from that night on, it seemed as if he was getting drunk every single night. Now, he hardly even talks to me.

It's like we're strangers. We even started sleeping in separate bedrooms. He's refused to talk to Father Joseph," Martha said as salty tears leaked from her eyelids.

Naturally, Martha was worried about Neil's drastic personality change, so she started following him when he went out. During normal work hours, she expected to always be following him to the USDA offices, but he frequently went to the produce wholesalers at the farmers market. He never stayed long when he was there. Sometimes when he arrived there would be a refrigerated delivery truck backed up to the loading docks and she'd see him walk in and walk out within fifteen to twenty minutes. He looked to be filling out paperwork, as a Federal Inspector would, but Neil hadn't been working as an inspector for the past several years. He kept his licensing current, just in case he needed to do inspections as a side job for extra income, but as far as she knew, he never did. At least he never told her he was doing inspections.

Trish couldn't help voicing her opinion. "I don't think that you should go home until we have a chance to at least do a preliminary investigation."

"Part of me agrees, but in my heart I can't imagine him ever physically hurting me again," Martha said with pain in her voice.

Everyone at the table agreed that the most important thing was to find out if Neil was involved in criminal activity, and if so, what was he illegally doing to get flush with cash.

Martha correctly assumed that Shawna would be interested since he works for the government and because the agriculture business is so highly regulated. It only stood to reason that this was a news worthy story that deserved exposure.

"I understand that you want to know what Neil's involved in, but as his wife, aren't you basically turning him out to the wolves by calling us?" Wade asked. Being the photographer, this was the first time he spoke during the entire meeting.

Martha slouched in the booth and wiped the last of the tears from her cheeks as she thought out her response.

"Even if it means destroying his career or subjecting him to legal problems, as long as he's forced to stop whatever he's doing, I'd be satisfied."

Wade was disgusted with her lack of loyalty and it showed in his face. "You don't care what happens to him?"

"Of course I care! The Lord knows how much I love him. That's the point of this! Knowing Neil as intimately as I do, I'm worried that his stress or guilt will drive him to suicide. The way that I see it is that his severe personality transformation, along with his inability to cope with life, is a sign that he might go over the edge. He needs to get straightened out and find his way back to the church. And to me," she said with the resolve and strength that most women could never muster.

Wade nodded his head in understanding, feeling guilty that he had been so judgmental only moments ago.

"You're a strong woman Martha," Trish said admiring her convictions and sense of morality, even though she viewed Martha as overly religious.

Shawna and Alyson nodded in agreement with Trish's statement.

"Please, try to keep me out of it if you can. I know he'll think I'm betraying him if he finds out I went to you or got involved in any way," she pleaded.

"Sure. We don't need to tell him anything. We just need your help in supplying us information," Shawna assured her.

"Once this is over, hopefully we'll be able to repair our marriage."

"I'm sure you will," Alyson, the romantic one of the bunch said.

Shawna's thoughts were going a mile a minute without the benefit of tapping her pen or rubbing her temples. "Okay. So, basically, we need to find out where he's getting all of this extra cash. We presume it's coming from something to do with his capacity in the USDA. Presumably, something illegal..."

\\\\\\\\\

Alyson went to her hotel room and made arrangements with the car rental service to deliver each of them their own cars since they all came to the hotel from the airport in one vehicle. After the arrangements were made, she planned to catch a long nap. Shawna warned her that she may be up working late into the night. Everyone else would be doing investigative work, then, they'd report to Alyson. She would need to record and organize everything and would have a list of things to follow up on from each person.

Shawna and Wade went to the farmer's market area to scope out the surroundings. After lunch, they planned on gathering general information at the St. Louis office of the United States Department of Agriculture. Then, they would come back to the hotel and rest before staking out Neil Gentry for the rest of the day and night.

\\\\\\\\\\

"Extension 515, please," Trish said.

A few seconds of silence, then a low-pitched hum.

"You have reached 515," announced a voice that sounded computer generated.

"83, please."

A few seconds of silence.

"A.W."

"Avery? Avery Warner?" Trish asked even though she recognized the voice that she longed to hear.

"Trish?"

His heart melted.

"Yes. How are you?"

"Fine. And you?"

"I'm fine, but I could use a favor. Can you talk?"

"Right now?" he asked, hoping that she meant that she was in Washington D.C. and needed to meet with him.

Her heart was racing. Maybe this was a bad idea. After all, she still had other contacts in the FBI and he knew it.

"Sure, if you can," she said, wishing they were making plans to be together the way they used to be.

Avery thought about his answer as he read the note his partner set on his desk, directly in front of him. The note had an address in St. Louis, Missouri and a telephone number. He was disappointed and relieved at the same time. Could his heart have taken seeing her in person?

"I can talk."

The tension in her voice relaxed some when she asked, "What's this A.W. thing you answered your line with? It reminds me of the root beer... which I love, by the way!"

"My new partner, Abdul Samhiti, can't pronounce my name! He calls me A.W."

"You're serious?"

"Yes."

"Is everyone else calling you A.W.?"

"No. I just answered that way to patronize him. He was in my office when I picked up the line."

It wasn't true. Everyone he worked with in the office called him A.W. now. He just didn't want Trish to start because he always loved how she pronounced *Avery* with her diminishing southern accent, blending with just a hint of New York. He melted when she called him by name. It's funny, the things that can get to a man.

Trish was curious about how his life was going, but she didn't dare ask. At this point in her own life, there was no answer that would have felt right to her. If he was still alone, she'd feel pity for him and it would hurt her. Yet, if he had found someone else, her heart would be shattered. Again.

"The reason I was calling is because I'm working for Shawna Sanders..." she said, knowing he'd expect an explanation.

"Doing investigations for her stories?"

Her entire body tensed up. "Yes."

"When did this start?"

"Avery, please."

"Please what?"

"Please don't think that you can..."

"Forget it! It's your business, not mine," he said, knowing he didn't have a right to influence her.

That was how all of the problems started in the first place.

"I was wondering if you've ever dealt with anything involving the Department of Agriculture?"

"You're not working on some lame story about how pesticides are supposedly more dangerous than the critters they destroy, are you? It's been done a dozen times!"

"No. That's not what the piece is about. But even if it was..." Trish started fuming under her breath. At least his attitude allowed her to forget her yearning for him. Most of her yearning. Some of her yearning. Okay. So she still yearned for him. But still, it didn't take many words to remind her of their differences.

"Never mind. I'm sorry," he interrupted before she could start an argument by defending herself.

"Apology accepted," she said, not knowing if she meant it or not. She would decide later, when she was tossing and turning in bed instead of sleeping. Tonight would be another sleepless night thinking about where they went wrong.

"Anyway, I personally don't know anyone with the USDA, but try Caleb Anderson."

"Yeah?"

"He's in St. Louis working on something with the local offices there and it has something to do with the USDA," he said.

"Do you know what it's about?" her heart started beating rapidly. What a coincidence.

"No. But you ought to call him and see what he can tell you."

"Will you get a feel first, and see if he'll take my call?"

"Just call him."

"Would he talk to me? Please, give him a quick call and see if you can find out..."

"I'm not doing your investigative work for you. Let me give you his number," Avery insisted as he was thumbing through the A's in his Rolodex.

"Avery..." she drew out his name the way it drove him wild inside.

He ignored the stiffness under his desk.

"His number is 314-555-1056. Tell him you talked to me. That's the best I'm going to do for you," he said, hoping that he'd reach Caleb before she did. He had to tell him to act as if they never talked about her.

"Okay. Thanks," she said, not wanting to hang up. "It's so good to hear your voice," slipped out. She felt her face blush from the admission.

"Yours too."

"Let's don't go there," she said, holding back tears.

"Well, I'm here if you change your mind. I'm waiting for you."

Trish's heart felt like hot fudge poured over ice cream in a freezing dish. The heat spread through her, just like it always did when she let her thoughts drift to how she felt when they were together.

\\\\\\\\\\

Caleb Anderson returned Trish's phone call within ten minutes of receiving the message on his pager. His secretary surely sent the message promptly, hoping that Trish was a prospective date. She was always meddling in his private life. Always trying to fix him up with somebody. He never took her up on it and she never stopped trying. He'd wait to return Avery's phone call until tonight. His friend could wait. Trish's message said she needed to speak with him ASAP.

After Trish explained what her job is, who she now worked for and what information she was looking for, Caleb said he couldn't meet her at his office. They arranged to meet an hour later at a park near his rental house.

"It's so good to see you!" Trish lied, opening a dialog that was supposed to sound trusting. It's not that she didn't want to meet with him. Of course she did. She just didn't want to have to look at him. She didn't know how to look without staring or appearing as if she were grossed out by the burn marks on his face and the entire right side of his body. At least the surgeons improved his appearance as much as they could. Trish preferred him as the handsome, debonair FBI agent he was when they met. Who wouldn't? It's human nature.

Eighteen select people were in advanced weapons training together. Trish was the only woman. Not just in their group, but the only woman ever. Even until this day. Avery, Trish and Caleb were the boisterous ones of the bunch. Both men were sexually appealing to her, but she never showed her interest. It wouldn't have been professional and it would have been dangerous. They all needed to keep their mind on their objectives... learning to safely deploy every kind of weapon made available to the FBI field officers, the SWAT team and the 'go to' people, including hostage negotiators.

Of the eighteen people in training, two would be selected to spend the next full year training other people coming through the program. No one in training wanted the job. Everyone wanted to be working in the field where there was at least a chance for some action besides using their brains and other skills. Avery, Trish and Caleb talked about the fine line of passing with flying colors [when it came to proving that they could safely and effectively use any and all weapons that they may need to use in the field,] yet, not be so good that they were stuck training other agents in the future. How were they going to distinguish themselves with honor and not end up with a job they would hate?

Caleb got out of it the hard way. He improperly handled a live CHS-1, a mechanism that is similar to a hand grenade. He accidentally set himself on fire right in front of everyone. It was horrible, especially for Trish. She thought the reason he was reckless was because he was flirting with her at the time he was handling the CHS-1. Later, she found out that he wasn't interested in her at all. The woman he had been dating for some time had agreed to move in with him. Caleb was so excited that the relationship had finally moved to that level, he wasn't thinking on his feet that day.

Unfortunately, Trish blamed herself for his tragic accident for almost a month. Avery told her that Caleb's girlfriend broke up with him because she couldn't deal with his burn marks and all of the skin grafts he was going to be going through. That's when she asked about when their relationship started. The pieces came together enough for her to realize that she didn't distract Caleb. Of course, she still felt bad that he was burned, but at least it wasn't her fault!

Today, they gave a friendly hug the way people who talk to each other all of the time do. That was just their personalities. Faking any and all kinds of emotions helped them be good agents. They actually had training on how to try to distinguish real feelings from acting. It was one of the most difficult things to deal with on the job once you were working undercover or working on a case that you had to appear to befriend a snitch or an informant. Usually, the relationship with these people lasted for extended periods of time. It was easy to fall into a situation where you didn't know your own feelings.

Caleb was frustrated with his career right now, especially since out of nowhere he was completely left out of the loop and kept in the dark on the case with the USDA and with the Murphys. He was insulted, confused and determined to find out what was going on.

Normally, he wouldn't have told a private investigator anything at all, but this was his old buddy, Trish. When she was still at the Bureau, she ranked higher at the FBI than he ever hoped to be. Besides, he needed someone to share his frustration with about being shut out of the operation. It wasn't legal, ethical or professional, but Caleb disclosed to her almost everything he knew.

Seventeen

It was Wade's ingenious idea that Shawna wear the auburn colored longhair wig. Once the tresses were adjusted on her scalp, she applied triple the amount of eye makeup as usual, going for the Tammy Fay Bakker look. Topping it off, she drew on a deep-pigmented lip liner and slathered herself in lipstick reshaping her mouth to be fuller and more sensuous. The disguise would probably even fool her husband if she were somewhere out of context when he passed casually near her. Shawna loved being incognito for investigations, and every once in a while for her husband.

Wade, the ever-accomplished driver who took racecar-driving classes at the Bonderaunt School in Northern California, tailed Neil, starting from the entrance of the Gentry's subdivision. Shawna didn't want to drive anyway, she told him. For a half an hour on the interstate, they speculated about where Neil was heading. They were in the heart of the Downtown St. Louis Historic District before Neil finally pulled into the city owned parking lot. Fortunately for Wade and Shawna, there was an ample number of parking spaces and Neil didn't seem to be watching out for whether or not he was being followed. Because both sides of the street are lined with restaurants, bars and coffee houses, they followed him closely so they didn't lose him.

Briskly heading toward his destination, Neil appeared tense, but not paranoid.

Inside the historic brick building, which had once been a train depot, Neil walked with purpose to a booth in the bar where he joined an unshaven man who looked as if he'd slept in his clothing. They didn't show any signs of friendship; in fact, they were hostile toward each other.

Wade approached the women in the booth immediately adjoining the side where Neil sat carrying on a nervous sounding conversation. He tossed a crisp hundred-dollar bill in the center of the table where three women were seated with empty beer mugs and a half eaten platter of grease drenched chicken wings.

"Take this," he said, obviously referring to the money, "And clear the table without saying a word right now. My partner and I need your seats," he explained in a hush. He nodded toward Neil and added as if he were disgusted, "This jerk's screwing around on his wife. I'm a detective for the wife. Get it?"

The heavy set woman with a wedding band quickly snatched up the hundred dollar bill and gave a thumbs up sign to Wade. She was the first to rise. Her friends giggled and proceeded to follow her to the bar where there were plenty of vacant stools. When the women looked back over toward Neil, they realized that it was two men sitting across from each other. They debated about whether they were conned out of their booth or if the men were gay.

Unsteady on her spiked high heels, which clicked as she walked across the plank wood floor, she tried not to be self-conscious of her petal pink cleavage showing short dress. Trying not to expose too much leg, Shawna slipped into the booth arranging herself in position to be back to back with Neil. Wade scooted in right beside her and they acted like a couple on a date, cuddling and whispering. To their benefit, the background music was soft and the minimal crowd wasn't loud yet, enabling them to overhear most of Neil's heated conversation.

Before the waitress even noticed that the three ladies had been replaced by the affectionate couple, Neil jumped up from his seat, slammed his fist on the table and in an animated voice that rose in pitch, he said, "You don't think I'm serious, do you? I'm going to D.C. if you don't get me out of this! I'm not doing it anymore!"

Neil turned on his heels away from the table and bustled out the door.

In response, the man with a beer gut hanging over his belt pulled a ten from his shiny money clip and threw the bill on his table to cover his drink and a tip. His bright gold and diamond pinky rings and thick gold chain necklaces looked out of place with his wrinkled clothing. Instead of following Neil, he hobbled to the far end of the bar. As he was making his way there, he was pulling up his slacks a couple of inches toward what should have been a waistline.

Wade followed Neil trying to remain inconspicuous.

Shawna stayed to see what the greasy skinned man would do. She watched him use his short stubby index finger to dial a number on the old rotary telephone.

Unexpectedly, everyone in the bar froze from the vibrations and resonant sound of an explosion. Oblivious to how unbalanced her high-heeled shoes made her, Shawna ran outside toward the commotion and headed toward Wade who was feverishly approaching Neil. Neil was pale white and nauseous looking and appeared as if he were going to collapse thirty feet from his new car, which was in flames that were obviously intended for him.

Wade rushed to support Neil under his arm to keep him from melting into the asphalt pavement. A warm tingling sensation of guilt spread through him while he contemplated getting his video equipment in order to film the aftermath of the explosion. His self-restraint felt good… for once, he was helping someone instead of recording their trauma as evidence of something they would probably rather forget.

"It looks like you could use some help," Shawna offered when she approached the stunned man that she had heard so much about.

The dazed look still hadn't vanished from his face. Neil stared at her as if he were trying to understand the meaning of a nightmare. Her kind eyes spoke to him. He realized it was Shawna Sanders at his side.

Eighteen

The blazing fire that engulfed Neil's car roared in the background as Shawna attempted to convince him that he needed help; not the kind that you can get from the police. Wade suggested that they at least talk about it before the authorities arrived. Neil was so shook up that he agreed to at least go back into the restaurant with them and try to gather his thoughts.

As the waitress served their coffee, the threesome tried to ignore the sirens outside and the police that were cordoning off the area of the explosion. An outsider looking into the window of the pub would think they looked like any other paying customers.

Neil calmed down enough to think semi-rationally; he really couldn't go on like this any longer. "Why do you even want to get involved with my problems?"

"We think there may be a good story in this, to be perfectly honest," Shawna confessed.

"Story? I'm in trouble. Somebody just tried to kill me! I'm not going to be your story!"

"Neil, we can probably help you if we understand exactly what has been happening. Your wife is a nervous wreck about how you came into so much money and..."

"Martha? Martha doesn't know anything. Leave her out of this!"

"Oh," she hesitated. "Yes. In all the commotion, I guess we didn't tell you. We've been in contact with her. It's how we found you. I'll let her explain it," Shawna said, not wanting to interfere in their marriage.

"Found me?" Neil said, confused. He just assumed it was a coincidence that Shawna and Wade were in the parking lot.

"Your wife wants to help you and she didn't know where to turn. She contacted me, hoping..."

Neil didn't give her a chance to finish her explanation. "I told her to stay out of this. It's my problem, not hers. I'll take care of this... somehow."

"Someone just tried to kill you. Are you sure you want to take a chance that you can deal with this alone?" Shawna asked.

"It's all become so complicated and too many people are involved. If I turn myself in, I'll go to jail!"

"Tell us about it. Maybe we can help."

"Actually, I think I'll be okay now. I just met with someone else involved... I insisted that he leave me alone and that he get me out of all this mess. I threatened to go to the authorities if he didn't get me out of it," he rambled.

"This is serious. I think you're underestimating your problem. What are you involved in that someone would try to kill you?"

"It's a long story. Things got out of control."

"Maybe you should call an attorney," Wade said, thinking he was being helpful.

Shawna spoke up before Neil could reply. "Wade! We're not the authorities. Anything that he tells us can't be held against him! I'll get his story first and then *he* can decide if he needs legal representation."

"If Neil works with us, you can't even pursue the story without someone knowing what he's told you..."

She interrupted. "I certainly can. All I have to do is tell whoever I'm speaking with that an unnamed source gave me information..."

Bewildered, Neil slumped in his seat, listening to the two 'professionals'. His mind wandered away; did he fail to think of any options that he hadn't considered before?

"You wouldn't sound credible..."

Despite the weight of the heavy Tammy Fay Bakker eye make-up, her eyes opened wide. "Credible? I'm Shawna Sanders! How much more credible can anyone get?"

The color drained from his face, although his argumentative tone didn't falter. "That's not what I meant. I meant that the people involved will probably be sophisticated. They aren't going to chance that you're tricking them into giving you information or evidence. You'll have to use his name to show you really do have some credible proof and a basis for your inquiries."

Shawna relaxed her posture, lowered her chin and sunk back into her chair. She was embarrassed for having overreacted and she felt awkward for having appeared as if she thought she was so high and mighty.

"Let me think about it. We can still get the story from his side before he calls an attorney. Maybe he can just go to his boss and they'll let the USDA handle it internally."

Shawna and Wade spoke as if Neil weren't present, until he finally interjected one detail. "My boss knows. That's who I was here with. I've been giving him a cut of the action."

"How deep does this go?" Shawna asked.

"I'm not sure. I think I should call Martha and my attorney," Neil said, almost resigned to the idea that he'd probably end up in prison over all of this.

Wade didn't give Shawna a chance to open her mouth again. He gently kicked her on the leg as if to say *be quiet*. "That's a good idea. They'll both need to know everything eventually anyway."

Neil stood up, exhaling a sigh of relief now that everything was coming to a head, even if he was going to be in serious trouble. "Did you see a public phone?"

Shawna shot up straight as if she were mildly shocked. "The bar. But don't use it!"

She bustled over to the bartender nearest to the phone. Following their instincts, Wade and Neil trailed close behind, not really knowing why.

"Excuse me... do you know if anyone has used this phone since the explosion outside?" she asked the bartender with a sense of urgency.

He looked at her as if she were crazy, but just a little familiar looking. "Sorry. I didn't pay attention."

"Please, don't let anyone touch this phone," she told everyone within earshot as she pointed to the ancient bulky beige piece of plastic.

The bartender was trying to place where he knew her from. Was she a regular? He didn't think so. Did she teach one of the sociology classes at the college he was attending? No, he didn't know anyone who would dress like that or wear so much make up... yet... it all almost looked like she were playing dress-ups, like a little girl trying to look like someone else. She didn't carry herself or speak in a manner that was consistent with how she appeared.

Shawna motioned for Wade and Neil to come closer, not wanting anyone else to eavesdrop. She directed her words to Neil. "It just dawned on me that the man you were sitting with used that phone immediately after you walked out. I was watching him while Wade was following you. He dialed, then the explosion sounded. I ran outside without even relating the two until now."

Wade had a revelation. "His boss could have detonated the bomb by the telephone."

Neil trembled, thinking about how close he was to his car when it went up in flames. If he hadn't stopped in the parking lot to let two cars pass in front of him, he would have been hot amber ash now.

"We need to tell the police," Shawna said.

"How can you without blowing cover?" Wade asked.

Shawna gazed up toward the copper pressed tin ceiling panels and thought for a moment.

She leaned close to the bar again and got the bartender's attention. "Can I talk to you privately?"

"Sure," he said, trying to place the voice that suddenly sounded familiar.

"Listen, I can't be involved in this, but I really need for you to go outside and tell the police that you just realized a man dialed the phone and then the explosion went off. Tell him you obviously have no idea if one thing has anything to do with the other, but if they want fingerprints or can trace the call, they'll need to look into this. Make sure not to touch the phone or to let anyone else use it before the police decide what they want to do."

Now he knew. "Sure, Ms. Sanders. I'll get outside right away," he said through a wide grin. "Amy... keep an eye on this phone and don't let anyone, I mean anyone, touch it!" he called to the waitress who was lazily rolling silver for the evening crowd.

In the wide hallway between the bathrooms stood a bank of pay phones and cigarette machines. Neil called Martha from one phone and Shawna called Trish from another, leaving three phones in between at an attempt for privacy.

"I just walked in!" Trish said into the phone, anxious to tell Shawna what she was able to find out from Caleb. She threw her purse onto the bedspread and kicked off her shoes.

"We're with Neil Gentry. We need you to meet us..."

Trish gasped. "Are you all right? What's going on?"

"Wade and I are fine, but Neil just missed being blown up in his car... we're with him now and I want you here."

"Are you in the historic district?"

"How'd you know?"

"Driving back to the hotel, I heard on the radio that a car exploded in a parking lot in the historic district and that they didn't know if anyone was in it. The last I heard, it was still on fire."

Shawna looked out the window to confirm what she thought. "The fire's out, but we're not talking to the police. Not yet, at least."

"Good idea. It would only slow everything down. At least Neil's alive! Otherwise, we'd never get the story out of it that we're going to..."

"You are cold! I can't believe you said that," Shawna admonished her, almost in a whisper. Deep inside, she was thinking the same thing.

Wade heard Shawna attempt to give Trish driving directions; he couldn't resist snatching the phone right out of her hand and making a silly face at her. He got on the line with Trish and gave her directions to meet them, then he added, "Bring a tape recorder and drive carefully."

Neil was still on the phone with Martha when Shawna and Wade went to sit back down at their booth. They saw Neil break down crying once he was alone. He was nodding his head to the phone as if he thought Martha could hear him, Wade supposed. To him, it looked as if he were relieved to be able to unburden himself by confessing to his wife.

The bartender returned to the bar with three stoutly built men who were officially working on the car explosion. One of them took fingerprints as the other two began questioning each person in the bar about whether they had observed anyone who looked suspicious. Wade and Shawna said they hadn't seen anything unusual.

Neil returned to the booth with a dry face; it was red from crying. With a sense of calm, he told them that Martha was on her way to come hear about everything. She thought that they should wait to call an attorney.

It was going to take at least a half an hour before Martha and Trish arrived, so they ordered appetizers and tried to make conversation while avoiding the subject of his problems. Shawna and Wade learned more than they ever wanted to about the redevelopment of the historic district.

Trish arrived before Martha. True to her nature, she sized up Neil Gentry as she approached the table filled with dirty food plates, empty water glasses, and three full cups of coffee. "You ate without me?" she asked as a greeting.

"We needed to do something to pass the time. You can order, but why don't you wait a few minutes and see if Martha wants anything," Wade suggested.

"I'm Neil Gentry," he said as he held out his hand in a gesture to offer a handshake.

Trish didn't offer her hand back. She had no intentions of shaking hands with a man who had struck his wife.

"Nice to meet you. I'm Trish Hart," she said, concealing her true feelings towards him.

"Ms. Hart, you may as well order yourself some food now. Martha never eats when she's nervous or preoccupied," Neil said.

"Just call me Trish. I wish I didn't eat when I was nervous. If my body worked like that I wouldn't have to jog everyday and work out with weights four days a week."

The waitress came by and asked Trish if she wanted coffee or anything else to drink as she handed her a menu.

"Can you clear this mess first? I can't eat or drink around all of this," Trish said.

The waitress was put off, but cleared the plates from the table, ignoring the dirty silverware that remained. She returned with a stained cloth that smelled like bleach, and proceeded to wipe around the utensils, the cups and the cream and sugar. Her sloppy job still left a mess and she didn't speak.

"Do you work for tips?" Trish asked her.

"Yes."

"Try acting like it! Can I give you my order now?"

The waitress wished she had a different station. Different customers. Actually, a different job. She didn't go through four years of private college, and then law school, to do this. She swore to herself that after she took her bar exam she'd never serve anyone anything else again. One more week until the exam and her life would change forever. Her father will be proud; she'll join his law practice. In the mean time, he wanted her to work in the real world where common people existed. He wanted her to see what the struggle of life was all about until she joined one of the most influential law firms in the mid-west.

"Do you have any private rooms available, like a small banquet room or anything?" Trish asked the waitress.

"Yes. As a matter of a fact, we do," she said as she pointed to the far corner of the restaurant. "It seats twelve people. Would you prefer to go back there?" she asked, finally not acting as if her customers were a burden.

"We would. Yes. Can you have it set up for five with fresh water and a water pitcher for refills. And if you have a pot of coffee you could leave with us so that we can have some privacy...and I'd like to order a grilled sesame chicken salad."

The waitress perked up and showed that she was in fact working for tips. "I'll make sure everything is set up for you by the time your fifth person arrives. We don't have that salad on the menu, but I'm sure that I can get the cook to make it up for you. We have a great ginger dressing that we use on an oriental dinner item. Would you like that on the side?"

Trish was glad she finally got her point across to the waitress. "Sounds great. Thank you."

Shawna and Wade were a little embarrassed at how Trish treated the waitress at first, but by this time, they were glad she spoke up and were impressed that she had thought of the idea of a private room.

"Shawna, can I talk to you in the room for a few minutes before Martha comes?" Trish asked, eager to share what she found out from Caleb.

"Sure," she answered as she struggled to get out of the booth without her dress hiking up her thighs any further.

"By the way, you look like a whore from the seventies."

The bartender overheard Trish's comment and laughed out loud.

"Speaking of styles, you look a little too sexy for being on the job! You've over-dressed yourself," Shawna said clearly as a complement rather than a put down.

"Thanks. I met with a guy I knew when I was with the Bureau. He's single. I knew he'd be more forthcoming if I was sexually appealing to him. As you can see, it doesn't take much work for me to have the perfect combination of professionalism and seductiveness," she explained as she tossed her hair in mock exaggeration. "I don't look like a tramp though, like you. I just look as if I've got pride in my wardrobe and my body... it shows that I care about style and fashion. And proper use of cosmetics!"

Shawna's face was overcome with a sanguine smirk. How many times had she done the same thing when she was younger...and single?

She didn't need to defend herself but she wanted to keep the light mood going a little longer. "I'm not trying to attract a man or keep my husband interested. I'm just disguising myself!"

"You could have chose any number of disguises. I think this is how you really want to look, but the network and Loren won't let you..."

"Shut up!" Shawna said letting out a laugh that she needed.

"Make me!" Trish dared her.

"Speaking of Loren, remind me to call him after we're done here. He paged me about ten minutes after Neil's car blew up," Shawna instructed.

The small banquet room was quiet and perfect for their meeting.

"Loren's got FBI and USDA contacts doesn't he?" Trish said, serious again.

"I think so. It seems like the man has a phone book full of contacts and informants."

"Good. We need someone higher up than Neil or his boss in the USDA. Let me tell you what I found out from Caleb," Trish said as she pulled out a chair from under the solid oak table. Limber as a gymnast, she raised her leg so that her heel rested on the back of the chair. She reached forward, easily stretching her fingers to touch the toes on her raised foot, stretching as slow and as far as she could. She counted to thirty in her mind and then switched legs to stretch.

Shawna wrote on her yellow pad of paper adding to her notes as Trish detailed what Caleb told her regarding the USDA and the Murphys.

"We definitely need to get to the bottom of this. If Loren doesn't already have a USDA contact, he'll find a way to get inside for a story like this!" Shawna already knew that having Trish on her team was a wise decision, but this confirmed it.

"Caleb sounded sincere when he said he didn't know anything else, but my gut is telling me that he knows something he's not sure he can trust me with," Trish added.

Shawna thought about what she would have done if she were unmarried like Trish. "Can you casually invite him for a drink tonight... try to get him to open up more?" she suggested as she feigned the helpless woman look as an example of what she thought Trish should do.

"You mean lead him on to get him to loosen his tongue a little more? That's not decent or professional!" Trish acted put off in an exaggerated manner. "In other words, yes, that's exactly what I plan to do tonight!"

Shawna grinned. Who said women didn't have the advantage in the work place?

"Good."

Trish held out all five fingers and began counting off the informants they had and that they needed. "Okay. We've got Caleb with the FBI. Neil with his local end of the USDA. Loren will get to someone deeper in the FBI and the USDA. And you should get to the market manager at the farmer's market, and we need to get with the Murphys."

"Sounds like we've got a solid start," Shawna said enthusiastically.

"We've got a hell of a first story... or we will when we get to the bottom of everything," Trish answered just before Wade, Neil and Martha walked through the door into the banquet room.

Nineteen

Ryan Sanders settled himself into a Chippendale chair in the reception area of the production offices for *Insight with Shawna Sanders*. The receptionist had left for the day, which was reasonable since it was already seven in the evening. Always prepared with reading materials, Ryan brought a novel, *The New York Times* Bestseller, *Never Enough!* to read while he waited. It was rare that Shawna was really ever ready to leave when he arrived to pick her up at work. He had learned to be patient and have something to do, whether it was reading for pleasure, reviewing contracts for his business, or studying his monthly profit and loss statements.

The noise from Loren Blackstone's office was muffled due to the thick carpeting, solid walls and heavy eight-foot tall door. Ryan couldn't understand anything that was being said, but it was obvious that Shawna was going to be awhile. He came to pick her up for dinner, then take her home since she went directly to the studio from the airport. Once she was engrossed in an investigation, it was next to impossible to get her to break stride. He was the same way with his work, especially when he was filming a movie or getting a Broadway play going, so he couldn't complain.

An hour later and four chapters into the novel, Ryan was getting hungry and wondered if Shawna was aware of the time. Usually when he waited for her she would at least pop her head out the door and apologize for keeping him.

When the second strong hunger pang punched him in the stomach, which in his personal opinion was relatively firm for his age, he knocked on the door just below the engraved marble name plate that read *Loren Blackstone, Executive Producer*.

Based upon how loud the muffled sounds coming through the closed door were and that no one answered, he assumed that they didn't hear his knocking. He took the liberty to swing the door open wide enough to stick his head in, hoping to get Shawna's attention. The moment the door was open a crack, the noise level was amplified at least a hundred percent. The words he heard made it clear that the group was in a heated discussion. He recognized Trish's amplified voice trying to be heard over everyone else. She was saying that in her opinion, she should meet the Murphys without telling them what it was about before the meeting. Everyone else adamantly disagreed.

Wade spotted Ryan standing at the doorway looking uncomfortable about intruding. "Shawna, your husband's here," Wade told her loud enough to stop everyone from talking.

Her eyes darted toward the door, flustered. "Hi honey, is it seven?"

Ryan gave her a patient smile. "It's eight. But that's okay," he said sincerely, spotting what appeared to be cold pizza on the table in front of them. "It looks like you've eaten. Should I just meet you at home later?"

"No. I only had one piece to tide me over. I'll just be a minute or two," she promised.

"I'll be out here," he told her acting as if he really believed her estimate of timing. May as well start another chapter, he thought.

As he was closing the door behind him, he heard the words Johan and Jordan. At first, he didn't think anything of it, but his subconscious stored it. Twenty minutes later, another chapter finished in the novel, the name Murphy popped into his head. Yes. He heard them saying the Murphy brothers, then a minute later saying Johan and Jordan. Did the Johan Murphy that bought Love Letter have a brother named Jordan?

For the next half hour Ryan tried to concentrate on reading more, but he was getting hungrier by the minute and his mind kept flashing back to hearing the names. Finally, to pass the time since he couldn't concentrate on reading, he used the receptionist's telephone to call his farm manager in Santa Barbara.

"Hi. It's Ryan. Am I interrupting anything?"

"No. Just watching the idiot box," she said.

"How are the horses?"

"Fine, we just finished feeding them dinner."

"Do you know Johan Murphy?"

"The guy that bought Love Letter?"

"Yes. That one."

"No. I don't. I only saw him at the auction and read about him, why?"

"Just curious. Do you happen to know if he's got a brother?"

"I have no idea."

"Okay. Thanks."

"Anything else?"

"Not now. Call me if you need anything."

"Yes sir, Mr. Sanders." As always, her voice rose in pitch as she said sir, sounding as if she were in the military.

Ten minutes later, Ryan dialed the same phone number and his farm manager picked it up before the first ring completed.

"Hi. It's Ryan again. Am I interrupting anything?"

"No. Still watching the idiot box," she said.

"Hm. Sorry to bother you, but are you friendly enough with Greg Bordeaux to call him and ask him if Johan Murphy has a brother named Jordan?"

"Not really. I barely know the guy."

"Okay. Thanks."

"Anything else?"

"No."

"Are you waiting for your wife?"

"Why do you ask that?"

"Because you only call me with nothing to say when you're waiting for her. You never noticed?"

Ryan smiled. "No, I never noticed."

"What's all this about Johan Murphy?"

"It's nothing. Don't worry about it. I was just curious."

There was a silence as Ryan wanted to ask her if she'd call Bordeaux anyway. It had only been a couple of month's prior that she'd shown Greg his foal crop by his stallion that he'd imported from Poland. He couldn't imagine that Greg would care if she called and asked a quick and simple question.

"I could call Brian Pondergrass."

"About what?"

"About whether or not Johan has a brother."

"Would he know?"

"Maybe. Brian and Dean brought Johan to the auction. I assume that they were his agents."

Ryan temporarily forgot about his pending starvation. "Really?"

"Yes."

"Can you call now?"

"Now? Aren't they on the same time zone as you?"

"Yes."

"No, it's almost nine o'clock. It would be a little rude."

That's your specialty, he thought to himself.

"Ten o'clock is rude. Nine o'clock is slightly inconsiderate. Please, give him a call and I'll call you back in a few minutes."

"Yes sir, Mr. Sanders," she said in a tone she knew he wouldn't like too much but would tolerate. After all, technically, her workday was over and this was his second call. Typically, her official workday started at 6am before it got too hot out, and she wasn't usually finished until five or six in the afternoon. During the four months of foaling season, it was a twenty-four hour a day on-call rotation with two other people.

His hunger pains returned. He couldn't resist rummaging through the receptionist's desk drawers looking for something to eat. When he was introduced to her, he guessed her to be at least thirty pounds overweight and pictured her eating more than three meals a day to maintain status quo... that would mean that she ate while working. Everybody that worked a desk job kept some sort of snack foods in their desk, didn't they? Wow! An entire drawer dedicated to preservatives that posed as real food. He normally didn't eat processed foods with ingredients that he couldn't pronounce let alone know what they were, but sometimes a guy just didn't have a choice. This was one of those times. Bar-B-Q potato chips, sour cream and onion potato chips, cheese curls, cheese flavored crackers, processed cheese… he was ready to puke and afraid that if he kept looking he might find a can of Spam. Should he risk it? He took a deep breath, considered how hungry he was, and decided to take a chance. BINGO! The candy stash! He knew exactly what was in each wrapper and every ingredient was perfectly acceptable. He took a Nestle's Crunch Bar and replaced it with a dollar. As he savored the first big bite, he contemplated the Snickers Bar. Good idea. I'll leave two bucks for that. This woman is going to think the tooth fairy came when she goes back into this drawer. Oh look! A giant Hershey's with Almonds Bar. He didn't have any more dollar bills; better leave another five bucks.

He licked his fingers after finishing off the last of what just might turn out to have been his dinner. Hoping there was no chocolate on his face, he dialed the phone again.

She picked it up during the first ring.

"He has a brother named Jordan. They live in St. Louis. They're in the produce business and own it together."

"Thanks!"

"Yes sir, Mr. Sanders."

Shawna finally escaped from Loren's office and caught her husband red handed, stuffing the candy wrappers neatly into his jacket pocket, trying to conceal the evidence. He didn't know she saw him because his back was to her at the moment.

"Hungry?" she asked.

"Starving! I haven't had a bite since breakfast. I was too busy."

"You poor baby. I'm sorry I kept you so long. This story's going to be incredible. We're all arguing about where to go from here. Sorry."

"That's okay. I've just been reading," he said as he tucked the novel under his left arm and gave her a peck on the cheek.

"I'm starving too," she said, not intending to tell him that she had two more huge pieces of pizza after he had popped his head in earlier.

He debated whether he should tell her that she had damp looking pizza sauce caked on her chin since he knew she'd check herself in the mirror to put on fresh lipstick before they went inside the restaurant. Surely, her A-Team spotted it too but intentionally decided not to tell her. It was one of the ways people that work with her brought her back to earth and made her remember she was just a person like everyone else.

She didn't tell him that his breath reeked of chocolate and that she knew where he got it. Shawna was just grateful she never caught her husband smelling from another woman's perfume.

"Should we go to Vito's? Italian sounds good to me and you only had one piece of pizza a couple of hours ago," he said as she checked herself in her compact mirror while they rode the elevator down to street level.

He saw this pizza sauce on my face, she thought. "I'm not really in the mood for Italian. Why don't we go to Uptown's. They've got a little bit of everything and delectable chocolate desserts. We can eat a light supper and then splurge on our diets and have a big piece of chocolate cake… for each of us!"

Ryan couldn't think of another restaurant or a reason to turn down dessert.

After the server took their orders, Shawna pondered over whether or not she should discuss this story with her husband. Technically, everything really should be confidential until the story is aired, but this was her husband, who she trusted with her life. And it was her first story on her own in ages.

"When I interrupted your meeting I heard someone saying something about Johan Murphy," Ryan said, testing the waters. He didn't want to be intrusive, but he was particularly curious.

Shawna lightly bit her lower lip, blasé about why Ryan would care about the name. She sipped her Bloody Mary and decided she had to tell him about the story.

"This story I'm investigating…"

"Your team is investigating," he corrected.

"Yes. You're right. The story *we are* investigating is incredible. I want to tell you about it, but I need to remind you everything is confidential!"

"That goes without saying," he said, just barely insulted that she even felt she needed to remind him. Was she intentionally ignoring his inquiry about Johan Murphy?

"This is the story about the man whose car was bombed?"

"Yes. He's who I told you about on the phone last night. Anyway, this man, Neil Gentry works for the USDA. He's been making money on the side by doing a variety of fraudulent things. When the FBI got wind of it and assigned an investigator to look into it, the FBI investigator and his own boss at the USDA insist to get in on the action rather than exposing the wrongdoing! Apparently, it goes even deeper in each organization. We're going to get to the bottom of it and break the story wide open," she started explaining enthusiastically.

"What kind of fraudulent things did this Neil guy do?"

"There's a long list. First, it started out small. This international produce company offered to pay him a couple of thousand dollars to sign a Federal Inspection Certificate stating that a huge truckload of berries was bad and needed to be trashed because the refrigeration unit in the truck wasn't operating properly. In reality, the berries were in great condition and the produce company accepted the truckload from the driver, who apparently was on the take already, and they sold the berries like normal, netting about thirty thousand dollars."

"Don't they pay for the shipment in advance?"

"No. In fact, the grower never really knows how much he's going to get for the shipment. There are so many variables with every load. What happens usually is that the grower sets a per pound price based upon the delivery being accepted in the best possible condition... assuming that's the condition that it left his farm in, that is..."

"What do you mean?" Ryan asked after he swallowed the buttered fresh baked warm sourdough bread he was chewing.

"Well, not every crop is the exact same quality or even ideal quality, but hypothetically, if the crop left the grower in top perfect condition, that would be rated a 10. The produce buyer agrees to buy it for '*x*' amount of dollars per pound, based upon a '10' rating. But with refrigeration and evaporation and its resulting shrinkage, the weight changes during transport. Sometimes, so does the quality of the produce. Like, maybe there are crushed boxes or there are parasites, or some mold forms on the berries, or they lose their plumpness or something..."

"I never thought about it, but that makes sense."

"So, by the time it arrives to the buyer, the broker or wholesaler at the loading dock goes to inspect it. He's got a right to call in a Federal Inspector if he doesn't think that the shipment is the quality he expected and/or if the weight is changed more than about 10% from the shipping statement from the grower. If it warrants it, the inspector will downgrade the load or give it a totally failed inspection," she explained.

"What about number of cases? Do they count those, or just go by weight?"

Shawna knew the answer. "Well, they know how many cases of each standard size fits in a certain area, so they calculate from that in addition to a manual count when they physically unload."

"I get it. But what I don't understand is how they can say an entire shipment is bad."

"That's where the Federal Inspection comes in. If the person who is refusing to pay for the load claims it is bad, of course, he probably wouldn't be believed, so the inspector does a written certified report. What can the grower say?"

"Why wouldn't the grower tell them to return the load to him then?"

Shawna had asked Neil the same thing. "Because then the grower would have to pay for the shipping both ways, which is very costly. If it were in fact bad, he would have to throw it away himself. It would be stupid of him to take the chance."

"That makes sense. So they just trust the inspector?"

"Right. What else can they do? Things happen. Of course, the same broker or wholesaler can't do it very often to the same grower. And the grower has to have a lot of trust in who he's doing business with, but every once in a while, the broker or wholesaler can make out like a bandit with each grower he does business with. The more growers they do business with, the better."

"Can't the grower get insurance to protect against his product being delivered in unacceptable condition?" Ryan asked.

"It's too expensive. Same thing for the trucking companies. None of them are insured for their refrigeration going out or not working at peak function. It's just a risk of the business," she told him.

"Wow!" he said as he shook his head in amazement.

"It's a crazy industry," Shawna told him. In her mind, she was thinking it was as crazy and risky as the Arabian horse business, but she didn't dare say a word about that.

"What were you saying about downgrading the shipment? What's that mean?"

"Well, '10' is the ideal and '3' is not acceptable at all by USDA standards. But say the shipment turns out to be a '7'. Then, the wholesaler or broker pays the grower a certain percentage based upon the '10' price in comparison to the '7' price. I guess it's like a sliding scale," she said, hoping she explained it as well as Neil had to her.

"That makes sense," Ryan said as their waitress served them their Caesar salads and another loaf of sourdough.

"Neil didn't know it, but the guys who bribed him the first time took a home video of the whole thing and backed it up with a cassette recording of it," she explained. "Then, the next week they told Neil they needed another favor."

"What kind of favor?"

"I'll get to that in a minute. Neil tells them that he can't do anything else again because it's illegal, he felt guilty and he was worried he'd get caught. Then, they blackmail him and tell them they've got a tape. What else can he do? He goes along, afraid of losing his job and of being prosecuted."

"So then what did Neil do that was fraud?"

"The same thing, but with about two dozen other growers from different parts of the country and the world!"

"Are you serious?"

"Yes. And if that wholesaler is doing the same thing in every market that they're in, they're really making a killing!"

Ryan was confused. "What do you mean, every market?"

"This wholesaler, they have markets in every major city in the U.S. and in seven other countries. In some places, they do brokerage, others they're the wholesaler."

"Sounds like they'd have a lot of influence," Ryan said, comparing it to the motion picture industry in his own mind.

"You wouldn't believe the kind of things that go on."

"Like what else?"

Shawna confided in him. "Well, when a wholesaler is big enough, they can get into price fixing, which is another thing that this wholesaler did. And, they paid off other people to get government contracts..."

"Government?"

"Yes. The deal that Neil Gentry was involved in, which he assumes is only one shady government deal, was that they paid off the buyer for the entire U.S. Federal prison system to buy all of the produce the prisons use from them."

"From who?"

"From Murphy Enterprises, the wholesaler/broker I was talking about," Shawna clarified.

Ryan almost choked on the last bite of his salad. "Johan Murphy?"

"Right. And his brother Jordan… how do you know?"

Ryan used his white linen napkin to wipe any traces of food from his face. "I overheard the names when I opened Loren's door to let you know I was waiting."

Shawna picked at her salad while she tried to put two and two together. What meaning would Johan Murphy's name be to Ryan. She nodded her head, letting him know she was listening and waiting for him to elaborate.

"Did you know that Johan Murphy bought Love Letter?"

"What are you talking about?" Shawna gave him a look as if he were speaking a foreign language.

"Love Letter. The mare that's the only Triple Crown Winner. Remember…I went to Scottsdale and bid on her at the auction?"

She didn't know whether to be honest or not; she really didn't pay too much attention to what he did in the Arabian horse business. "Refresh my memory."

"I told you last February. I was going to buy Love Letter if I could get her for one million, but I doubted that she'd go for that low. We almost got in an argument about it because you thought it was stupid for me to even pay a million for a mare that wouldn't be able to have any babies," he said, wishing in one way that they weren't going to rehash it.

Suddenly, she relived the conversation in her mind. "Oh. Yes. I remember now! You ended up bidding to a million two hundred thousand and then finally had the sense to stop…"

"Right."

"So… so you're saying that Johan Murphy, the same one that I'm talking about, is who ended up buying the mare?"

"I'm sure of it," Ryan said.

"Well, the guy is a world-class crook. I haven't told you half the things he and his brother did and got Neil Gentry involved in!"

Ryan laughed even though it wasn't funny. What was funny was the way in which his wife said it. It didn't matter to him what the Murphys did or didn't do. He never did horse business with them and obviously wouldn't in the future.

"So what exactly did they do with the prison system? I mean, they have to buy produce from somewhere, I'm sure there are payoffs all of the time. The government doesn't pay its people anything. It's got to be tempting to take a bribe to buy from one guy over another when you need the product anyway," Ryan said, as if he would have been the guilty party if he were in their shoes.

"It's still illegal. On top of that, the buyer overpaid for the produce because there was no one checking him. Then, to top it off, the contracts said they were getting top quality produce when in fact the Murphys were delivering only product that no one else would accept, but it wasn't quite bad enough to be graded as garbage!"

"That's rotten!" he laughed to himself. "Pardon the pun! What else did they do?"

She pretended to laugh and he could tell. Sometimes things are only funny in your mind. Then once they slip out of your mouth, it loses it.

"Lots. Keep in mind, what I'm telling you is only what we know about through Neil. Who knows what else the Murphys have done that we're not aware of."

The waitress served their quiches and refilled their waters.

Ryan wanted to hear the dirt. This was all very interesting to him, regardless of whether or not the Murphys had Arabians.

Shawna didn't really remember what kind of transactions came in which order, but she remembered this next one for sure. "These guys paid people to remove labels from fruits that were grown in Chile, and paid them to replace the labels with ones that said the fruit was grown in whatever place made the best quality fruit, like Texas grapefruits, Florida Oranges... you get it."

"And that was worth while?" Ryan asked, thinking it sounded bogus.

"Apparently. When they got caught, there was enough money to pay off the guy to not turn them in and let them continue."

Ryan thought about the concept for a moment, relating it to people being able to claim a horse was sired by a stallion that it really wasn't sired by. If the people really liked the horse and they weren't going to breed it, even though it was wrong, and illegal, it wouldn't really hurt the buyer. It was just perception.

"That wouldn't hurt anyone at least," he said.

Shawna needed to make him understand. "No. It doesn't actually hurt anyone, but two things happen. One, they make much bigger profits because the fruit from a prime growing area sells for more than it does if it's labeled as being from Chile. The other thing that happens is that for the consumer, the produce from Chile doesn't usually taste as good, so they aren't getting what they thought they'd get. But who bothers returning fruit? No one. It's just a fact of life that some fruit tastes better than others, regardless of where it's really from."

"Yeah," he said as if it were no big deal.

"Ryan, the point is that these guys are international crooks!"

"You're right, but it doesn't seem that important in the big picture," he said, bursting her bubble. He dug into his food like a football player after a tough game.

His statement flustered her and she lost her appetite. "Want to know what else they've done?"

"Sure. Hit me with the big stuff!" he said as if it were all a joke.

She was starting to get defensive. "It's illegal to import avocados from any other country..."

He interrupted her. "Why?"

"The avocado growers in California have a strong organization and they have influence in Congress. They were able to actually get Congress to pass a law to make it illegal to import avocados whenever California growers have them available for sale."

"In other words, the California growers want the right to control the market?" Ryan asked accusingly.

"Yes. But that's not the point. The point is, it is in fact illegal for anyone to import avocados. Your friends…"

Ryan laughed. "They aren't my friends just because they have Arabians!"

"You're defending them!"

"I'm not! I'm just giving you a hard time. Trying to keep you passionate about the story. You know I love messing with your mind… and other parts!"

Shawna rolled her eyes and made a face.

"Anyway, as brokers, the Murphys, go and buy semi-truckloads of avocados from Mexico. They already have a contract with one of the biggest chain stores in the U.S. to provide them their avocados. This chain store knows they are illegally buying avocados from Mexico. On top of that, it's the chain store that's sending their trucks to Mexico to off-load from the Mexican trucks onto theirs. The Murphys paid off an inspector to say that each truckload was clay pots for gardening. That's how they got them into the U.S. The chain store delivered the avocados directly to their warehouses since they have a good shelf life, considering it's produce. The Murphys paid fifteen cents each and sold them to the chain store for fifty cents each. The store put them 'on sale' to the public in their stores for a dollar forty-nine each."

Ryan wasn't phased by the discovery. "Ready for dessert?" he asked.

Completely deflated by her husband's indifference to the importance of her investigation, she pushed her plate away and answered, "No thanks. I'm full. I haven't even finished half of my quiche."

Without comment, Ryan finished his wife's food in a few quick bites before responding. "I think I'll watch my waist line tonight," he said as if he were proud that he had self-control at a place known for their desserts.

Able to separate her career from their marriage, she stretched her hand and rubbed his neck in an affectionate manner.

"You have such self-control!" she said, then slid her hand into his jacket pocket. Out came a hand full of candy wrappers.

"How'd you know?" he said, blushing and with a wide grin he couldn't hold back.

"Your breath!" she said smiling seductively.

"You had pizza right before you came out of Loren's office!" he said as if it were a game, which it was.

"How'd you know it wasn't from a couple hours before?"

"It was still moist looking on your face!"

The waitress cleared the plates and served them the decaffeinated coffee they ordered.

"So, is your investigation into the Murphys business practices or into Neil Gentry taking bribes?" Ryan asked. In his mind, he thought about what the plot of the story would be.

Shawna sat back, astonished. She hadn't really thought about it and no one else, including Loren, brought it up.

"Well?"

"I don't know. We haven't gotten far enough to know the slant we'll be taking," she said insecurely, not feeling at all like a seasoned investigative reporter.

"What are the other issues?" Ryan asked, wanting to help her gel everything in her mind.

"Neil works for the USDA and he took bribes, but after the first time, it was because he was forced to. When his boss found out, his boss insisted on part of the action. Then, his boss went directly to the Murphys to get in on more money, and to force Neil to continue. We don't know yet if it goes any further than that within the USDA. Then, the FBI investigator finds out about it, and the exact same thing happens. Caleb Anderson, Trish's FBI contact, is helping us with the FBI. He was pulled off of the case, but he told Trish that the FBI agreed to give the Murphys full immunity to turn States evidence against other people in the produce business... people who are doing the same thing on both larger and smaller scales. And to turn States evidence about who they were able to bribe from the USDA and the FBI and how they did it."

Ryan was very interested again. "So the Murphys are getting away with everything they've done?"

"We don't know now. That's a big issue in the investigation. Caleb was on the case, in St. Louis, when he was abruptly pulled off of it with no explanation. He was instructed not to talk to the Murphys ever again. He said that in the office, no one's even talking about the case any more, as if it never even existed."

"That is really strange. At least he's helping you get to the bottom of it," Ryan told her as he took her hand into his, caressing it in a supportive manner.

Shawna was glad that he was interested in this part of the drama. She drank the rest of her coffee as she thought everything out. "Caleb is helping to the extent he can. So far, he hasn't gotten anywhere, at least not that he's told us. Loren is going to use some of his contacts in the Bureau."

"Whatever direction you take it in, this *is* going to be a great story," he assured her.

"I know. I'm just in a hurry to get all of the facts to put together the pieces. It's just a huge puzzle right now."

"That's what a great story is," he reminded her.

"You're right. I guess I'm just tired. Can we go home now?"

Ryan pulled out his wallet, looked to see how much cash he had and decided to use his credit card. While they waited for their server to process it, he changed the subject.

"Do you need to work this weekend?"

Shawna thought for a moment. "I don't think so. They'll be doing investigating that I can't, and I could definitely use some rest and to step back from this for a few days. Why?"

"How about coming to Santa Barbara with me? Just relax at the farm. The foals are all being weaned… it's fun to watch them discover their independence and watch them playing together in the pastures."

"I don't know, let me think about it tonight," she said, hoping she wouldn't disappoint him when she told him she didn't want to go.

Ryan knew she'd have a reason not to go with him. She never really had much of an interest in the farm or the horses. In fact, she really only tolerated his passion for the horses because she was so busy with her career and circle of friends.

"Whatever you want, honey. You don't mind if I go either way though, do you?" he asked.

"Not at all. I know you love it there," she said, wishing she did too. It would have made their marriage even stronger.

Twenty

Greg was sound asleep, completely unaware that there were droplets of drool escaping from his mouth, forming a wet spot on his silk pillow case. Marcie sat up in bed trying to distract herself by attempting to name all of the movies that she knew of that were produced or directed by Ryan Sanders. It was futile. She couldn't concentrate on that any more than she could on anything else. Wide-awake at four a.m., she wrote a note on their monogrammed stationary in her usual calligraphy style printing. The note was left leaning on the coffee maker for Greg to find when he woke up. *G- Took Flash to Payson. I'll call if I'm not coming back tonight. Love, M.*

Her husband would understand that she needed time for herself. An hour and a half north of Scottsdale where the land was in complete contrast to the arid desert she lived in, she'd haul up to the lush green countryside where the hills rolled and the air was fresh and clean. A leisurely trail ride and a place to go full out cantering to get her adrenaline pumping would facilitate her being able to think things through and sort out everything that was happening in her life.

In the peaceful quiet time that separated night from morning, Flash, her bright copper colored gelding, had his head and long arched neck hanging like a pendulum out of the top half of his Dutch style stall door when she entered the barn. Excited to see her and the bag of carrots she was carrying, he quickly nodded his head up and down repeatedly until she arrived at his door with an offering of a cold crisp thick carrot. The other dozen horses in the small back barn, the original structure on the property, knew the routine. Flash was always first for treats, but his friends were never ever left out, no matter what. Even though Flash was her personal trail horse, she couldn't just give him the carrots and get on with whatever she came to do...the five pound bag had to be distributed *almost* equally to every horse in this barn that housed the pets of all the Bordeaux family members. These were horses never presented to the public. Each horse in this barn was like a family member of a particular Bordeaux clan member; everyone was attached to all of the horses here, like having cousins you enjoyed the company of and knew you could depend on, no matter what.

Of course, she had to feed Flash a noticeable amount more bites than everyone else got, to remind him that he was not only hers, but also her favorite. Marcie was sure he knew when he had been short changed on carrots. Somehow, the horse has a sense about knowing if he was rewarded with more than everyone else. If his opinion was that he didn't get what he deserved, he fidgeted in the grooming rack and would refuse to stand still while being tacked up with his saddle, bridle and splint boots.

Marcie stepped into the deep pine shavings in his 14 x 14 stall to remove his custom fitted flysheet that protected him from head to tail. As she told him that they were going to Payson, she promptly folded the sheet and hung it on the brass blanket rack outside his stall, next to the matching hook that hung his halter and lead rope. He lowered his head for her to put on the walnut color rolled leather halter with his name engraved on a brass nameplate on the left cheek piece.

The other horses whinnied in apparent jealousy as he followed her out the barn to the two-horse trailer that was in view to most of the horses. Flash pranced as he looked back over his left shoulder at the noisy horses, as if to say *I'm going for a ride and you're not! Na na na na na na!*

An arrogant horse from the day he was born, it was what Marcie admired most about him. That, and his emotional stability. Six years ago, at precisely two in the morning, Greg was with Marcie from the moment the colt's front legs pushed out of his dam's womb onto the thick soft straw bedding. Flash looked confused that his world of eleven months floating backwards and upside down in a warm cushioned sac was over. Marcie cleared his nostrils for his first breath and helped him the first time he tried to stand up on his wobbly legs an hour later. Even though her husband had more experience with newborns than she did, she insisted to be the only one inside the stall to imprint the colt. Two and a half hours after he was born, Marcie urged him to find his mother's udders by trying to point his nose under her massive belly. Flash was much more interested in getting to know Marcie and mouthing his mother's dirty tail than he was in nursing.

As if the newborn comprehended the human language, immediately after Greg suggested that he call the vet if the colt didn't nurse soon, Flash finally went nudging and nibbling her belly, her chest and then her shoulders in search for her colostrum. Eventually, to his delight, he found what he was looking for. From lack of experience, he drooled more milk out of his mouth than he actually swallowed. He caught on by nightfall. Together, Marcie and Flash's dam, Fladdiar, laid in the stall next to him when he took his first nap after his first meal in the world of humans.

Even before Flash was actually born, she knew she would have a lifetime bond with him just as she planned to have with Fladdair, her first Arabian broodmare. The mare, imported from Sweden, was given to her as a wedding present from her husband. Fladdair died and left Flash to be an orphan at ten days old. Without any external signs of problems, no one knew that the mare had twisted a part of her intestine during the birthing process. Ten days later it caused a serious case of colic. Their regular veterinarian was in the hospital with a case of appendicitis, so they had to use a different local veterinarian who ended up handling the colic so poorly that the mare died.

It didn't matter that the farm had plenty of barn help that could have dealt with the orphan. It was Marcie who mixed the Foal-Lac milk-replacer every two hours and handheld the bucket for him to drink from for his first two weeks. After that, he was willing to drink from an unattended hanging bucket with Foal-Lac, so Marcie shared the job of preparing it and serving it with Greg and the other family members taking turns, which wasn't so bad after they got him on a schedule of feeding every four hours. She couldn't let herself trust the barn help with something so important even though no one had ever failed in their responsibilities with any of the other horses before.

Marcie turned on the exterior lights of the horse trailer before she opened the back door and lowered the ramp for Flash. He didn't like step-up trailers so she bought this trailer with a loading ramp to accommodate his preference. He seemed to appreciate it. There wasn't a time that he didn't just see the open door and walk right on without being led. If he could have, he probably would have tied his lead rope to the front of the trailer and set out his own hay in his manger area. Flash was like a dog that loved car rides.

"Good boy!" Marcie told him as she hooked the butt rope across the back of the trailer.

He whinnied, waiting for another carrot and his hay that he knew would be coming when she was ready to tie him.

"Just a minute!"

He pawed at the rubber-matted floor, not minding the hollow sound underneath him.

"I'm coming! I'm getting your water. Give me a minute before I forget. You don't want to go thirsty, do you?"

He was silent, waiting patiently as if he understood the reason he needed to wait.

Marcie ran the hose to the bed of the truck and filled the forty-gallon water container. As the hose ran, she gave Flash his carrot and his hay, then closed the exterior feed door. Just as the water container was full, Flash whinnied in a way that bothered Marcie. Something was wrong. What could it be? She opened his feed door to make sure everything looked normal. The horse was already breaking a sweat. Was he sick? No. She'd forgotten to open the air vents for him. He was hot and the air was still. As she opened the side windows and the rooftop air vents she doubted her capabilities of doing anything right today. She was so distracted. She'd be fine, she thought. She just needed to get out on a trail with the cooling landscape of evergreen trees surrounding her and a clear sky above her.

"Okay. There's your air. Sorry about that," she told him as she was ready to close his feed door once again.

Before the door closed, he stretched his neck as far as he could to reach his soft muzzle to her hair to nudge her in a way that let her know he forgave her and that everything else would be fine.

"Thanks buddy, I've got a lot on my mind."

He made a soft whinny.

"I'll tell you about it when we get to Payson."

His soft eyes looked into hers and told her he'd listen for as long as she wanted to talk.

Two hours later she pulled into the horse trailer parking area closest to the trailhead of the National Forest trails system. At first she was surprised that there were only three other trailers parked, then she realized in was only six in the morning. Sane people didn't start until eight or nine o'clock. Well, she wasn't sane. She had so many things to sort out.

"Okay Flash, we're here!" she told him as she opened the back door of the trailer.

There were two normal consistency piles of manure in the trailer. That was a good thing, along with his body being dry, rather than damp. Flash waited for her to let down the butt rope and tell him to step off. She finally unhooked the rope, but was silent in her own thoughts as she unlocked the tack compartment to retrieve the brushes and her saddle and bridle. Flash stayed on the trailer even though he was unrestrained front and back.

In her mind, Marcie was going over the details of the claims in the lawsuit that was filed last week and recalling the short list of people that bid on Love Letter. When he gave a loud whinny, she remembered to get Flash a bucket of water so that he could drink before their ride in case she didn't get to the creek or river waters edge in time to satisfy his thirst.

Hanging the bucket on the side of the trailer, she realized that she hadn't given him permission to get off the trailer.

"Sorry Flash! Step off."

He concentrated on backing down the ramp straight so that an outside leg didn't go off the trailer ramp. When he was young, he used to be so anxious to get off he didn't think about anything else other than going backwards. Now, he was grown up and knew better. He had to watch every step he took, wherever he was, especially out on trails, but he loved it.

Flash walked himself toward the water bucket and drank the entire five gallons down as Marcie tied him and brought over a hoof pick.

"Want some more?"

He responded with a quiet whinny.

"I'll get it. How are you feeling today?"

He pawed the ground once and arched his long neck.

She poured another five gallons into the bucket, which he only took a few sips of.

"I'm doing shitty," she said as she picked up his hoof to clean it out and check for rocks or anything else that shouldn't have been embedded in his foot.

He looked around at her as if to say, *what's wrong?*

"You know all that legal stuff I told you about before? Well, the jerk's actually filed the lawsuit! He's actually suing us! His attorney is holding depositions with everyone that bought at the last auction *and* every single person who bid on the horses!" she told him as she checked his last foot. All four were still clean.

He twisted his ears to listen to her better until she came around to the front of him with a soft face brush. Lovingly and gently, she brushed his face, going in the direction his hair grew.

"Our phone is ringing off the hook with people wanting to know what the depositions are all about. Ryan Sanders is the only one who doesn't seem furious about it. In fact, he's flying out here a day early to meet with us before his deposition. I guess he's the first to be deposed since he bid on Love Letter in particular. I don't know! I don't even know Ryan Sanders and neither does

Greg. He was just a wealthy bidder," she said, still amazed at times about the type of people they were surrounded by in the Arabian industry.

Flash lowered his head to her torso and nudged her to show her he was there for her.

"I can't believe Johan! He's trying to get twenty-five million bucks including punitive damages!"

As she looked into her horse's soft eyes, she thought that he seemed to be listening carefully as if analyzing whether he thought the dollar amount seemed as unreasonable as she thought it was. In reality, he was wondering if she remembered to bring him any treats, like carrots or apples. He loved Golden Delicious and Granny Smith the most, but any fresh crisp juicy apple would be greatly appreciated.

"You're right, Flash. The guy will never win," she said as she brushed down the rest of his body in preparation for being tacked up.

He nonchalantly stared at the big patch of grass near the picnic tables. *That grass looks good enough to eat,* he thought. He hoped she would let him have a few bites if he kept still and listened attentively.

She was positioning the Western saddle on his back, slightly behind his high and sloping withers. "I was with my mom and dad last night until after midnight, then I stayed up and cried on and off until four this morning. That's why I came to get you... for us to go on this ride."

He glanced back at her as she slowly and gently tightened the cinch.

She went back to the tack door of the trailer and got his bridle and a carrot. She fed him the carrot as a tear rolled down her face.

"I told my parents a little of what was going on about the lawsuit and they totally freaked out... without even knowing a fraction of the reality or potential consequences."

He wanted one more carrot before she slid the snaffle bit with copper rollers into his mouth.

"My parents think that we should sell the farms and just start training horses for a living. Then, Greg would probably want to have a baby and raise a family… which is what I really want."

She dipped the bit in his water bucket to get it wet, then slid it into his mouth after he dropped his head down for the inevitable.

"I want a baby so much, especially now, with all of this going on. It would be so nice to have a child to distract us."

He pawed several times, creating a fine dust. That was his way to tell her that he was ready to be able to move after standing still so long on the trailer, and now here.

She locked up the truck and the tack area of the trailer, untied him from the side of the trailer, then unexpectedly, she stood directly in front him and wrapped her arms around his neck to hug him as she broke out crying.

He raised his head and neck so that she'd be more comfortable as he wondered if she was crying because she was out of carrots for him. He hoped not.

"I've wanted a baby for so long, but I want one even more now that I found out I was adopted," she confided to him as she lead him to the patch of grass she noticed he had an eye on.

He couldn't wait to sneak a bite or two even though he had his bit on. He could chew it good enough, he'd promise her if he could talk in human language. *Just give me a few bites,* he thought.

"I really want to love someone with my genetic pool. I want to have a baby," she said as she tightened the cinch again.

As soon as she was finished tightening the cinch and was ready to mount him, he was able to sneak a bite of grass. *Wow,* he thought, *she's so distressed she didn't even try to stop me!* Marcie just sunk into the saddle, contemplating life and he kept nibbling, trying not to let even one blade of grass get stuck between his gums and the snaffle bit.

"I want to see and touch my own flesh and blood. It's normal. Anyone would," she said as she finally gently drew up the reins in order to get his mouth off the ground.

Fine. That patch was kind of tough anyway. And not very tasty, he thought.

Flash waited for some hint of a cue, but none came. He walked off in the direction of the nearest trail even though she was so distracted she really wasn't even guiding him. She seemed to just be along for the ride.

"I wonder if I look like my mom… my biological mother that is," she said as if her adoptive mom could hear her and have hurt feelings from the word 'mom'.

"You don't look anything like your mother, Flash. She was a big gray mare with dark eyes and a gorgeous black mane and tail. She was beautiful, but you're even prettier," she said as she patted him on the neck, suddenly realizing that it was him that got them onto the trail rather than her.

He perked up and quickened his walk just a tad in response to her compliment. He looked at the running water up ahead, hoping she didn't plan to ask him to cross it.

She still wasn't guiding him, so he took the fork in the trail that headed left in order to avoid crossing through the water.

"Maybe I should just stop using birth control and not tell Greg. If I get pregnant, surely he'd want our baby."

Flash smelled the strong scent of pine. In one way he liked it and in another it irritated his delicate nostrils.

"That's what I should do. He loves me and he loves kids." She brightened up and saw that she had no idea how she and Flash got to where they were. In fact, she didn't even know how long they'd been gone. It couldn't have been that long. She wasn't thirsty or hungry yet.

He decided to go off the trail and into the open meadow that he could see through the trees up ahead. The ground would be softer and more comfortable on his hooves. *Maybe she won't mind me having a little grass if she gets off to stretch her legs or go pee,* he thought.

It only took him a minute to get to the meadow. Flash wished she wanted to pay attention to their ride right now. Surely she'd want to canter through this gorgeous open meadow. *This must be at least fifty acres of soft grass and pretty wild flowers that would be fun to ride on,* he thought. He couldn't resist but to break into a slow trot, hoping that she'd get the hint that he'd love to get some real exercise.

"But that damn lawsuit! I've gotta deal with that before I go and get pregnant. Uncle Dolan and Jessica think we should offer to settle before it goes any further and becomes public knowledge. Greg and I need to decide right away and make a settlement offer or fight it."

You're such a good rider, you post my trot without even thinking about it... can I canter too without you thinking about it? I better not try, he thought.

"You're so lucky to be a horse... a cherished horse. Life's so simple for you."

Flash saw some deer in the distance. He veered the opposite direction but kept at a slow trot while considering if he could get away with trotting faster and raising his knees higher.

He decided to return to a walk and try to spot some birds or squirrels or something interesting in the trees that were at the perimeter of the meadow. If something would give him an excuse to act like he got just a little spooked, maybe she would finally pay attention to their ride and want to canter.

"I feel like I'm going to lose it sometimes. Just totally collapse."

A squirrel! Yeah! Flash reared up just enough to get her attention, faking a small spook.

She pat him on the neck and said, "Flash, it's just a squirrel, you've seen a million of them!"

Oh manure! It didn't work. I'll have to find something else, he thought.

Marcie finally took real notice of the breathtaking meadow they were in and wondered if there was any river or creek water nearby to offer to Flash.

Flash felt her actually take control of the reins, like a rider should... soft handed and gentle, but definitely doing the directing. She was obviously paying attention now. He'd step up a little higher and extend out a little faster hoping she'd realize he wanted to trot then canter. If he just broke into a trot while she was paying attention, she'd rein him back letting him know she was the one in control of their speed and direction, not him. He picked up his walking pace without breaking into a trot.

"Hey boy! You want to trot? Actually, I bet you'd love to canter this, wouldn't you?" she said as she gently asked him to stop by lightly pulling back the reins and leaning a couple of degrees backwards.

She dismounted him, stepped back as far as she could while still holding his reins, and took a pee. Then, she gently tightened his cinch, which had loosened up considerably. After double-checking that his bridle was adjusted correctly and double checking the off side of the saddle for any problems, she remounted him.

Flash knew that all the steps Marcie just went through meant that they were going to canter. He wanted to jump for joy. Not literally of course, because he wasn't a jumper. Marcie was afraid to jump, except over a little creek if it was too rocky on the bottom for him to walk into. All his life as a riding horse he always had wanted to try jumping or going in a big fancy show like the horses in the other barns. Oh, well, they have pressure and stressful lives and he doesn't.

Marcie took up the reins a tiny bit and barely squeezed her legs into the sides of her mount as she dropped her heels down into the stirrups. As she requested, Flash went into a smooth but animated trot. It felt great. After about three or four minutes, she sat deep into the saddle and squeezed her legs just a slight bit tighter as she said "Canter!", the word he'd been waiting for forever.

They cantered the perimeter of the gigantic open meadow twice in each direction, then she put him in a slightly collected body frame and took him into figure eights and serpentines at random through the entire field. Flash was perfectly balanced and responsive to every subtle cue. Finally, she did flying lead changes across the entire long length of the field. Flash felt invigorated to be doing everything he loved in such a magnificent setting. Marcie felt as if the weight of the world was lifted off of her shoulders...even if it was only a temporary reprieve.

She slowed him down to a trot for several minutes and then back to a walk to cool him down before she overworked him. Staring into the distance in each direction from the middle of the meadow, she tried to identify where the trail was that led them into that slice of heaven. To her frustration, she couldn't see it.

"Where's the trail buddy?" she said as she let the reins rest over his withers and reached her hands over her head to stretch.

In response to her inquiry, Flash casually turned ninety degrees to the left and walked with the confidence and purpose of a tour guide who loved his work. Never doubting the direction he was heading in, a couple of minutes later, he was back on the trail they came in on.

She pat him on the neck. "Good boy!"

I'm not just good, I'm very smart too, he thought.

"Where's the water? Are you thirsty?"

Ten minutes later they were at a crystal clear running water stream. Marcie dismounted, loosened the cinch of his saddle and gave him his head to have all the water he wanted. It looked clean enough for her to drink, so she cupped up her hands and dipped them in the water as she bent low to refresh herself, drinking down all that she could. She splashed her face to freshen up. When she stood up, she felt as if she had been christened and was ready to start a new life.

When Flash made it clear that he'd had enough to drink, Marcie could see that he was yearning to eat some of the tender young grass that was sprouting about twenty feet downstream. How could she deny him his pleasure? She couldn't. They walked side by side, both with the heightened awareness of the sounds of wilderness. The cool clean air that was effortless to inhale deep into their lungs refreshed them. Flash found the exact section of greenery that he had in mind. Marcie removed his bridle from his head and attached a single rein to the halter that she'd left on him for occasions such as this. She sat in the grass next to him, spread her legs into a V and stretched the muscles that would be sore the next day if she didn't stretch within an hour of cantering or trotting. Methodically, she used her thumbs to massage the insides of her knees in a counterclockwise circular motion to prevent lactic acid build up that would also contribute to sore muscles.

Flash was content with the grass and Marcie was exhausted from having been awake for over twenty-four hours now. She sprawled out in the grass intending to take a catnap while holding the rein turned lead rope in her right hand. If Flash went to wander off, she'd feel it and wake up.

The chilled air abruptly woke Marcie out of a deep sleep. Covered in goose bumps, she realized that it was almost dark. Her mind was hazy as she realized that she was no longer holding Flash and that he'd had access to the grass for the entire day. The adrenaline rush caused her to jump up in a panic, a frantic moment of searching for her horse. It turned out he was standing at the trail that would lead them back to the truck and trailer. It appeared as if he were guarding her by not letting anyone else through and into the area.

Marcie laughed as her head cleared up.

"Flash! Come here, boy!"

Flash jogged over to her and lowered his head and nudged her to let her know everything was all right.

Twenty-One

Ryan flew from Santa Barbara to Scottsdale in his private jet. Now, he was in a rented emerald green Jaguar XJ-S and on his way to Vintage Arabians.

He didn't want to leave his Santa Barbara farm before he absolutely needed to, but he had to admit to himself that he was curious to find out directly from the Bordeauxs why he was being deposed. After all, he personally never bought horses from them or sold horses to them. Within ten minutes of being served the subpoena, he telephoned Greg, a man he only casually knew from the industry, and certainly didn't know well, to find out what it was all about. Greg told him that Johan Murphy, the successful bidder on Love Letter, was suing him. Following his attorney's advice, Greg was humble and brief, not voluntarily offering any additional information. Consequently, Ryan told Greg that he wanted to meet with them the day before his deposition, which was today.

Marcie and Greg were preoccupied in an emotional conversation behind closed doors in the barn business office when the guard gate called to announce that Mr. Sanders had arrived. Quickly, Marcie concluded the conversation with her husband.

"Hello, you two are looking well," Ryan lied. They looked worn, stressed and exhausted.

"Thanks. And thanks for coming to see us. You're the only person who suggested we meet before their deposition. We appreciate it," Greg said.

Ryan didn't think he would have recognized Marcie if he weren't at the farm and she wasn't standing next to her husband. Of course, Ryan had never seen her in natural looking makeup (versus the way women wear makeup to look dressed up) and wearing shorts and a tank top. He'd only had occasion to see her in horse show attire and in formal wear. Today, she appeared a good ten years older and noticeably fatigued. Not that he saw her all that often, but she'd always looked like a vibrant woman, a perfect picture of health and a carefree life.

Marcie made an effort to smile, but she was so preoccupied with her troubles it didn't work. "Can I get you an iced tea or a soft drink or anything?"

"Actually, do you have any sparkling water?"

"I'll check, we usually do," she said as she opened the refrigerator door behind the full bar in the lounge. Her nose crinkled and she said, "No. I'm sorry, we're out of it."

Greg joined his wife behind the bar and gave the bottles a once over. "Actually, it's almost five. How about a glass of wine or a mixed drink?"

Ryan normally didn't drink alcohol unless it was with a meal, but he thought it might loosen their tongues if they relaxed a little with a libation. "Sure, I'll have a glass of wine."

"We're really not drinkers normally… except in February during the auction season. Otherwise, we'll maybe have a glass or two of wine with dinner or a cold beer after work on a hot day, but that's about it," Marcie explained.

"Same here," Ryan concurred, glad they had no intentions of getting drunk.

After a few minutes of small talk and a couple of sips of wine, Ryan got to the point.

"I don't know what this lawsuit is about, but this must be a tough time for you."

Tears glassed over Marcie's eyes. "It's the worst thing we've ever been through. We didn't even do anything illegal," she said melodramatically.

Greg didn't want to correct her, but he had finally accepted that a lot of what they had done was illegal, even though they didn't intend to do anything wrong at the time.

"I've had the same thing happen more times than I'd like to think about. People knowing I have money and then fabricating a bogus claim. They think I'll just settle it to get them to go away and leave me alone, which is what I used to do," Ryan admitted.

"It's all bull shit. The legal system and the attorneys who take cases that aren't even really legitimate cases. They turn the simplest thing into something that looks bad, whether it's true or not. That in itself should be illegal!" Greg said, growing agitated just thinking about it.

"So what's this lawsuit about? Or supposed to be about?"

Greg and Marcie looked at each other before either of them spoke. They hadn't discussed exactly what they would or wouldn't tell Ryan and now neither of them knew how to answer.

Someone had to say something, so Greg stepped up to the plate. "Johan Murphy, or I should say 'Murphy Enterprises' bought Love Letter. The lawyers say that he claims that he overpaid for the horse."

"He did pay a hell of a lot of money!" Ryan said.

Greg didn't take Ryan's response as him agreeing that Johan overpaid for the mare. He elaborated. "It's very suspicious to us, because a few weeks before the attorneys got involved, he called me and told me he was having cash flow problems and asked if I could work with him. He said he really loved the mare and didn't want to jeopardize his ownership in her."

"Did you believe him when he called you?"

"Sure. He sounded sincere to me. He was very nice on the phone, and before that we talked a few times on the phone when he called to see how she was doing," Greg said and then paused for emphasis. "In fact, during one call, he asked me if I knew anyone in St. Louis who boarded Arabians that would be able to take good care of her. Johan said he wanted to be able to see her frequently and the only way he could do it was to get her to St. Louis."

Ryan thought about whether he knew anyone there or not. He didn't. "So, do you know of any place?"

"Sure. Well, actually, the farm I know of is about an hour from St. Louis, and he said that wouldn't be a problem. I told him I didn't have the phone number handy but that I'd write it down and put it in my wallet. I suggested that he call me back another day. Then, when he called me back I could give it to him."

Marcie finished the story. "He never called again, except to try to make arrangements for delaying his payment. Then, at that time it didn't even come up about the place to board the mare near him."

As if he were the attorney taking a deposition, Ryan questioned Greg. "Did you work out an alternate payment plan with him?"

"Not me. I told him that he needed to call my accountant because he's the one who handles something like that," Greg said.

Marcie drained her wine glass and stood up to pour herself a second. "The next thing we know, Greg was served a subpoena! And now, here we are," she said dejected.

Ryan thought about where to take it from this point before he spoke. He took the last sip of his wine. When Marcie looked to him questioningly with the raised bottle, he covered the top of his glass with a flat hand to indicate that he didn't care for a refill.

"Why are his attorneys deposing me?" Ryan asked straight out. He wasn't usually one to beat around the bush.

Neither Greg nor Marcie knew what to say. Ryan wasn't one of the people that they made the offer to about bidding up the horse because he wasn't a client of theirs. They couldn't reward him by giving him services or eliminating commissions on horses that they sold for him. Besides, they hoped that he would have gotten carried away bidding and end up buying her.

The silence lasted too long. It was conspicuous that they had no intentions of telling him the complete truth.

Finally, Marcie spoke up. "We have no idea!"

Greg knew the way she just answered sounded ridiculous and was obviously a lie, so he needed to give a little something in order to attempt to gain Ryan's trust.

"Actually, they think that some of the other bidders on the mare were shills that were bidding her up."

Ryan sat back in a relaxed posture. "Well, I wasn't a shill, I have no problem with that! I can prove I own a herd of horses and my own farm."

"I know. It won't be a problem," Greg said, even though he was in fact very concerned about where the questioning in the deposition would really go. Apparently, Ryan mistakenly only thought of shills as people not associated with the business at all, as people just planted in the crowd being paid to bid up a horse.

A disturbing thought crossed Ryan's mind. "Did you have any shills?"

"No!" Marcie and Greg said at the same time and a little too boisterous to sound honest.

At that moment, Ryan knew they were both lying. The way they answered too quickly, too adamantly for the conversation, and most importantly, they both lowered their eyelids as the single word left their lips. Immediately after the word passed their lips they both opened their eyes just a little too wide and looked him straight in the eye as if that was the proof that they were telling the truth. He knew liars and bad actors when he saw them.

"What else do you think they'll ask me about?" Ryan said, testing the waters for a grain of truth.

Greg thought for a half a minute. "I'm sure they'll want to know if I offered you anything in exchange for your bids. And they'll probably ask about any history of a business and a personal relationship… which we have none."

Ryan decided to put Greg in his place since he'd already been lied to. "Actually, in a round about way, we have had one transaction," he said in a manner intended to make the Bordeauxs nervous.

"What do you mean?" Marcie asked.

"Venttada. *I* actually bought her," he said with a sly grin.

"Pardon me?" Greg said, confused.

"Remember when you showed her to me and priced her at $75,000?"

The blood drained from Greg's face. "Vaguely."

"I told you I'd pass. A few days later I flew my niece over and she told you she was buying her first horse and that she was looking for an amateur show horse prospect to show in just local shows in Arkansas. When she spotted Venttada in her stall she asked about her. As you recall, you sold her to Missie Phelps for $10,000."

"Missie Phelps is your niece?" Greg said, thoroughly embarrassed, while at the same time, obviously angry that he had been deceived.

Ryan wanted to make Greg feel even more humiliated. "Didn't you think it was a little odd that an eighteen year old girl carried $10,000 cash with her? A complete stranger?"

"As I recall, yes, I did. But how would I have known you were going to take advantage of me and practically steal the horse?" Greg said defensively.

Ryan couldn't believe what Greg just said! That he was taking advantage of him! But, he didn't dare respond to that thought. Instead, he acted as if he weren't phased by the accusation.

"I've bought quite a few of my horses that way. Everyone over prices their horses to me, although I must admit, you were without a doubt the boldest ever! From $75,000 to $10,000 in less than a week!" Ryan said it as if he were giving Greg a compliment, or at the very least, humored by the whole thing. It was business dealings like this that gave Shawna good reason to think the Arabian horse business was crazy. He learned to quit telling her what she didn't need to know.

Greg proceeded to talk as if he were an excellent and honest businessman. "Are you intending to disclose this tomorrow at your deposition?"

Ryan is in fact an excellent businessman. He thought quick on his feet. Or his ass, as it was in this case. "No. Short of outright blatantly lying, I definitely won't say anything which would tend to harm your reputation, insult your way of doing business, or hurt you in any way whatsoever."

"Thank you. I appreciate it," Greg said, relieved.

"I have to be honest, I have nothing against you personally, but I'm not particularly fond of you. My objective is to avoid doing anything that would assist their case because I don't want them to put you out of business..."

Greg interrupted. "Again, thanks."

"Don't thank me. By protecting you, I'm protecting myself and the tons of other people heavily invested in this industry... and all the small people in the industry," he said as he stood up and stretched his legs.

"What do you mean?" Marcie asked.

Ryan casually looked at an original oil painting of a group of mares from Poland. Sounding fatherly he answered. "Whether I like it or not, you are the market leader. The price setter, the trendsetter, the guru. If you go out of business, there won't be a market for Polish Arabians at a decent price let alone the inflated prices people, including you and I, are getting now."

Greg was complemented yet extremely distressed at the idea that Ryan put forth. "There are other big people in the business..." his voice trailed off as his thoughts wandered.

"Sure there are. But without you, the market will crumble. No one takes responsibility for the Polish Arabian horse industry except you. Everyone else reaps the rewards of following or imitating you. At best, they align themselves with you. At worst, they turn over their money to you and expect you to make the money for them," Ryan said bluntly.

Greg was turning pale. "No one just turns over their money to me!"

"Sure they do. They buy the horses you tell them to buy for the prices you tell them to pay. They pay you for the training or showing, and show in whatever classes you tell them to. Or, they breed their mares to any stallion you suggest. They buy syndicate shares in whoever you're promoting. Then, they pay you for your marketing and then pay you the commission for selling their horses. They do absolutely nothing but claim ownership of the horses and the profits. You do everything else for them!"

Greg defended his clients. "You've got it all wrong. A lot of them go to other trainers and breeders. A lot of them have other trainers resell their horses or the foals of their mares for them."

"Because you directed them to. You have alliances with those other trainers and breeders! You're really the mentor of the top trainers... they do what you suggest..." Ryan said slyly. "The breeders follow you too, hoping they'll get their horses in your auctions or that you'll host an auction or event with them or send buyers their way."

"It's friendly competition," Greg said without much conviction.

"Only because you can't personally handle all the business. You and your brother and your staff can only handle so many horses. The other trainers base their prices and the amounts they sell horses for solely upon the prices you get!"

"No, they sell them for what the market will bear," Greg said, looking at the dust on his boots.

"You set the market though! You know it! Sellers flat out tell people things like *'Greg Bordeaux sold a full sister to this horse for X'* or they'll say *'Greg Bordeaux says this horse is worth at least X'* and chances are, you never even saw the horse... but people follow. This is a business of followers and no leaders... except you!"

Of course, from the first day they met with Jessica and Dolan at their offices, Greg knew they were personally at great risk of losing everything, but he never thought about how it would affect anyone other than he and Marcie, and his parents and brother. He hadn't ever truly considered the impact he personally made on the industry. It was just a hobby... then he wanted to make money from it... then he wanted to provide even more financially for Marcie...now it came to this. How did this happen?

Ryan helped himself to the refrigerator behind the bar as the Bordeauxs absorbed what he was saying. They were obviously both lost in their own thoughts.

Greg broke the long silence. "You'll help us?"

Marcie looked at Ryan with pleading in her eyes.

Ryan wanted to instill a little fear in Greg; he waited to answer. "I don't know if I'd call it 'helping' you. All I can promise is to do my best not to say or do anything that may help *them* with their case against you."

"That will help us a lot," Marcie said, wanting to believe it would actually solve everything. Deep inside, she knew it wouldn't.

Greg decided to be bold. "Hypothetically, if you really wanted to, do you think that there is anything that you could do to actually help us? To get us out of this?"

"I don't know. Let me get to my hotel room and give it some thought overnight," Ryan said, not wanting to make any commitments or raise their hopes.

"Sure. Anything. We'd appreciate anything," Greg said, humbled more than he had been since his high school years when he didn't make the football team.

Marcie decided to change the subject. "Where are you staying?"

"The Hyatt Regency. I understand they have a beautiful swimming pool with a man-made beach where the sand actually goes into the water, just like a lake would."

"You'll love it. The pool has waterfalls too. The rooms are very nice also," Marcie said as if they never discussed anything of any importance.

"How about if we meet you for breakfast in the dining room there at about eight?" Greg suggested. Meeting that late would still give him ample opportunity to check on the stallions and all the show horses and touch bases with his brother about the day's training regimen.

"Would that give us time to get to your attorneys' office by ten?" Ryan asked.

"It's only about a half an hour away," Marcie answered.

"By the way, how did you get them to do the depositions in Phoenix?" Ryan asked.

"Believe it or not, if we don't offer to settle this in the next couple of days, there are depositions scheduled every work day for the next two months! We offered to pay opposing counsels expenses to stay in Phoenix so that we didn't have to leave the operation here for two months. At least we'll be able to work early in the morning and late in the afternoon and in the evenings. If we went to St. Louis, it would be a killer on our business."

"That's got to cost an arm and a leg. To put up a lawyer for two months! You have to pay for his meals also?"

"Actually, the General Manager of The Pointe Resort is a client of ours. He's comping the rooms for both attorneys and giving them free meals at the restaurants on the property. We gave him a couple of breedings to our stallions...If you ever noticed, all of our auction materials suggest that people stay at The Pointe. In the past, they paid for the promotion, but we're not going to charge them next year," Greg explained.

"Good deal! You lucked out!"

"It's all a matter of establishing relationships. I'm sure your business, your film business, must be like that also," Greg said.

"It is. By the way, did you say two attorneys?"

"Two!" Marcie confirmed as if it were ridiculous.

"Of course! Why use one lawyer when you can use two?" Ryan said sarcastically.

Twenty-Two

Breakfast consisted of strong Kona coffee, fresh squeezed orange juice, a chilled platter of exotic fruits, and a basket of miniature croissants. The trio ate heartily; Ryan, because it was his habit; and the Bordeauxs because they were nervous about the first deposition being held. True to form, Ryan kept them in suspense about any ideas he had about their legal issues. He glanced at his watch. They were half way through their breakfast before Ryan brought up anything about the lawsuit.

"I spent most of my evening last night thinking about Murphy's claim that he overpaid for Love Letter, " he finally said.

Marcie and Greg nodded, anxious to hear his thoughts. As interesting as it was to hear about the motion picture that he was in the process of getting financing for, they were there to talk about a possible solution, not Ryan's business.

"First, to be honest with you, my gut is telling me that there must be more to the lawsuit than what you've told me," he said, looking Greg straight in the eye, man to man.

Greg swallowed hard. "Why would you think that?"

Marcie stayed silent, not wanting to say anything that may be taken the wrong way or say anything that would open a potential can of worms.

"I think that if that was all there was to the case, your attorney would have hired two or three appraisers to appraise the mare. The varied appraisals would clearly explain that the nature of the business is that the value of a horse is very subjective." He gathered his thoughts as he took a plump red grape into his mouth and bit just once to feel the texture and savor the sweetness. "I think you would have offered to compromise and settle with him, maybe perhaps allow him to reduce the amount owed and delay the payments to accommodate his cash flow problems."

"Our attorneys said we couldn't speak to Johan because he retained an attorney," Marcie said.

"Your attorneys would have made the offer to their attorney. You know that," Ryan said in a manner that indicated that they needed to stop assuming he was naïve.

"No one thought of it," Greg said.

"Of course not. That's because the lawsuit is really much more complicated than you've told me." He tapped his index finger on his juice glass, trying to create more tension by hopefully annoying them. "By the way, are the consignors of Love Letter being sued also?"

"No. Not that we're aware of," Greg admitted.

"That proves my point. If you were only being sued because Johan thinks he overpaid for the horse, they definitely would have sued the actual previous owners of the mare," Ryan said accusingly while still tapping the glass.

"Okay! So we didn't tell you everything! It's really none of your business. Anything that doesn't relate to your deposition is none of your business," Marcie said defensively and with an attitude. She wanted to tell him to stop making aggravating noises, but at least had the sense to keep that to herself.

Greg quickly put his hand on her bicep. "That's no way to speak with Mr. Sanders! He's here to try to help us," he scolded her. Then he looked over at Ryan apologetically. "I'm sorry. This is all just so mortifying and disgraceful for us. Especially since all of our auction buyers and bidders have been brought into it. I'm sorry."

Ryan expected Greg would apologize but didn't expect him to have the tears in his eyes that he could see were forming. "I understand. It's human nature not to divulge all of your problems, but sometimes you just have to."

Greg suddenly felt as if he were talking to a priest or a therapist. They didn't have time this morning to make this a confession.

"Have you thought of anything that could help us? I mean, I know you don't know everything involved, but do you think that you could actually help?" Greg asked with a growing desperation in his wavering voice.

Ryan asked the obvious. "Have you contacted Johan and tried to work things out? To work it out quietly without a lawsuit?"

"Our attorneys said not to," Marcie said before Greg could.

Ryan shook his head. "Like you said, I don't know everything that this is about. But if I were you, after this mornings deposition, out in the lobby or the parking lot or somewhere, I would corner Johan and ask him if the three of you could sit down and talk this through before it goes any further."

"I can't imagine he would. His attorneys gave us a settlement offer demanding twenty-five million bucks," Greg said.

Ryan laughed at the outrageous figure. "Yeah! Sure! Write him a check..."

Greg wasn't laughing. His stomach was tied in knots and his temples started to tighten. A quick glance at his watch revealed that it was time to leave. It was already nine-thirty and Ryan hadn't offered a solution. He pulled two twenty-dollar bills from his wallet and slid the money under his coffee mug where the waitress wouldn't miss it so that they wouldn't need to wait for the check.

As an afterthought, Greg asked Ryan if he could ride to the law offices with him in his rental car, suggesting that they'd have more time to talk, and Ryan wouldn't be concerned with following close behind their car.

"Sure, if Marcie doesn't mind being alone right now," Ryan said.

She bit her lip as she gave it some thought. "I don't mind. I could use some time to myself to get my head in the right place. I can't stand the idea of facing that fat pig!"

Ryan looked at her with a questioning face.

"He's very overweight. She's not tolerant of people who don't watch their health and appearance," Greg explained.

\`\`\`\`\`\`\`\`\`\`

The receptionist walked Greg, Marcie and Ryan back to the conference room where the deposition would be conducted. The room was empty, so they selected their own seats for the time being.

Jessica and Dolan entered together, greeted their clients, and each introduced themselves to Ryan Sanders. Jessica told him they appreciated his time and apologized for any inconvenience that may have been caused.

"We're waiting for the court reporter. She was stuck in traffic, but she'll be here any minute," Dolan explained.

"The attorneys are conferring with each other in a spare office. They'll come in as soon as the court reporter gets her equipment set up," Jessica elaborated.

"And where is Johan? Still trying to fit in the elevator?" Marcie said sarcastically.

"I'm afraid that he was unavailable today," Jessica said.

"Good. I don't want to see that triple chinned flabby face before I have to!"

"Marcie. Calm yourself down and act like the respectable young lady that you are. You are completely out of line, especially with Mr. Sanders present," Dolan said, speaking as her uncle and her attorney.

"I'm sorry," she said as she looked toward the ground, much like a young child being scolded for bad manners.

The receptionist brought in a tray with coffee, cream, sugar, cups and saucers and napkins. The court reporter walked in and expediently set up her equipment as she apologized for keeping them waiting.

"I'll get Alec and Garth," Dolan told them.

"Marcie. Greg. I want you to be professional, calm, and as quiet as possible. No sly remarks or rudeness. Keep all of your emotions to yourself during this," Jessica insisted.

The couple didn't respond.

"I'll be a good boy too!" Ryan said, trying to break the ice.

They all faked a chuckle and pretended to smile.

Dolan returned to the conference room with the opposing counsel.

"Gentlemen, you've met Jessica. This is Greg and Marcie Bordeaux," he said, gesturing toward them. "And of course, this is Mr. Ryan Sanders, here from New York."

"Actually, I live in New York, but I came directly from my farm in Santa Barbara," Ryan clarified, wanting to show that his tone would be friendly.

"I'm Alec Douglas," he said as he sat down across from Ryan.

"And I'm Garth, Alec's associate," he casually said, hoping that no one caught the fact that he hadn't used his last name.

\\\\\\\\\\

"Lily! Wake up honey, it's almost noon... are you sick?" Davis sat on the edge of their king size bed and rubbed her back in a circular motion.

She was barely able to open her eyes, which were puffy and swollen. "Noon?" she said, stretching her neck to the right and then to the left, trying to wake up.

"Yes... almost. It wasn't that hot out and there was a light breeze, so I decided to go out and shoot video's of the horses."

She looked at him, but didn't respond. Tasting the slime in her dry mouth, she hoped that her breath wasn't terribly offensive.

He showed her the videotape in his hand. "I lost track of time... at first I just planned on shooting scenery and group shots, but then I decided to make it more like a sales tape where people could really see one horse at a time. I ended up taking each of the younger horses in the arena, one at a time, and having Raul use the shaker bottle to get them trotting and cantering. I think I got good footage of everyone."

Lily finally found the energy to sit up in bed and comprehend what he was saying. "Why did you do that?"

"There's something we need to talk about. Are you okay? It's not like you to sleep so late!"

Lily rubbed her eyes and put her hands behind her head. "I'm not ill. I was up most of the night. I couldn't sleep."

"How come?"

"I have a lot on my mind and I was wide awake, so I went to the barn and groomed everybody that was inside last night…"

Davis interrupted. "That's why everyone looked so great! When I went to feed them breakfast, everyone was glistening clean for a change. That's what made me decide to do the video… they were already immaculate and needed to be turned out anyway. "

"I'm sorry I haven't kept them groomed up. It's just been so hot and humid I can't make myself do it often enough. Although, I have to admit, it was really comfortable doing it in the middle of the night!"

"You said that you have a lot on your mind. Anything you want to talk about?" Davis said, hoping that she'd get it off her chest.

Lily was glad it came up this way. "As a matter of a fact, yes. I do want to talk to you about it. How about if you make lunch with the leftovers from dinner and I'll take a shower and get dressed."

"Sounds good to me," Davis told her. He leaned over and kissed her on the forehead. He had his own news to tell her. Trying to protect her, he hadn't even told Lily yet that the case that Garth was working on was against Vintage Arabians.

Davis wished he didn't have to give her the bad news about them needing to sell off their horses as quickly as possible before the Bordeauxs went under. She was going to be heartbroken. Their lives practically revolved around the horses since Garth had moved out.

He just finished preparing sandwiches made with pork tenderloin, sliced onions, homegrown tomatoes, red leaf lettuce and cheddar cheese. The stone ground whole wheat bread was slathered with honey mustard oozing onto the thick crust. When Lily walked into the kitchen, he was slicing fresh peaches and placing them on the plastic coated paper plates.

"Looks good, honey."

"You must be starved. You barely touched your dinner last night."

Lily took the plates from the counter to the table and set them down in front of the cups of coffee and ice waters. She sipped her coffee as Davis methodically washed his hands and returned the condiments to the refrigerator.

The temperature rose in her chest and throat as she searched for the words. "Honey, there is something I have to tell you. A secret that I've kept throughout our entire relationship," she said, not feeling as scared as she thought should would.

Davis didn't think about touching his food as he watched her eat a bite of peach. "Go ahead," he said lovingly. He'd waited for this moment for years. His curiosity was finally going to be satisfied and hopefully unburdening herself would relieve her of the depression that she endured all of these years.

She got right to the point. "When I was nineteen, my stepfather raped me." Her chest heaved and the tears began gushing out as she said the words.

Davis stared at her, not knowing what to say. He automatically held her hands in his. She was obviously feeling strong and wanted to continue.

"When I told my mother that he had raped me, she was so distraught, she killed herself."

"Oh my God. You've been carrying this around all of these years? You should have told me. I love you, Lily. You should have shared this pain with me," Davis said as he went down on his knees and wrapped his arms around her and began crying with her.

"Can we go in the family room?" she asked, barely able to catch her breath.

Davis rose to his feet and helped his wife who was trembling from the memory. They eased into the couch and he held her close, rocking her like a young child cradled in his arms.

Lily tried to hide the quiver of her lips, but it was impossible. "He started having sex with me when I was fourteen, right after they got married. I was afraid to deny him. He said that it was me or Jennifer... I couldn't let him touch her! She wasn't even a teenager! And she was still so sad about daddy leaving us. I couldn't let her go through more..." she faded off.

"So you let him have you to save your sister?" Davis asked sympathetically.

"Yes. He said that if I told my mom, she'd never believe me and he'd divorce her and we'd have nowhere to live... he said we'd be living on the streets begging for food," she said, now easier to understand. The tears had temporarily slowed and it was if she were telling the story of someone else.

"You believed him. You were just a child yourself," he said, imagining how she must have felt.

"Of course I believed him. He was the Mayor of our town. He said everyone respected him and no one would believe a stepdaughter whose own father abandoned her."

His heart was aching for her. It was bad enough what had happened, but to have no one to share the pain with all of her adult life was too much of a burden on her.

"You should have told me," he said, waiting for a response. None came. "I can't believe he raped you at all, let alone at only fourteen years old!"

"It wasn't rape then. I consented to his advances because he said it was me or my sister. He told me to pick," she said.

"That's still rape to me and it would have been to the police also. How did it happen the first time?"

She played the movie back in her mind. "I had ridden my bicycle to a park to meet some friends. My mother told me I wasn't allowed to ride that far away, but I did it anyway, thinking she'd never know. Then, my bike got stolen, or somebody used it without telling me. I had to get home by a certain time and now I had to walk. I was walking along the road trying to think of a lie that my mom might believe, a reason why I was so late and why I didn't have my bike anymore, and a lie about where I had been."

"Kids do things like that all the time," Davis said.

She closed her eyes tight and held her clasped hands pushed against her chest. It was the only way that she could continue the story. "My step father was driving by, slowing down to go around the hair pin curve in the road when he saw me on the side. He pulled over and stopped. He demanded that I get in his car, then he grilled me about where my bike was and why I was so far away from home. Finally, he said he wouldn't tell my mom if I would do a favor for him too. A few minutes later, he pulled his car down a small dead end road."

Davis waited in silence. Lily kept her eyes closed tight and raised her head as if she were looking toward the ceiling. The tears streamed down her face and neck, but she didn't seem to notice. The white knuckles of her clenched hands looked out of place with her dark sun tanned skin. Davis couldn't help but think about how frail and delicate she looked.

"The Mayor pulled down his zipper, opened his pants and gently pulled me by the hair. I thought I was going to throw up all over him, but I didn't. I kept gagging and he kept pressing my head down toward him. Finally, he let loose of me and told me he'd teach me to do it right when there was more time," she said, terrified by the memory.

"You poor baby," he said, now understanding why she wouldn't have oral sex.

"He sexually abused me from then on. My mother never seemed to notice that I rarely talked to him and never wanted to be around him."

Davis shook his head. "How could your mother not notice?"

Lily had stopped crying again, her eyes were open and looking at him. "After she married him, she entered into her own little socialite world. She bought a show horse and was always taking lessons and showing her horse, or she was playing bridge with a ladies group, or entertaining people at our pool, or going to political fundraisers. She was in her own little world, which unfortunately included a lifestyle of drinking. She really wasn't there for my sister or I once she married the Mayor and didn't have to worry about money or working anymore."

"What a horrible mother!" Davis said, thinking that saying it out loud would make her feel better. He caressed her back as she leaned forward in contemplation.

"Well, I guess she was horrible in one way, but she must have loved me," she said in deep reflection and with a longing in her voice. "The night I told her that her husband raped me, and I mean a real rape..." The pitch of her voice got higher and emotional with anger. Her heart started beating wildly as she remembered. "For the first time I refused him. I absolutely told him not to touch me ever again and I pushed him away as hard as I could. He threw me on the floor and pinned my hands and brutally forced himself on me!"

He looked at her in shock, but she didn't see his face. She was lost in thought, staring out the bay window at the pasture full of horses. Speaking calmly again, she finished telling her dark secret.

"Mom was supposed to be gone for the weekend at a horse show, but her horse turned up lame. She came home unexpectedly. Of course, when she saw me, she asked why I was all bruised up and had a bloody lip; she assumed that I had fallen off of my horse. When I told her the truth, she held me and cried and cried and apologized. Mom started guzzling down Scotch or something, saying it was to calm her down before she got a gun and shot him. Finally, she went in the kitchen, saying she was going to get us a snack... she never came out."

The words hung in the air. Lily was tortured to continue.

"I went in to get her, afraid that she was searching for another bottle of liquor, which she didn't need," Lily said. Her mind drifted to the scene she had tried to block out. "Mom was draped over the kitchen table with blood all over her wrist and hand… and laying on the table next to her head, there was a sharp knife dripping with blood. My mother was dead," she described with little emotion, as if it weren't real, even though she knew it was. A coping mechanism.

Lily looked into her husband's eyes for an answer to the question that haunted her. "She must have loved me to have done that… don't you think?"

Davis could see the helplessness and pain in Lily's face. He couldn't answer her. He pulled her toward him and held her tight, feeling her beating heart against him; feeling the heat of her tortured body and soul. Lily was obviously longing to be sure that at least her mother loved her, even if she didn't protect her from that monster, and even if she didn't give her enough attention after she married him. It seemed that Lily wanted to believe so badly that her mother loved her so much she died for her. Anyone else would know that if her mother loved her the right way, she would have stayed alive, got them out of that house and helped her daughters through everything.

"Did it happen in the late summer or early fall?" he asked.

She looked at him, not understanding what he meant.

"Your mother killing herself, what time of year was it?"

"It was a week before Christmas. Why?"

Davis weighed his words before he spoke. "You're always so sad in the late summer and in the fall. "Now that you've told me this, I thought that your mother dying related to it."

Lily took the box of tissues from the end table and blew her nose with one and wiped the tears from her face with another as she thought about how to tell him what she really needed to reveal.

"Davis?"

"Yes?"

"The reason I'm so depressed at this time of year is because when he raped me, I ended up pregnant. I had a baby girl and gave her up for adoption."

Davis felt queasy. They had always wanted another child, a daughter hopefully, but she was never able to get pregnant again after Garth.

"I'm so sorry. I wish you had told me. I love you no matter what, honey. You should have shared this with me. You shouldn't have suffered like this alone, keeping all these secrets buried inside with no one to share it with."

"I know, but the time never seemed right. When we were dating, I couldn't tell you. I was afraid you wouldn't have wanted me. Then when you proposed marriage to me, I was afraid of the same thing. After that, I knew I had deceived you by not having told you before, so I just couldn't find a way to tell," she said as if she were the only person to have had a deep dark secret.

Davis took her face gently into his hands. He looked her straight in her eyes, then delicately kissed each of her puffy wet eyelids as they closed. "I would have married you if I knew, Lily. I've loved you with everything I've got from the day I met you."

"Thank you. I love you too."

He sat back in the chair and guided her head onto his shoulder and held her tight.

"Tell me why you've decided to share this with me now," he said in almost a whisper.

She took a deep breath and looked into his eyes. "I want to find my daughter."

"I'll support you with anything you want to do. I think we should tell Garth though. He's certainly old enough to understand, and maybe he could help us in locating her and contacting her."

With the weight lifted from her shoulders, Lily looked ten years younger and happier than Davis had seen her in ages. She sat up straight with purpose and felt the rush of new life from her head to her toes.

"Garth is a gentle hearted young man. He'll understand, I know he will," Lily said, sounding at peace with herself.

"Of course he'll understand."

They sat for a few minutes, holding each other and calming down.

"Now that we're confessing secrets, there's something that I have to tell you too."

His eyes shifted from left to right. She waited, not knowing what to even imagine. Lily looked at him with an unspoken question lurking behind her face.

"Remember that day I rushed to Garth's place after I hung up the phone? The night we almost got into an argument because I wouldn't tell you what it was about when I finally got home?"

"The night you came home drunk and wouldn't say where you were until almost ten o'clock at night?"

"Yes. But I wasn't drunk. I told you, I only had one beer. You only smelled a beer on my breath..."

"You were gone for hours after you left Garth! He called here looking for you at seven and you weren't home until just before the news started!"

"I drove in through the back entrance. I needed time to think, Lily. I was alone out in the pasture with the horses. There was a full moon, so I could see well enough."

The sinking feeling in the pit of her stomach returned. "Are you seeing someone else? In love with someone else?"

"No! Of course not. I've never wanted anyone else since the day I met you. That will never change."

"Even after what I told you today?"

"Nothing will change how I feel about you. Nothing."

"So what are you trying to tell me?"

His mouth was suddenly parched. It took only a moment for him to come back to the present. "Garth is in Arizona in depositions right now, as we speak. The lawsuit that he is working on is against Greg and Marcie Bordeaux..."

She unconsciously grabbed his thigh and dug her fingers in. "That's a conflict of interest. He can't work on anything against them..."

"When it all started, he didn't know we did business with Vintage Arabians at all, let alone that we have a million dollars invested in their program."

She pushed herself onto her feet and began pacing and biting her fingernails. "Does he know now?"

"Yes," he said somberly.

"Well, tell him to drop it!" she said knowing they were only words, and not a command that would be followed.

"He can't drop it. *He* could walk away from it, but Alec Douglas isn't going to, no matter what Garth says. "

She stood above him and faced him. He slowly took in a breath and let it out gradually as he looked up at her familiar face, willing to lose everything in the world except her. She watched the man she was growing old with, wanting to embrace him and melt into him. He started to stand up but she sat down to meet him first.

\\\\\\\\\\

Ryan's deposition was over before lunchtime. After Alec and Garth left, Dolan suggested that he treat everyone to lunch. Jessica declined; she wanted to take the remainder of the day off to rest. She'd been putting in incredibly long hours, even working at home at night. Ryan declined, anxious to return to his own farm. Greg and Marcie declined; they needed to tend to business at the farm.

Like the gentleman he always was, Greg opened the car door for his wife and waited until she arranged herself in the deep leather seat. She reached over to put the keys in the ignition as quickly as she could in order to start the air conditioner on high speed as Greg went to the driver's seat.

"What did you think?" Marcie asked.

"I don't think his deposition hurt us, do you?"

"Not really, but you never offered him any incentives to bid."

Greg changed the subject, knowing exactly what he was guilty of and what was sure to cause them irreparable problems.

"I loved it when Alec's side kick asked Ryan…"

Greg completed her sentence, mimicking the young attorney. "Do you think that the value of a horse is whatever the buyer is willing to pay?"

Marcie broke out laughing.

"Did you see the look on Alec's face? I thought he was going to grab his own co-counsel by the collar and throw him out of the room!"

"Whose side is that kid on, anyway? I felt like we should have been paying him for his help!" Marcie said with a broad smile showing off her polished teeth and the results of four years of braces and retainers.

\\\\\\\\\\

After eight more depositions over the course of four days, Greg called Ryan and asked him for advice as to whether or not they should throw out a reasonable settlement figure. Even though Ryan's deposition didn't harm them, it didn't help either. In contrast, all of the other people deposed hurt the Bordeauxs. At Greg's request, Ryan returned to Scottsdale since the weather forecast predicted rain in Santa Barbara for the next several days.

They met in the heart of Scottsdale at The Back Stage Restaurant at one-thirty. After everyone agreed, Marcie ordered an extra large lavosh topped with Dolfino cheese, mild green chilis, mushrooms sautéed with garlic, diced Bermuda onions and diced vine-ripened tomatoes. Since the Armenian cracker bread took a fair amount of time to be prepared with its toppings and then to bake, they ordered individual appetizers of tiger prawns, and they each ordered peach flavored sun tea on crushed ice.

"So, Marcie, were you able to contain yourself and be polite around Johan?" Ryan asked, starting the subject of the lawsuit casually.

"He still hasn't been there. Alec said *'He's not available at this time',*" Marcie said mockingly.

"It was odd that he didn't show up for my deposition, especially since it was the first one, but not to show up all week?"

Greg agreed. "I know! And you'd think that he'd have wanted to meet you. Most everyday people wouldn't miss an opportunity to meet you in person."

"I know. It's ridiculous. I'm just a human like everyone else, but people are weird when it comes to famous people!"

"I'm *glad* the pig wasn't there," Marcie said, disgusted by the vision of him.

The men ignored her crassness. There were probably medical reasons why Johan was obese, but she was too angry to consider the likeliness of that.

"I understand that he probably wouldn't sit through two months of depositions and leave his business, but I thought he'd at least come to the first several, just to see how they went. And to face us," Greg said.

"That's the key. Just the fact that he hasn't been there might mean that he feels that he can't face you after what he's started. I think I should call him on your behalf. Maybe he'd settle for something reasonable if he heard me out," Ryan suggested.

The Bordeauxs looked at each other hopefully.

"I guess you're allowed to call him. We're just not, because of the attorneys," Greg said.

"Right."

"You would do that for us?" Marcie asked.

"Like I said, it's not just for you," Ryan said. He didn't intend to tell them anything about Shawna's investigation and the USDA and the FBI, but because of what he learned from his wife, he was curious to meet Johan and Jordan Murphy in person himself.

Ryan ate his six prawns in record time, and then suggested that he use the pay phone to call Johan, right then and there.

"Now?" Greg asked, stunned by the very idea.

"We're at a restaurant. In public," Marcie added.

"No one's going to pay attention. I'm just going to call and ask him if I can fly him here to Scottsdale to discuss the idea of a potential settlement. I'll explain that you don't want attorneys involved since they inevitably complicate everything."

"Now is as good a time as any I guess," Greg said, feeling ready for just about anything after all they've been through recently.

"I have his phone number. I called information last night and got it," Ryan said as he stood up from his seat and pushed his chair back under the table. He folded the cloth napkin into thirds and placed it next to his fork.

When Ryan walked away, Marcie and Greg talked about how Ryan took the initiative to get involved. They speculated as to whether or not he had an ulterior motive, other than 'wanting to protect the industry', as he claimed. They couldn't come up with any ulterior motives.

Marcie studied her make-up mirror and drew with a stick of lipstick to touch up her full lips. Wishing he could hear what was being said, Greg watched Ryan's body language while he was talking on the phone. It was obvious that Ryan must have been talking with Johan, because this was taking much longer than it would have taken to just leave a message with a secretary. Ryan was shaking his head, raising his eyebrows and crinkling his forehead as if he were amazed by what he was hearing.

The waitress rearranged the table to clear the center and placed the lavosh in the middle.

"Bring us a bottle of your finest champagne!" Ryan told the server as he approached their table.

"You already convinced him to agree to a settlement? On the phone?" Greg asked, hopeful but doubting.

"Nope."

"Well, then what?" Marcie said.

"Let her serve the bubbly, then I'll tell you so that we can make a toast!"

Frustrated, but playing along with what Ryan was turning into a game, the couple didn't ask anything else. Marcie dug in and took a slice of lavosh and savored her first bite. Her husband and their new friend took pieces for themselves and raved about how delicious it was.

The waitress brought the bottle of champagne and nestled it deep into the bucket of ice. "I'll be right back with your champagne glasses," she told them.

"Okay guys. Wait till you hear this!"

"What?"

"The FBI thinks that Johan and Jordan Murphy have fled the country," Ryan explained.

Greg and Marcie looked confused rather than excited.

"That's what his office said?" Greg asked.

"No. When I called his number, no one answered and there wasn't a machine on. I called my wife and asked if she knew how to reach him…"

Marcie interrupted. "How would she know?"

"It's something I can't discuss, but she's investigating a story that he's involved in. I thought she might be able to give me a different number than what's listed with the operator."

"Yeah? Go on…" Greg said, still confused.

"Wouldn't you think that if they fled the country, that Johan's not going to be pursuing this litigation? His attorneys probably don't even know!" he said, then immediately took another bite of the lavosh.

"Are you serious?" Marcie asked with a huge grin.

Temporarily speechless, Greg sat back, the muscles in his neck and shoulders finally relaxed for the first time in ages.

"I'm as serious as a heart attack. I'd love to see the look on those attorneys faces when they find out they don't have a client anymore!" Ryan said laughing out loud.

The waitress wasn't in sight, and she hadn't brought champagne glasses yet. Ryan took the full iced tea glasses, one by one, and slowly poured them into the potted plant that was on a ledge next to their table. Marcie and Greg burst into hysterics. Greg refilled the glasses with the bubbly and they guzzled down the first glass without anyone even making a toast.

Twenty-Three

After he left the Bordeauxs and checked back into the Hyatt Regency, Ryan and Shawna had a long telephone conversation. She said that she didn't want to join him at the Santa Barbara farm, but she'd come visit him in Scottsdale if he could get a deluxe villa at the John Gardner Tennis Ranch and if he could arrange for a series of private lessons for her. He agreed, wanting to spend time with her anywhere away from New York City.

The next morning he picked her up at Sky Harbor International Airport. She always insisted to fly commercial airlines when she traveled without him, not wanting to waste the money on private jets, although she did insist on the luxury of first class.

"What do you have in here besides tennis clothes and swimming suits?" he said, exaggerating the weight of her carry-on bag.

Shawna grabbed it off his shoulder. "I have work-out clothes, dress clothes for the evening and cosmetics! It's not too heavy for me."

"Fine," he smiled and let her carry her own bag all the way to the car.

"I love the desert," she said once they were away from the airport area.

"It's pretty, but I couldn't live here. I like the greenery of Santa Barbara."

Shawna suppressed a frown. He loved the quiet country and she loved the hustle of New York City. This wasn't the time to talk about it again. She wished he'd sell the farm and spend more time with her.

Just about the time they could see Camelback Mountain in the distance, Ryan asked her if she was upset that her story was killed.

"Yes, and no," she said with little emotion.

Ryan playfully rolled his eyes, but she was looking out the passenger window and didn't see it. "You're a woman of many words!" He affectionately reached over and squeezed the back of her neck. "Especially for a journalist!"

"Thanks."

"Thank you for thanking me," he said.

"Thank you for thanking me for thanking you," she said.

It was a private joke from when they were in Jamaica on a vacation. They both laughed out loud, glad to be together somewhere without the distractions of their careers.

"So, what's 'yes and no' mean?" he asked. He wasn't the type to make small talk with his own wife. Silence was golden unless they had something of interest to say… or of affection.

"I'm upset it was killed because we put a lot of work in on it and it was our first team project. The morale has gone down, as you can imagine," she said as she riffled through her purse looking for her sunglasses. "We were all anxious to get our first story together on the air."

Ryan nodded in understanding. "You just found out yesterday morning. Everyone needs time to adjust to the news. They'll be fine by the time you get back. So will you."

"I know. You're the one who asked!" she said, then put her natural colored lip-gloss on without using the mirror.

"So, in what way are you glad?"

Shawna smiled with pride. "I showed Loren that I still have a nose for a great story, and we obviously got a really good start on putting the pieces together. He said he was impressed."

"Will you ever be able to pursue it and run it?"

"They said we will, but we don't know how long it will be. I've never been involved in something so big that the FBI asks us to delay investigating and running a story so that they can pursue an internal investigation deeper into the organization," she said, still astonished.

"What exactly happened?"

"Loren called his FBI contact and gave him the basics of what we've already got. That guy called who knows who and a couple of days later we've got five men waiting at Loren's door when he gets to his office!"

"Yeah?"

"Right. So, it turns out, one's a big honcho with the Teamsters Union, one's a big honcho with the USDA, and the other three are with the FBI. They tell Loren that they've worked this case for two years and the deeper they dig the more corruption they find. Obviously, they want to get to the bottom of it. If we keep investigating and run the story, whoever is involved is going to cover up what they can or they'll disappear."

"What exactly is the big deal about people in the produce business being fraudulent? Lots of businesses do fraudulent things!"

"Because the Murphys are *only one business* doing this. It's a rampant problem in the produce industry that's practically as bad as organized crime, even though they haven't traced anything to the Mafia. What's even worse is how deep the pay-offs are going in both the USDA and the FBI to keep the wheels greased. That's probably their biggest concern. The dirty people in the USDA and the FBI. They've got to flush them out with good solid evidence and they have to get to whatever the highest levels are," she explained.

"I get it. Like in the drug business, you've got to bust the user that gets caught, but you really want the source of the drugs. Not only the dealer the user bought from, but however deep it goes, even if it's to Columbia or wherever."

"Right. And in that scenario, like this one, there are lots of people just letting things slip by because they're being paid off. Like the workers at the airport or whatever. Everyone needs to get identified and caught. Some will get immunity to roll over on other people," she told him.

"We'll be there in a minute, do you need anything before we check in?" he asked.

"No. Thanks."

"So, I thought the Murphys had immunity. Why did they flee?"

"Allegedly flee?"

"Yes!" he laughed.

"Probably because they're looking for the FBI agent who froze their bank accounts..."

"What? You've never said anything about bank accounts!"

"This agent froze their business bank accounts until they provided the evidence and testified at the hearing. Apparently, the agent stole the money from the Murphy's accounts!" she said as if she was amused.

"No shit?"

"No shit!"

"Isn't the FBI liable to the Murphys for how much was in their accounts?" he asked.

She fluffed up her hair as they drove up the steep driveway of the tennis resort. "The agent stole all the files that had to do with them and never gave them anything in writing. On top of that, he never gave them a written contract or anything they could use as evidence that would be proof to them that they were to get full immunity in exchange for cooperation, let alone proof that they acknowledged the bank accounts were being frozen."

"And the Murphys have no credible witness that this was happening?"

"Not alive," she said as the valet opened her door. "Thank you," she told the young man.

Ryan gave him a twenty-dollar bill without saying a word. He was engrossed in the conversation.

"What do you mean, not alive?"

"Their attorney, Nathan Burger, was gunned down. Murdered. He's the only one that knew what was happening with the Murphys and the government," she confided.

"Did the FBI agent kill him?"

"That's what they think. They don't have any evidence though," she said as they entered the lobby of the resort.

Ryan was becoming sympathetic toward the Murphys even though they were crooks. "I guess that's why Johan couldn't make his payment on Love Letter," he surmised.

"That makes sense," she said.

"Can I tell the Bordeauxs the reason why Jordan couldn't make his payment?"

Shawna stared at her husband in disbelief. She thought she could trust him, but a tiny part of her, deep inside, had a doubt. Especially after he asked a question like that.

\`\`\`\`\`\`\`\`\`\`

"Victor says that my serve is radically improved. Maybe you and I can play together tomorrow morning."

Ryan looked across the lunch table at his wife who was glowing from the heat and exercise. "What's he going to tell you? After three consecutive days of working on your serve, you haven't learned a thing!"

"You've been watching me play?"

"No. I mean that for all that they charge for the lessons and clinics, they've got to tell everyone that they are improving or they may as well tell you that you're throwing away your money."

"I know I'm improving."

"Good. I know you definitely needed the break from work. And I'm glad we're together," he told her without much conviction.

She could see his mind was elsewhere. "I know it's been great to be together, but you've been really distracted. Do you want to talk about it?"

"I do. This lawsuit against the Bordeauxs is getting worse. Johan's lawyers don't believe the Murphys fled the country and they're proceeding full force. They said there isn't a warrant out for their arrest and they are entitled to pursue the litigation. I want to talk about it, but not here," he said, glad she asked.

"I've got a yoga session after lunch, then a massage. Why don't we talk about it after that. I should be done at about three-thirty."

Ryan pictured a written appointment book filled in for the day. "Aren't we having those Reiki masters to the villa at five?"

"You're right. We'll talk about it after that."

"Sounds good," he said just as a young woman from the front desk escorted a man with a Federal Express envelop to their table.

"Mr. Sanders?" the uniformed man confirmed.

"Yes."

"I need you to sign here," he said, referring to the receipt for the package. Ryan thanked him as he scribbled his signature and placed the unopened package on the table.

"What's that?" she asked.

"It's an inventory list of all of the horses and the farm's assets, along with valuations and a cumulative profit and loss statement," he said quietly.

Shawna looked at the package, as if it would elaborate on its own behalf. "What for?"

"It's information that I need to study. I'm thinking about selling out."

Shawna tried to keep her smile to herself. "Selling the horses and the farm?" she said, trying not to sound hopeful.

"Yes. That should make you happy," he said, unable to look her in the eye.

"Ryan..."

"It's not because of you. I'm sorry I said that. It's got nothing to do with you."

"What's this about?"

"We'll discuss it when we have more time. Don't worry, I'm fine."

"You don't look fine. You look like you've lost your best friend. I'm canceling the rest of everything scheduled today," she said as she stood up to leave the table. "Sign the bill and I'll meet you in the lobby. The front desk can cancel everyone for me."

Ryan took off his shoes and socks, pulled back the bedspread, piled four pillows against the headboard and arranged himself comfortably on the bed.

"Yesterday, Greg said that the last five depositions were really hurting them and each of the five clients have informed them that they have no intentions of paying the notes due from the horses they bought at the auction."

"Why? What does the lawsuit have to do with people paying the payments on their horses?"

"They're angry about how Greg basically had them serving as shills in the audience bidding up the horses… the horses these people bought. They think… they know… they got screwed. They overpaid for the horses. At least for the contract amount, in their opinion. He said they each told him that they refuse to pay the balance and if he doesn't like it, he can sue them. They know that Greg would lose the case. He committed fraud and they have plenty of proof."

"I don't understand why this legal action is even being continued. How can his attorneys proceed without a client?"

"It's bull shit. But they can. I suppose eventually, if Johan never does come back before the actual trial, they'd have to drop it, but at this point, it's not legally necessary for him to be present."

"It's crazy! I guess because the FBI doesn't have any actual evidence that the Murphys fled the country, and because there isn't actually a warrant out for their arrest. I don't know."

"What's all this got to do with you selling your horses and the farm?"

"If Bordeaux goes under, we'll all lose money. I can see it coming. I'm not an idiot. I love the horses, but I don't need a hundred and ten horses and a six million dollar farm for just a hobby that doesn't make any money. I'm going to liquidate before all of this becomes public knowledge and the market collapses. I'll keep a handful of horses and take them back to the farm in Connecticut."

"You don't think you're overreacting?"

"No. I'm not jumping the gun. Greg's already got a new client to buy out his parent's twenty horses..."

"To protect his parents from financial loss?"

"Yes."

"Is he getting cash? Surely, if he finances the transaction, he'll never collect the balance owed once these newest buyers find out Vintage is going to lose their business."

"He's getting cash. He offered the new buyers a 20% cash discount and free board and training for ninety days in order to get them to pay within seventy-two hours. This buyer is in the oil refinery business. I'm sure he's just writing a check like it's nothing to him. He's got a couple thousand-acre farm in New Mexico, so he's got the place to take the horses once he puts up another barn to accommodate the new horses. That's why he got ninety days of free board and training. It'll take him about that long to get everything perfect at his place, including enough cross fencing and everything."

Shawna joined him on the bed, sprawling out and stretching her spine.

"So, back to you selling out. Aren't you rushing things?"

"I'd be stupid not to follow Greg's lead. He rushed to protect his own parents..."

"That's true."

"It's been like a two by four slapping me upside the head."

She leaned into him and tickled his stomach affectionately. In a Southern accent she teased him. "Since when did you start talking like that?"

"I don't know. Hopefully I haven't. It just came out of my mouth!"

"Why don't you try to get Greg to sell your most expensive horses for you?" she asked as she wrapped her arm and leg over him.

He pulled her close and held her tight enough to feel her heart beat on his rib cage. "I was thinking about that, but I don't know if I feel comfortable asking him."

"Why not?"

"I've never even bought a horse from him. I bought most of my valuable horses directly from either Poland or Sweden. And of course, I bought a few from Celia Vanders. The rest, we really bred ourselves," he said, subconsciously thinking about his ex-wife who had passed away. They got into the Arabian horse breeding together, before she had gotten ill.

"Surely the real estate won't lose any money no matter when you sell. There are always people wanting gorgeous farms."

"That's true. Maybe I shouldn't even deal with thinking about the farm in Santa Barbara yet. One thing at a time. I'll deal with liquidating the horses first."

"You're really sure that you need to do this?"

"Pretty sure. You don't like the horses or the farm anyway. It will give us more time together when I'm not on location if I don't have the operation and don't go to the major shows."

"But it makes you so happy, Ryan. I hate to see you give it up," she said as she looked into his sad eyes.

"It's not my choice. I either give it up and make money, or I wait to give it up and lose a ton of money. My only choice is the timing."

"I'd ask Greg to help if I were you. After all, you're helping him."

"Not really."

"Sure you are. On some level, you must be or we wouldn't be here in Scottsdale still. And he wouldn't be confiding in you about what trouble he's in."

"Last night, when Marcie went out to the barn to check the horses, Greg actually broke down in tears. I barely know the guy. I felt so bad for him."

"So, he does need you in his own way. You're helping him in your own way. Why not ask him?"

"I did broach the subject last night. He suggested that I show him my inventory list and valuations."

"Then do it."

"I am, but I can't count on him. Once he thinks about it, he'll realize he's got plenty of clients that are probably just like his parents... clients that can't take the loss without it destroying them."

"Why don't you have Dan liquidate the herd?"

"I can't tell him what's happening. Trainers are the first people to start gossiping. It will spread through the business like wildfire and the market will just collapse sooner. All I can do is tell him I want to move ten or fifteen horses as soon as possible to help with some expansion plans. Maybe I'll tell him I want to build a state of the art breeding lab or something. That would get him excited and motivated."

"What's wrong with how you're breeding now?"

"Nothing. I wouldn't really do it. It would just be a story that justifies why I want to sell a lot of horses right away. He wouldn't suspect anything about me getting out of the business."

"It's worth a try. If not, what about calling some of the agents that deal with your farm? It's their business to sell horses. Offer them an added incentive to get it done right away."

"That's a good idea. But I'll have to be careful." Ryan thought about the added incentive that Greg offered the bidders in the audience at the auction.

"Careful?"

"Yeah. People never deal directly with me. They always deal with Dan or Marty..."

"Speaking of them, will they be able to get other jobs if you shut down?"

"Dan will. A successful national level trainer with a track record like his will always have work. I doubt if Marty will be able to be a 'marketing director' for anyone. I really just created the job because there was so much marketing and advertising done that I could justify creating the position."

"What does she do besides give the farm tours and general PR?"

"She follows up on people to see if they're interested in buying horses... if they didn't show a clear interest while they were at the farm. If they show a clear interest at the farm, she introduces them to Dan and he takes over."

"So she doesn't actually do the selling?"

"No. Dan's really protective about it. I suppose he wants all the credit for the income generated. Of course, Marty and I know that if she doesn't do her job well, there are a lot of sales that would never happen."

"Dan needs his ego stroked?"

"Everyone wants to feel important and indispensable. It's human nature."

"You're right. I've got to remember that. You're so good at bringing out the best in people."

"Marty was a quick study. She develops our marketing campaigns and hires the ad agencies and coordinates with the professional photographers... she's great. She knows horses too, but is careful not to step on Dan's toes. She lets him do all the selling. I should say, he insists on doing all the selling and she doesn't mind."

"I can see why it would be strange if you contacted the agents then, but there must be a way."

"I think I'll just call the one who sells the most for us."

"Good idea."

"Do you mind if I try to get together with Greg tomorrow after the depositions, now that I have the inventory list?"

"Of course not. Maybe I'll join you, if you don't mind."

"I don't mind. I'd love for you to be involved," he said,. *Even if it's for the liquidation rather than building up the program,* he thought.

\\\\\\\\\\

Friday evening Greg and Marcie looked as if they'd been through the ringer. Shawna hadn't ever met them before and they were trying too hard to make a good impression, conscious that she knew whatever Ryan knew.

"I wonder if I should even bother making the payment for the property taxes in Kentucky... I'll probably just be throwing away our money," Greg said.

"The mortgage holder will have to pay it if you don't," Ryan said.

"I'm sure we'll eventually be foreclosed on there. Dolan arranged for the investors who hold the mortgage... I can't believe we'll be embarrassing him like this."

"Why not propose to the investors that they give up their position and become a majority partner in the farm and all of your horses? Then, everything would be protected from creditors and you could conduct business as usual... you just wouldn't be the sole owners anymore," Shawna suggested.

Marcie's eyes lit up. "That's an idea! Let's ask Jessica and Dolan what they think of that."

"While you're at it, why don't you see if you could get the investors to buy out most of my herd?" Ryan said lightly.

"Why?"

"I've decided to get out of the horse business. Shawna doesn't like the horses and we really don't have enough time together. When I'm not on location working on a movie, I have to divide my time between staying in New York with her or going to Santa Barbara. It's a major conflict that I'm tired of dealing with," Ryan explained, acting as if this has been in the planning for sometime now.

"You have a farm in Connecticut also don't you?"

"Yes. But it's not nearly large enough to operate a commercial business, and all the money on horses is spent here in Scottsdale or in California. No one pays the prices anywhere else. You know that."

"You're right. Even in Kentucky we don't get the big prices! We bring the same horses back to Scottsdale and sell them for quadruple. Our plan is to get the prices up wherever the horses are, but it's been hard. We don't understand it ourselves..."

"Anyway, of course, I'd be happy to pay you a 20% commission for selling the herd if you can get it done quickly."

"I'll work on it. We could use the money from a big sale like this. Maybe we could use the commissions to offer a settlement with Johan," Greg said, seeing some light at the end of the tunnel.

"Ryan has an inventory list and valuations. We can help you put together a proposal to the mortgage holders," Shawna said without having talked about it with her husband.

Marcie couldn't imagine Shawna, as important and famous as she is, would want to take her time with this, but she thought it was exciting. She'd obviously get to know her if they spent time putting together a proposal.

"Should we start now... the brainstorming at least?" Marcie asked.

"Sure," Shawna answered.

Ryan and Greg sat back, impressed how the women were taking charge.

"Greg, I assume that you know how to contact the mortgage holders?"

"I send my payments to a company in Florida. Hopefully I can find out from them who the principals are that actually hold the mortgage."

"Make that a priority. We have to know who we're dealing with," Shawna said.

"I think the proposal should be simple," Marcie started. "We propose that we retain a 49% interest in the enterprise which consists of all of the horses except the stallions, here and in Kentucky. They'll also get 51% of the real estate here and in Kentucky... and the business name. Greg and I continue to operate the business as usual. It can be self supporting, paying us a salary and commissions on sales. The mortgage holders are contributing the real estate and any business expertise that they have in exchange for their interest. The only thing that they need to do is the legal paperwork and pay for your horses, whatever amount that comes to..."

"Why don't you want them to get ownership in the stallions?" Shawna asked.

"We'll keep that income for ourselves," Marcie said.

"I would doubt that they'd go for it. The stallions are the biggest money makers, aren't they?" Shawna asked, trying not to sound like she was gathering information for a story.

"Yes. But they don't need to know that. I can't imagine that these people know anything at all about the horse business. We just won't put the stallions on the inventory list. We'll form a syndicate for each stallion that's not syndicated yet and tell them that the syndicate owns each of the breeding stallions..."

"That's deceptive," Shawna said.

The men just sat back and listened since the women seemed to forget the men were even there.

Greg couldn't believe his wife was in the middle of a lawsuit about fraud and misrepresentation and was still thinking of new ways to commit more fraud and misrepresent something else. He leaned over and whispered to Ryan that he would set her straight when they were alone.

"Don't worry. We'll find a way to do it. Besides, they'll own 51% of anything we do with any future stallions or syndicates," Marcie said, oblivious to any ethical considerations.

"You'll need to talk to your attorney about how to do everything legally, Marcie. The main objective will be for you to stay in the business but be protected from creditors. Also, if you have a majority partner, hopefully they'll be able to force your clients to pay on their existing notes so the cash flow and profits continue. You'll need to talk to your attorney about those kinds of issues also," Shawna said.

The more she thought about it, the more she really didn't want to be involved, especially since Marcie's instinct was to take advantage of someone else.

"You know, really, Ryan and I don't have time to deal with this. Of course, he'll provide you with what you need to try to sell his herd of horses. You obviously need professional legal advice in proposing a plan and knowing the various consequences of different scenario's," Shawna said, trying to dig her way out of the hole she started.

"You're right, " Greg interjected, knowing he had to step in and stop his wife who seemed not to be able to face reality.

Ryan handed him the overstuffed folder of documents. "Here are copies of registration papers, production records for the broodmares, and a complete inventory list with valuations. Of course, the syndicate members will have to vote on where they want to stand Brighton," he said. "I'm taking a few of the mares and Farroah to Connecticut."

Brighton is the first stallion he owned. He purchased him as a weanling, then after his show career took off, he syndicated the Multi National Champion for fifteen million dollars. Farroah, the last stallion he imported from Poland, is sentimental because his deceased wife selected him, saying that he was her dream horse.

"Do you know the Macdermots?" Greg asked as he thumbed through the inventory list and looked at the total dollar figure.

"The name sounds vaguely familiar," Ryan said, racking his brain.

"They just got into Arabians through the Pattons up in Seattle. I understand that they own some sports team and a chain of upscale retail stores. Would you mind if I contact them first and see if I can sell them your program?" Greg asked.

"Of course I wouldn't mind, but it needs to be confidential that I'm selling out. Dan doesn't even know. I don't want it getting back to him or anyone until there is a done deal. Completely finished, cash in hand and registration papers signed over," Ryan said seriously.

"I understand. I could try to call the Macdermots now if you want. I have their home number. I do know they own a beautiful five hundred acre farm and only have a few horses on it now. You know Patton... he only sells a few horses a year and he's overly particular about who he'll sell to."

"Sure. That would be great, we can wait," Shawna said.

Greg hesitated. "Would you be willing to pay a thirty percent commission if I could get this done within the week?"

"No. I wouldn't want it to come back to haunt me later," Ryan answered without even giving it a thought.

"What do you mean?" Marcie asked.

"Twenty percent is the industry standard. I don't want anything to appear fishy. Whatever sale goes, it will be disclosed in writing that you've been compensated twenty percent. The contract will be between me and the buyer, and the money will go directly to me. I'll disburse the commission to you when I receive good funds from the buyer," Ryan said in a tone that meant there was no negotiating on the point.

"That's not how I usually do business," Greg said.

"That's the point... and why you're in the position you're in," Shawna said.

Marcie and Greg ignored her comment. They needed the commission if they could get an important sale like this accomplished quick enough.

Greg went into his office and closed the door behind him. Marcie chattered on about local restaurants and decided to see if they could get into Chez Nous without a reservation.

Not ten minutes later, Greg came out of his office, hopeful. "Mr. Macdermot is very interested in acquiring an existing program. He assured me that he would keep it confidential that you were interested in selling out. He and his wife can fly to Santa

Barbara tomorrow afternoon and meet us at your farm. I told him we'd be there," Greg said, trying not to sound arrogant.

"Great!" Shawna said.

"I'll call Dan and tell him I need him to come here to look at a couple of mares for sale. Can you arrange to have your brother show him some mares?"

"Sure," Greg said, confused.

"That way, Dan won't be at the farm getting suspicious about what's happening," Shawna explained for her husband.

"Oh. Good idea," Marcie said, relating to the deception.

Twenty-Four

Shawna and Ryan returned to New York, not knowing for sure how their lives together would be now that the herd of horses was sold and the farm was listed for sale with a real estate agent. Both of them hoped that they'd still enjoy each others company now that they were going to have so much more time together when Ryan wasn't on location.

The couple debated about the ethics of their transaction and discussed having a guilty conscious about selling out to the Macdermots, knowing the events that were sure to come if the Bordeauxs couldn't settle the lawsuit.

As it turned out, the mortgage holders on the farm in Kentucky were Japanese investors who said they weren't interested in striking a deal to enter into a partnership with the Bordeauxs for the real estate or their horses. They had every intention of foreclosing on the property if they needed to. They planned on keeping it operating, thinking that one of the American educated sons could run the business. The Japanese family insisted that they wouldn't need Greg or Marcie; they could hire other people and make the farm profitable.

"Do you think that Greg will really let us know what's happening?" Shawna asked.

"I think he will. They were more than grateful to us. I think they were sincere when they said they didn't know what they would have done without us," Ryan said.

"Let's hope so."

\`\`\`\`\`\`\`\`\`\`

Trading Paper

George Powers, Davis and Lily Windsor's life long friend and personal attorney, joined them at their farm for dinner. Davis became close friends with him in college. George is who inspired Garth to go to law school. They sat on the screened-in porch now that the weather had cooled. After dinner, Davis told his friend the real reason he had invited him out.

"I have a couple of things that I need to consult with you about, but I'd rather do it here instead of your office... of course, I'll pay you for your advice," Davis offered.

"Don't be ridiculous. What's happening?" he said casually.

"We're in a very uncomfortable situation. I can't explain everything because Garth shouldn't have told me what he knew about..."

"You're not making any sense. Start over or leave out the details!" George said as he sipped his martini.

"Sorry. We're selling our herd of horses, except our two pleasure horses," Davis said, his heart feeling empty. "The people are paying cash..."

"I thought everybody financed the horses with the sellers," George interrupted.

"Normally, they do, but we offered a substantial cash discount. Very substantial," Lily said.

"Did you talk to your CPA about doing that? You could end up with a tax burden."

"No. A tax burden would be better than the alternative," Davis said.

"Explain yourself," George said.

"Garth is involved in a lawsuit against the farm that we rely on to make our money in the horse business... at least the big money. We bought a stallion from that farm and paid a lot of money in advance for a promotional program. I don't want to go into detail, but let it suffice to say that if that farm goes under, so will we," Davis said.

"I'll trust your judgment on that. Go ahead, continue."

"I found a buyer who obviously doesn't know that Vintage Arabians is being sued. I'm supposed to get a cashier's check in the next couple of days for two million dollars," he said, feeling guilty and relieved at the same time.

"Great!" George said.

Lily got to the point. "What we're worried about is that if we go through with this sale and accept her money knowing that Vintage Arabians might go out of business, can we be sued?"

"For nondisclosure?"

"I guess. Or for anything? Can she sue us if she finds out the real reason why we sold the horses?" Davis asked.

"No. You're the seller, not their agent. You have no fiduciary duty to them," George assured them. "I wouldn't worry about it."

"Oh good. We were so worried. The woman we're selling to can afford to lose the money. She's an heir to a major candy company. She has fortunes to play with. We sold her a horse a couple of years ago and she just happened to call to see if we had any full siblings for sale. We have three full siblings and still own the dam of those horses. The next thing I know, I made a proposal that she buy out our herd, and after I sent her my new video of the horses, she agreed!" Davis said.

"Two million is play money to her. She's nice, but filthy rich and didn't work for a dime of it," Lily said, not feeling guilty at all about the prospect of the woman losing every dime on the horses.

"Sounds like you lucked out. I wouldn't worry about it," George said. He finished his martini and reached for the pitcher to refill his glass.

"One other thing we want to ask you about," Lily said.

"I hope it's as easy as the first," George said.

Davis reached over to Lily's hand and held it as she organized the words in her mind. She was remarkably stable, in fact, she was almost enthusiastic.

"When I was nineteen, I gave a new born baby up for adoption. I'd like to locate her and hopefully meet her. At the very least, I'd like to know how her life has turned out."

George hid his surprise. "Do you know who adopted her?"

"No. But I did go through a private attorney," Lily said, hoping that the fact alone would simplify the process of locating her daughter.

"I'll see what I can do. Before I leave, give me his name and where he was the last you know of," George said, acting as if this was no big deal. Now he understood why Lily had always paid so much attention to his own daughter, who was now thirty and had three children of her own.

The next afternoon, George unexpectedly showed up at the Windsors. "You guys are too easy. I was hoping that this would have taken more time so that I could send you a bill!"

Lily hugged him and her eyes lit up like a child seeing the presents from Santa under the Christmas tree. "You've already found something out?"

"I called the adoption attorney. He's kept excellent records. As we're speaking, he's trying to contact the adoptive parents and talk to them. He'll call us here and let us know the status. It should be soon. I hung up from him about a half hour ago," George explained, always the hero.

The three of them tried to make small talk, but they were all on pins and needles waiting for the phone to ring.

"Hello," George said as he picked up the phone.

"This is Michael Warren. The adoptive parents are going to call you at this number in a few minutes. They don't want me to tell you who they are at this time, but they are willing to talk to you. They're very nice. This is a good start," he said.

"Thank you. We'll wait for the call," George said. "Send the bill for your services to my office. You've got the address."

"There won't be a bill. Good luck."

Within moments of George telling Davis and Lily what was happening, the phone rang again. Lily picked up the extension closest to her. Davis rushed to the telephone in the kitchen.

"Hello," Lily said.

"Hello," Davis said.

"Hello. My wife and I are both on the phone also. This is very uncomfortable for us, as you can imagine," he said.

"I understand. Thank you so much for calling us... especially so quickly," Lily said.

"Please, don't think we're cold or trying to be difficult, but we don't want you to know who we are or our daughter's name at this time. We didn't expect a call like this and we haven't had time to consider how to handle the situation," she said.

"Certainly. I really appreciate that you'll at least talk to us. Is my daughter healthy?" Lily asked, not really knowing exactly what to say or how to word it.

"Yes, our daughter is. She's never had any health problems. May I ask, have you or anyone in your family ever had any health problems that our daughter should be aware of?" she said.

"No. None at all," Lily said, not considering that depression was a health problem.

"Good. We've always wondered. The adoption records say that there weren't any, but health problems can obviously develop," she said.

"Is your daughter married?" Lily asked.

"Yes. She's happily married, but they don't have any children yet," she said.

"At least she's happy though. I'm so glad. I'm sure you're wonderful parents. I can tell by your voice and the fact that you've contacted us so quickly," Lily said.

"Are there any other general questions that we can answer for you?" he said.

"Well, did she go to college?" Davis asked.

"Two years, but she didn't like it, so she quit," he said.

"Does she have a job?" Lily asked.

"She and her husband own their own business," he said.

"That's wonderful," Davis said.

"I'm afraid there's not much else to tell you right now," she said, not knowing what to say to continue the conversation.

"Does she know that she was adopted?" Lily asked.

"Yes, she does," he said.

"Does she hate me?" Lily asked.

"No! She's a warm and loving person, she'd never hate you. In fact, I want to thank you for giving us such a lovely and wonderful gift. I couldn't have children of my own. You giving up your baby was a blessing for us," she said.

Lily started crying and was unable to speak.

"Would you consider letting us talk with your daughter? My wife and I would like to at least talk to her, if not meet her," Davis said.

"We have to think about it," he said.

"We don't want to cause any problems. I assure you. If she doesn't want a continuing relationship, we'd understand. We could play everything by ear...you can be part of everything."

He interrupted. "Like I said, we need to think about it. We'll keep your name and number and let you know as soon as we've made a decision."

"Your daughter is old enough to make the decision on her own. Would you tell her I want to talk to her?" Lily asked through her tears.

"Maybe soon, but right now is not a good time. She's happy, and happily married, but right now, they are going through some business difficulties. When things are settled down with that, we'll decide where we should go from there," he said.

"She's stressed right now?" Lily asked.

"Yes. It's nothing they can't handle. Part of life is stress and problems. They'll handle it fine, but for now, I don't want to bring another emotional issue into the picture," he said.

Lily was disappointed, but she completely understood. "When you do decide, would you tell her that I love her? That I've always loved her?" Lily said, still crying.

"Yes. Of course. I'm sorry, we've got to go now," he said.

They hung up their respective phones.

"Pretty soon, we'll have to tell Marcie about the call and let her make the decision for herself," Deirdre told her husband.

"I know. But now is not the time," Drake said.

Twenty-Five

Another week has gone by and several more depositions were hurting their case even worse. Dolan pointed out the obvious; there was a clear pattern that Alec would be able to prove in court. In fact, he even suggested the possibility that Alec may have the sense to try to put together a class action suit. After explaining the details about a class action and that criminal charges could very well be involved, Greg and Marcie were each feeling as if they were about to have a nervous breakdown.

Finally, Vintage Arabians received the commissions from the sale of the Sanders' herd of horses. They deposited the check in their account and placed the call to Jessica.

"The money is in the bank. Can you call Alec now and make a settlement offer?" Greg asked.

"I can, but I can't imagine that they'll go for it. They're asking for such an outrageous amount, a million dollars will seem like nothing," Jessica said, implying that Greg was wasting her time.

"Okay. Then tell him he can keep the horse, I'll pay off his note myself, and we'll give him the million dollars," Greg insisted.

"Grow up! You're in serious trouble and one horse and a million dollars isn't going to get you out of it. I'm fed up with how naïve you two act. Surely, you could have raised at least ten million by now if you really wanted to… the way you two conduct your business!"

"We need to use the money we already had as operating capital. Our overhead is incredible. You just don't understand!"

"I do understand how you two think. That's the problem!"

"Let me talk to Dolan. You have no right speaking to me that way," Greg said, trying to sound calm even though he was fuming inside.

"Fine. I'll transfer the call."

"Dolan, Jessica's being a bitch. We've got a million in cash to offer for a settlement and she's acting like it's peanuts."

Dolan tried to remain composed as he was thinking of a way to be tactful. "In this case, after what they've learned from the depositions, a million dollars is peanuts. I'm sorry. I know you don't want to hear it, but that's the fact."

"I told her to offer the money *and* to tell him he can keep the mare and I'll personally pay off the note," Greg said, as if it would make all the difference in the world.

"First off, how will you pay off the note?"

"I can make the money over the course of that much time, and remember, *half of the money goes to our sales company!* I can get Brian and Dean to take some other form of compensation..."

"Greg, I'm not trying to treat you like you're not intelligent, but haven't you thought about the fact that the Pondergrass brothers haven't been involved in this case up to this point?"

"I didn't really think about it..." he trailed off.

"Jessica and I did. I think that's where Alec got a lot of their initial information. Otherwise, they would have been the first people to be deposed. They received the huge commission."

"You're probably right. Anyway, I think I can offer them something substantial enough to work with me on the interest payments that I owe them. Somehow, I'll pay off the note to Ron and Claudia as it comes due. Please, make the settlement offer and see what happens."

Dolan sat back in his chair and rubbed his thumb between his eyebrows, trying to relieve the pressure of the headache that Greg was giving him.

"I have to make the offer if you insist, but I'm afraid that the insult will just inflame Alec even more. You've seen how cocky he acts. He knows he can bring you down to your knees."

"You talk to Alec and I'll call the clients that were deposed and made me look bad. I'm going to offer them some kind of compensation for them to sign a confidentiality agreement," Greg said as if everything would work out as long as he followed certain steps.

"You think they made you look bad?"

"Yes. Didn't you?"

"You did illegal things. You did it to yourself. They aren't the ones making you look bad... you made yourself... oh, never mind, you'll never get it, will you?"

"I'm sorry, I didn't realize," he said as if he were a teenager getting his first speeding ticket.

"Greg, we'll finish this case, but if anyone else goes after you or if criminal charges come out of this, I'm going to have to refer you to another firm. One minute you're panicked and the next day you act like you're the victim; Marcie always acts like she's the victim. I can't deal with clients like you two... especially since we're related. It's too difficult and it's not worth it..."

"You're just worried you're not going to get paid. That's it, isn't it? You're worried about your own damn money!"

"Not my money in particular, but Jessica's. She's had to come to me asking me to pay her out of my pocket... which she is fully entitled to do."

"What..."

"Your case is costing me all of my time and it's costing me my own cash to pay Jessica. The worst part is, you two don't think about anyone else but yourselves."

"That's not true..."

"It is true. Forget it," Dolan said, almost yelling. "I'll pay Jessica what she would normally receive for this amount of work and time. And, I'll call Alec and make the settlement offer," he said and hung up the phone just hard enough to let Greg know how aggravated he was.

\`\`\`\`\`\`\`\`\`\`

By the end of the day, Greg came to an agreement with each of the deposed clients. Everything would work out. Each person agreed to be compensated with unlimited breedings to Vintage Arabians owned stallions or stallions that they had syndicate shares in. They were also to receive free board for the mares being bred for whatever time period it took the mares to conceive and be checked sixty days in foal. And, of course, they would not be required to pay off their contracts on the horses purchased at the auction. All Greg had to do was put it in writing and they would each sign a confidentiality agreement.

Marcie and Greg were celebrating, dancing around, acting silly, relieving the built up stress their bodies had stored for so long now.

The phone rang and Greg answered as Marcie turned off the stereo.

"This is Greg."

"This is Jordan Murphy. Can you talk privately?"

Greg was excited, assuming that Jordan wanted to talk about the settlement offer directly rather than continuing dealing with the lawyers.

"Sure. No one's here except my wife."

"I'm sorry that I haven't called you sooner..." he told him. There was static on the line out of nowhere. "Can you hear me? We have a bad connection."

"I hear the static, but I can hear you. Do you want to hang up and call back?" Greg asked.

"Not if you can hear me. I've waited over an hour to get an overseas operator."

The static was getting louder, so Greg raised his voice. "Where are you?"

Greg thought that Jordan said they were in the Grand Cayman's, but he wasn't sure. The connection was getting worse.

"Marcie, get on the other line and see if you can understand what Jordan is saying… we have a bad connection and he's in the Caribbean, I think."

Marcie got on the extension phone.

"Hang up. It's worse," he told Marcie. "Can you hear me Jordan?" Greg practically yelled.

"I'll call back. Can you stay around? " Jordan said several times, hoping Greg could put it together.

Greg didn't hear anything, so he hung up the phone.

"He'll call back… honey. It's got to be good news if he called. Alec must have reached him and made the proposal; now he's calling to discuss it. Everything's going to be fine," he told her, all the muscles in his body having let go of their tension.

He grabbed her in his arms and hugged her and lifted her up and swung her around and kept saying "I love you!"

The phone rang again.

"Hello?" Greg said, hoping it was Jordan already.

"Hi Greg. I just thought I'd call and make sure that you received the commission check," Ryan said.

Greg was glad to hear from him, but was disappointed it wasn't Jordan. "Yes. Thank you. Dolan called Alec to make the settlement offer. I told him to also offer to let Johan keep the mare and I'll pay off the note as it comes due," he said.

Ryan didn't want to make judgments, but he doubted that Greg would really be able to satisfy the note, especially when he wasn't going to be getting paid from most of the other clients that bought at the auction…at least not from the ones that were already deposed. He didn't know that Vintage was supposed to get half of the sales price of Love Letter; he only knew that Vintage was keeping all of the interest and that they had agreed to pay it all out as an incentive to an agent.

"Good. I hope they accept," Ryan told him.

"The other good news is that I've worked out a confidentiality agreement with everyone who was already deposed. They're all getting free breedings and free board. It won't really cost me any money to speak of, and they'll be legally obligated to keep their mouths shut!"

Ryan was appalled at how disrespectful and cocky that Greg was sounding about the people that he cheated and misled.

"That's great. It sounds like things are going much better for you. How's Marcie?"

"Exhausted, but now that I've worked out the confidentiality agreement and the settlement offer is made, she's doing much better, as you can imagine," he said with enthusiasm.

"You sound as if you're pretty sure that Johan will accept the offer. That's great," Ryan said, glad he never did business with Greg, other than the inexpensive horse years ago.

"His brother Jordan called me directly, but it was a bad connection. I think he's in the Caribbean. I'm expecting a call back. We were disconnected. In fact, can I call you after I talk to him? I should keep this phone line open," Greg said.

"Why is Jordan calling?"

"I guess to negotiate. Johan probably feels too guilty that he sued us. Remember, the lawsuit is legally from Murphy Enterprises. Jordan has every right to accept our offer."

"I suppose...Well, call me later and let me know what happened. I'll let you go," Ryan said. *This would be a good movie,* he thought.

Marcie turned on the stereo again, although not nearly as loud as it had been. She started dancing around the room acting all silly and flashing her husband every once in a while. They laughed and kissed, and then dropped to the sofa in elated exhaustion. Just as Greg caught his breath, the phone rang again.

"Hopefully it's Jordan!" Marcie said as she turned off the stereo again.

"Hello."

"Hello. It's Jordan. I can hear you clear. Can you hear me?"

"Sounds like you're in the next room!" Greg said as if they were old friends.

"Good. Listen, I have something I need to discuss. Can you talk privately?"

"Yes. Go ahead."

"I know Johan owes you the third payment for that mare… or I guess it's due tomorrow…"

Greg motioned for Marcie to get on the other line. He was confused about where this was leading and didn't want to have to repeat anything to her.

"I understand that he told you that we've been having financial difficulties. It's a long story, but apparently Johan had a bank account in the Grand Caymans that he never told me about," Jordan said, angry that his brother had done this behind his back when he was the money guy in the business.

"Yeah…" Greg said, still not understanding where this was leading.

"Anyway, he really wanted to keep that mare, so we chartered a private plane a couple of weeks ago to fly down and get the money. There was so much turbulence, and Johan is afraid to fly. When we took a big drop out of a cloud, he had a heart attack… I guess from the fear. The pilot landed safely and we got him to the hospital, but it was too late to save him. We kept him alive on life support for almost ten days, but, finally his heart completely gave out…"

"He died?"

"Yes…and…"

Greg cut him off, not meaning to sound cold or indifferent.

"You aren't hiding from the FBI?"

"The FBI?"

"That's what I heard. That you and Johan disappeared because of some FBI investigation. Didn't you know they were looking for you?"

"No. We didn't know. We were flying to the Caymans to get your money. I can't believe the FBI's looking for us. We kept trying to contact them and we couldn't get anyone to acknowledge us. No one would talk to us!"

"Well, they want to talk to you now! But, Johan's dead?"

"Yes."

"I'm sorry. I'm very sorry for you and your family..." he trailed off.

Marcie looked so excited. She quietly said "Ask him if they're going to drop the lawsuit!"

He waved her off, as if telling her to be quiet.

"I don't understand what you're saying about Johan was going to get money. What about the lawsuit? I'm completely lost."

"Lawsuit?"

"Didn't you know Johan was suing us over the mare?"

"He wasn't suing you."

"Apparently he kept a lot of secrets from you. He didn't tell you about the money in the Caymans either."

"I know for sure that he wasn't suing you. He went to our attorney to find out if he could get out of the contract without us getting sued by you for being in default or for breach of contract or something."

"No. He sued us and has made our life a nightmare."

"Listen Greg, I know that he didn't. I was sitting right next to him when he fired our attorney over the telephone. Something about the lawyer wanting to go on a contingency instead of an hourly. I even heard him say that he didn't want to get anyone else involved just because he couldn't make his payment."

"Well, a suit was filed and we've had dozens of people in depositions and have lost a lot of business over it. You wouldn't believe what we've been going through."

"I know for a fact that Johan never authorized our attorney to file it. Why on earth would we be coming down here to get your money and why would he risk getting caught using hidden money to pay you? He didn't authorize any litigation! He fired the attorney!"

"You're serious aren't you?"

"I'm serious."

"Well, you better get back here, because all of this is in the name of Murphy Enterprises, which you're a principal in."

"I don't know what bank the money is in or any way to get to it. I've got to stay here and try to find out if I can get the money."

"You need to come back here and get this straightened out with my attorney, your attorney, and probably even the FBI... I don't know. Then, you can go back and try to find your money."

"All right. I'll catch a commercial flight tomorrow."

"Call me when you're in the States. I'm calling my attorney when we get off the phone."

When Greg hung up his head was spinning and he couldn't think straight.

Marcie took his face in her hands and looked him in his dazed eyes. "What on earth is going on?"

"We're not being sued."

"What?"

"Apparently, Alec and Garth did all of this without authorization! Those scum bags. We're going after their asses! We'll make so much money from this! They must have errors and omissions insurance or something that will cover what they've done. They sued us even though Johan fired him before the lawsuit was filed!"

"You mean that we've been through all of this for nothing?"

"Yes. Because those scum bag attorneys thought they could get away with something... who knows what they were thinking!"

"Call Uncle Dolan! He'll know what to do. I'll use the second phone line and call both of our parents. They'll be relieved."

\\\\\\\\\\

Greg hung up the phone from telling Dolan about his conversation with Jordan. Dolan was flabbergasted. He said he'd call Jessica, but he said he wasn't really sure how to handle what Alec and Garth had done. He'd have to wait until Monday and contact the Bar Association and see what they advised. He didn't know what else to do in the mean time. Of course, he was glad everything was over and that he wouldn't have to continue dealing with the case. At some point, soon, he'd have to have a heart to heart discussion with his niece about them finding ways to protect themselves from their past dealings and to learn what they legally and ethically can and can't do. From that point on, he had no intention of being involved in anything else about their horse business.

Marcie and Greg celebrated their victory with a bottle of wine and then made love in the living room. When Marcie fell asleep on the sofa, Greg called Ryan and told him what had happened.

"What a story! That's great for you though. Congratulations. I'm happy for you. Will you let me know what happens with Alec and Garth?"

"Sure. And thanks again for your help... and friendship."

"Yeah... sure. I guess I sold out for no reason. Shawna asked me more than once if I was jumping the gun. I should trust her instincts more..." Ryan said, deflated.

"I'm sorry. I guess I shouldn't have sold my parents' herd either. I couldn't think about anything other than protecting them."

Marcie woke up and overheard Greg saying goodbye to Ryan. Life was going to be back to normal again. Hopefully, better than normal. This was the right time of the month for her to get pregnant. In all of the excitement, she didn't use birth control. She'd keep her fingers crossed. Greg could never get angry with her for getting pregnant tonight. They were celebrating and both had an excuse not to be thinking of protection.

"Let's go to bed. I'm exhausted," she said, walking toward the stairs with an afghan wrapped around her naked body.

Greg followed behind, anxious to get a good night sleep. He'd already decided not to set the alarm clock. Neither of them had slept peacefully since all of this started.

Chapter 26

Shawna Sanders couldn't sleep that night. She kept rehashing the expression on Ryan's face as he was showing the horses for sale to the Macdermots. He hadn't looked that lost and lonely since his first wife, who he loved dearly, had died. When it was time for him to sign over all of the registration papers, he looked devastated, as if he were signing over his own life.

She couldn't bear knowing that Ryan may have held out to see how the aftermath of the lawsuit played out if only she enjoyed being with the horses or in Santa Barbara.

Not wanting to keep her husband awake, she went to the atrium with a steaming hot cup of Valerian herbal tea. Sipping her tea, a million things were racing through her thoughts. Ryan made plenty of money without income from the Arabian horse business. Not that it would be the financially prudent thing to do, but he could afford the financial loss of having the herd of horses for a hobby even if they didn't make a dime. Her income alone could support their lifestyle as they had become accustomed to living. Ryan always insisted that she keep her money separate; that he would pay for their vacations, the New York apartment and all of the expenses involved in running the household and daily living such as entertainment, dining out and buying clothes. If she wanted anything else, she could pay for it herself, which she did. She amassed an enviable art collection and investment portfolio.

Her charity contributions were not as significant as her husband suggested that she should do, but they were still substantial amounts to the charities that she did support.

Surely, now that the lawsuit was going to be dropped, and now that the Bordeauxs would have confidentiality agreements, Ryan must have gone to bed angry with himself for having sold the horses so quickly, she thought.

She didn't realize it, but it was five in the morning when she finally returned to their bed.

The bed was empty. There was a note by the nightstand which read, *'You were asleep in the atrium. I didn't want to wake you. I couldn't sleep. I'm going to the airport and catching the next plane, commercial or otherwise, for California. The horses are leaving for Washington next week and I want to spend the time with them before they go. Call me at the farm, or I'll call you. Love, Ryan.'*

Warm salty tears streamed from her tired bloodshot eyes. She couldn't bear to know her husband was in so much pain. If only he'd come to her so that they could have talked. She was sure that she wasn't asleep in the atrium; she rested her eyes while she laid down thinking, but she didn't sleep. Of course, he wouldn't have known.

Shawna fell asleep for a couple of hours, then called her office and left a message on the machine saying she wouldn't be in for a few more days. She told them to call her over anything, but not to expect her presence. Hopefully, she had a solution. She had to wait until eleven a.m., but hopefully her money would finally come in handy for something important.

It felt like an eternity until the clock struck eleven. She went to their home office and easily located the phone number in Seattle. She sat in the leather desk chair and dialed the phone. Totally unaware at the time she was doing it, now, dialing the number, she saw that she had bitten off all of her fingernails in the middle of the night.

"Mrs. Macdermot?"

"Yes, this is she."

"This is Shawna Sanders, Ryan's wife."

"Yes," she said, surprised by the call.

"I'm sorry to do this to you, but it was a big mistake that my husband sold you his herd of horses. Would you please let me buy them back from you since you haven't taken delivery yet?"

The woman was startled and didn't know what to say.

Shawna continued. "I'm afraid that my husband didn't realize just how important the horses were to him until he sold them! He knew he was attached, but I don't think he understood to what extent until the sale was actually finalized and the hauling arrangements made."

"I'm sorry…"

Shawna interrupted. "I can wire transfer you the money in full today. It will be into your account by the time you have lunch," she pleaded.

"I don't know…"

"I'll pay you double what you paid. Please. My husband needs the horses. The business. The money means nothing to me. Please…. will you take the money and cancel the contract?"

"The money doesn't mean anything to my husband or I either, Ms. Sanders."

Shawna didn't know what to do. Adding more money to the offer was obviously not going to have any influence on Mrs. Macdermot's decision.

"You don't understand Ms. Macdermot. It's my fault Ryan thought he should sell out. It will ruin my marriage if we have this hanging over us. I don't know what to do other than get the contracts canceled. I'm begging you," Shawna said through tears and with no concern for her dignity.

"Let me tell my husband and see what he says. Can you hold for a minute?"

"Certainly. Go ahead," she said as she wished as hard as she could that he would agree.

A minute later Mr. Macdermot came on the line. "Ms. Sanders, I'm sorry for the position you're in, it must feel terrible. Does your husband know you're calling us?"

"Of course not! He would have never permitted this. As a matter of a fact, he got up in the middle of the night and flew back to California to spend every day with the horses until they are to be shipped up to you…" she trailed off. "I found a note early this morning."

"I'll tell you what, we're obviously not attached to the horses and have very little time invested in looking at acquiring them. If you'll refund us all of our money, we'll cancel the contract… on one condition," he said.

"What's the condition?" she said, knowing that she'd do anything legal to accomplish this feat.

"You agree to personally speak to my daughter's high school journalism club about your career and answer any questions that they may have."

"Of course I'll do it! In fact, I'll even fly the whole club here to spend a week or two on an internship so that they can see everything first hand. Have we got a deal?"

"You've got a deal. It's nice to know two people love each other so much to do what you've done Ms. Sanders," he said.

"I do love him. Thank you," she said sincerely.

"I would only hope that my wife would do the same thing in the same situation."

"I'm sure that she would. Can you give me the wire transfer information? I'll call my bank when we hang up," she said with a pen in hand and a piece of paper to write on.

"No need. Just bring out a check when you come to speak to my daughter's club. Can you come in the next few weeks?"

"Yes, I'll make a point of it. I would feel better to know we have a done deal though… I'd like to return your money by wire transfer today," she said, worried that something would go wrong.

"I won't go back on my word, but if you'd feel better, I'll Federal Express a voided contract and a cancellation notice that states that we both agree to cancel the transaction. Just bring your check when you come."

"Thank you. Thank you so much," Shawna said with happy tears. If they had refused, she didn't know how she'd live with herself.

After she hung up the phone, she called the farmhouse in Santa Barbara. There was no answer, so she left a simple message.

"Ryan, it's me. I love you. Cancel the haulers."

\\\\\\\\\\

Marcie woke up at 10:30 that same morning and quietly crept out of bed, wanting her husband to sleep as late as his body needed. She slipped on her knee length moss colored damask robe and went barefoot downstairs to make a pot of coffee. As the coffee brewed, she stepped out to the patio and breathed in the dry warm air. She looked around at all of her plants and flowers and cactus. Life was fresh and inviting again. She would appreciate every happy and peaceful moment from this day forward.

Greg ambled down the stairs, wiping the sleep from his eyes. His head was too groggy to think about reading the newspaper yet, so he didn't bother getting it from the front porch. He went directly to the kitchen where his wife was pouring herself a cup of coffee.

"Pour me one too. I need to wake up. I can't believe I slept this late," he said as he kissed her on the top of her head.

Marcie glanced over to the table in the family room, which was still a mess from the night before. The telephone was off the hook. She replaced the receiver and didn't say anything about it. Before she even made it back to the kitchen, the phone rang. She turned around to pick it up.

"Hello," she said.

"Is this Marcie Bordeaux?" an unfamiliar voice asked.

"Yes."

"Do you have a comment I can quote you on?"

"Pardon me?"

"This is Paige Warner from The Phoenix Sun. Do you have a comment that I can quote you on?"

"I don't know what you're talking about," Marcie said, ready to hang up the phone and join her husband for coffee.

"Have you read the morning paper?"

"No," she said, then hung up the phone without thinking anything of it. She was so tired that her mind didn't comprehend any significance of the call.

"Who was that?" Greg asked.

"Some woman from the newspaper."

"Newspaper?"

"I don't know. I'm still half asleep. I have cob webs in my brain from the wine," she said, then took her first sip of coffee.

The couple each had a tall cup of coffee before Greg went to the front porch to get the newspaper. He carried it under his arm into the kitchen, sat down at the table and took the newspaper out of its plastic wrapper.

Greg turned stone cold and held back from vomiting. On the front page, there was a color photograph of the entrance to their farm, and a second color photograph of a promotional picture of one of the auctions. The headline read *"Trading Paper: The Legitimacy of the Arabian Horse Industry in Question."*

\\\\\\\\\\

Turner Lloyd finished reading the front-page article in the newspaper and the related stories. The reporter got almost everything right, and he kept his word. He referred to Turner as an unnamed source and didn't disclose where they got copies of the documents that they referred to as hard evidence. He would never tell his wife Jessica that he went to the press and told a reporter all the sordid details. He was sure that she would never suspect that he had been opening her briefcase at night to read her files and go through her notes, let alone that he made copies of the most incriminating writings. If he got his way, this would become a national story and destroy the Bordeauxs and all of the other greedy bastards involved in the Arabian horse business.

\\\\\\\\\\

In spite of the likelihood that he would be disbarred, Alec was delighted to wake up in St. Louis in his own bed for a change. He was tired of practicing law and his stock portfolio was worth a small fortune. With the success of his stock picks, he didn't need the money from practicing law anyway. He'd just sell stock as he needed money. Financially, everything would work out just fine.

His telephone rang and a reporter asked him for a quote. He assumed that the press had found out what he had done, so he hung up the phone without responding or giving it another thought.

After his long hot shower, without drying himself, he wrapped a thick towel around his waist before he entered his bedroom to dry off and get dressed.

To his astonishment, his wife was sitting on the edge of the mattress.

"This is a pleasant surprise... to what do I owe the honor?" he asked, unsure of whether he should drop his towel or not.

"You've been through a lot, haven't you?" she said with little emotion.

"Yes. I'm so glad you're here. I've missed you so much," he told her as he sat next to her, leaving his towel on. Forgetting he was still wet, he contemplated sitting closer and putting his arm around her, but he decided to take it slow.

"You've been through so much, and it's all been for nothing," she said.

Alec looked at her, hoping that she meant that she was coming back home.

"You shouldn't have gone through any of this," she said.

"I love you..." he said, and then started to kiss her.

She didn't let him kiss her. She slithered away from him and stood up to face him, her features turning hard and cold.

"That stupid idiot!" she bellowed as she became increasingly agitated.

He looked up at her, trying to decipher what she was talking about. He'd never seen her crazed before.

"That stupid idiot killed Nathan Burger instead of you!" she squealed, loathing his very existence.

"What are you..." he said in a staccato manner, trying to decipher what she had said.

"I know you were screwing that bimbo from the health club. She mailed me pictures you jerk! Two years and I never knew it!"

Alec stood up and started to approach her. Started to apologize.

She backed away from him as quickly as her legs would move.

"You just can't hire good help these days. When you want something done, you have to do it yourself!" she said, self-possessed and in a venomous manner.

She pulled the gun out of her jacket pocket, aimed, and squeezed the trigger.

\` \` \` \` \` \` \` \` \` \` \` \` \` \` \` \` \` \` \` \` \` \` \` \` \`